MW00941260

Fecha Para Retornar

OCT 0 1 2017

OCT 1 0 2017

NOV 2 0 2017

NOV 2 7 2017

APR 0 1 2019

DISCARDED

PRINTED IN U.S.A

Hodgkins Public Library District
6500 Wenz Ave.
Hodgkins, Illinois 60525

Copyright © 2016 Sabrina Stark

All rights reserved.

ISBN-13:

978-1539850397

ISBN-10:

1539850390

CHAPTER 1

I was in love with a maniac.

No surprise there. I mean, this was Jake, after all.

We were sitting at a table for ten near the front of a huge banquet hall. On a raised platform a few feet away, some famous sportscaster was entertaining the crowd with tales of player-exploits, both on and off the field.

With a toothy grin, the guy leaned closer to his podium and said, "So remember, people, when you're gonna spike something, make sure it's the ball." He winked. "And *not* the referee."

The crowd, nearly a thousand strong, roared with laughter. Around us, I heard glasses clinking and saw waiters moving. The way it looked, they were getting ready to serve dinner.

I frowned. I'd ordered Chicken Florentine. I liked Chicken Florentine. But I had a sneaky suspicion that I wouldn't be getting any tonight.

In fact, I was pretty sure that by the time the dust settled, we'd be dining somewhere else. And if things went *really* bad? Well, in that case, Jake would be dining in jail.

Again.

I leaned toward him and whispered, "You're kidding, right?"

He gave me a wicked smile. "Maybe."

I studied his face. His thick, dark hair framed his perfect features, those luscious cheekbones, those dark, intense eyes, and that mouth. Oh, my God. I swallowed. That mouth, those lips, his tongue – I couldn't see his tongue now, but I knew what it was capable of.

Damn it.

Focus, Luna.

From the look on Jake's face, there was no maybe about it. Something was definitely going to happen, because Jake was going to *make* it happen. I looked around the huge room. The place was jam-packed with sports fans, players, coaches, and management types, along with a scary number of burly guys in business suits – security, obviously.

This was the fifth annual Mid-Western sports award ceremony, and it had drawn a huge crowd, triple the size of last year.

I knew why. It was because of Dorian North. The guy's little brother was up for college athlete of the year, and everyone knew he was going to win it – not because he was the best, but because he was the brother of Dorian, the big, bad-ass brute who'd ditched the wrestling ring to become the latest, greatest thing in Hollywood action movies.

I looked to the far side of the room, where Dorian was sitting at a prime table with two brunettes and a blonde, along with the rest of his entourage. They'd arrived late – and loud. They were *still* loud. For the fifth time in the last half-hour, a cell phone rang.

The phone belonged to Dorian. I knew because the ringtone, if you could call it that, was his own voice, delivering his famous catch-phrase, "Suck on *that*, Jones."

God, what an asshat.

Dorian answered the phone and started talking. "Screw that," he bellowed to the poor slob – whoever they were – on the other end. "You get me double, or the deal's off. Got it?" Not bothering to say goodbye, he ended the call and tossed his cell phone back onto the table.

Next to him, the blonde squealed out, "You tell him, baby."

Grinning, Dorian leaned back in his chair. "Already did, sugar-tits."

I snuck a quick glance at the girl's chest. If her tits were sugar, they were definitely – How to put this? – in need of a bigger bowl.

Her halter-dress, some silver thing with sequins, was overflowing on all sides. She gave a little jiggle, and I saw the briefest flash of nipple before she quickly tucked it back in.

I heard a muffled moan and looked to my left. Sitting next to me was Trey, Jake's assistant. He was staring, hypnotized, at the girl's chest.

I leaned toward him and hissed, "Did you just moan?"

"It wasn't a moan." He straightened in his chair. "It was a sound of appreciation."

I rolled my eyes. "Oh, please." If he were any *more* appreciative, he'd need a change of underwear.

His face split into a huge, sloppy grin. "I think I saw a nipple."

"So what?" I said. "Me too. But you don't see *me* moaning about it."

"Yeah. Because you're not a guy." He frowned. "You can see them any time you want. Me? I've gotta take 'em where I find 'em."

My gaze dipped to his black button-down shirt. Trey did have nipples, right? But I got what he meant. Probably, his weren't nearly as interesting – or at least, I sure hoped not.

I looked to my right and studied Jake's face. Had *he* seen the nipple? Probably. But I didn't hear *him* moaning about it either.

Then again, Jake was never lacking in nipple-viewing opportunities. Everywhere we went, girls practically threw themselves at him. Every once in a while, they threw their clothes too, which, come to think of it, didn't exactly cut down on the nipple sightings.

Happily, Jake hardly seemed to notice – not since we'd been together anyway. From what I'd seen over the past few weeks, he was a one-girl kind of guy, which meant that *my* nipples were the only ones he paid serious attention to.

Thank goodness.

And just for the record, his attention was really, *really* good.

With an effort, I turned my attention to the stage and tried to focus on things *other* than ripping off Jake's clothes and jumping into his arms.

The sportscaster was still talking, louder now, in an obvious bid to drown out the latest interruption from Dorian and his entourage.

It had been going on like this for a while. Just as the sportscaster was hitting his stride, Dorian and his companions would knock the guy off his game with some new interruption – talking across the table, calling out for more booze, and yeah, taking more phone calls than a pizza delivery joint.

I snuck another quick glance at Jake, who was watching the scene with quiet amusement. As for the rest of the crowd, their amusement had faded fifteen minutes earlier, when Dorian had taken out his phone and ordered his driver to "be ready out front, the minute my little brother wins this piss-ant thing."

Recalling Jake's words from earlier, I leaned toward him and asked, "When you say 'be ready,' what exactly do you mean? Be ready for what?"

Jake flicked his head toward Dorian, but said nothing.

I didn't know whether to laugh or cry. "Don't tell me you're gonna mess with him."

Jake shrugged. "Alright."

"Alright? Meaning you're not gonna mess with him?" I paused. "Or, alright, meaning you're not gonna tell me?"

He leaned close and whispered in my ear, "Just be ready."

Again, I glanced toward Dorian's table. Across from him sat his little brother – although, to call the guy little was utterly ridiculous. Ronnie North was a head taller than his brother, and if the rumors were true, twice as mean.

Ronnie was a football player of some sort. What position, I had no idea. I wasn't exactly a fan. Still, I'd heard the rumors. Apparently, Ronnie wasn't nearly as good as he thought he was, and had gained a reputation for being, as Jake had put it, a piss-poor loser when things didn't go his way.

I glanced around. The odds of Ronnie losing anything tonight were slim to none. For weeks, rumors had been circulating that the whole award-thing was rigged, courtesy of Dorian, who'd been using muscle and money to boost his little brother's chances.

Why, I had no idea. I mean, a regional sports award wouldn't be the thing I'd rig. But then again, I wouldn't be using my own voice as a ring-tone either.

Again, I heard Jake's voice, low in my ear. "And keep your purse handy, alright?"

"For what?"

"To get out of here." Jake pointed toward the other side of our table, where a brawny, middle-aged man in a sports-jacket was watching the crowd with wary eyes. "If things get bad," Jake continued, "go with him, alright?"

I stared at the guy. Who was he, anyway? Yeah, he'd been sitting at our table, but so were a bunch of other people I didn't know. Other than Jake and Trey, I hadn't said more than a quick hello to any one of them.

And now, I was supposed to leave with that guy? A total stranger? Screw that. I was leaving with Jake. I hesitated. Well, as long as he wasn't arrested or anything.

When I said nothing, Jake spoke again. "You heard me, right?"

Again, I glanced toward the guy, whose eyes were still scanning the room. "Him?" I said, forgetting to lower my voice. "But I don't even know him."

Behind me, someone made a shushing sound. I turned and glared toward the unseen shusher. I couldn't even tell who'd done it, but that wasn't the point. Why were they shushing *me* when they should be shushing Dorian? He was a hundred times louder than *I* was.

I felt a familiar hand on my knee and turned to meet Jake's eyes. The humor in them was gone, replaced by a look I knew all too well.

"Yeah," he said. "*You* don't know the guy. But *I* do." He flicked his head toward the nearby side exit, and it suddenly hit me that it was probably no accident we were sitting so close to an easy out. Even at regular restaurants, Jake picked tables like this all the time, whether there was trouble brewing or not.

For all his easy ways, he had a paranoid streak that was more than a little scary.

Into my silence, Jake spoke again. "So if anything happens, listen to what he says, alright?"

"If anything happens?" I swallowed. "But you never told me. What's going to happen?"

"Eh, hard to say. Depends on Dorian."

None of this was making any sense. But by now, I should be used to it. With Jake, things tended to get a little crazy – because Jake was, well, Jake.

To me, he was the guy I'd been crushing on for years, starting when I'd been a bratty twelve-year-old back in our hometown. And Jake? He'd been the teenage bad-ass who, to my infinite frustration, had treated me like some sort of little sister – and not the dream-girl I wanted to be.

I met his gaze, and my stomach gave a funny little flutter. He was *still* a bad-ass, a tattooed, muscle-bound thing of beauty with a quick brain and wicked sense of humor. But these days, the sister-treatment was long gone.

I felt myself smile. He especially hadn't treated me like a sister this morning, when he'd given me three orgasms and waffles for breakfast.

Watching him now, I felt that thrilling warmth in all the right places. It was making it hard to think. Just above my knee, his hand drifted higher. It wasn't obscene, but it *was* a promise. I could feel it in his fingers, the hint of what might happen later, once we were alone.

My mouth grew dry, and I felt my tongue brush the back of my teeth. I liked being alone with him. In fact, I was kind of wishing I was alone with him now.

I gave my head a quick shake. Damn it. He was distracting me again. Probably, he was doing it on purpose.

Talk about devious.

Steeling myself, I tried again. "Seriously, what are you gonna do? You're not gonna start a fight with him, are you?"

"Me?" He grinned. "Never."

My gaze narrowed. Technically, Jake never started fights, but he had a funny way of finishing them. It was the reason he was rich, and yeah, famous if you knew where to look.

Unlike Dorian, who made his money on the big screen, Jake had built *his* audience on the internet, where he had twelve-million rabid subscribers, consisting of frat boys, mixed-martial arts fans, and slobbering groupies who sent him more suggestive pictures than I cared to think about.

I glanced to my left and saw Trey pulling out a small video recorder. He was grinning like he always did right before everything hit the fan.

Mentally, I braced myself.

The way it looked, our night was about to get a whole lot more interesting.

And I still hadn't gotten my chicken.

CHAPTER 2

On stage, the sportscaster finished his talk and turned the microphone over to the emcee, who started doling out the awards one-by-one. With growing nervousness, I watched as athletes from virtually every kind of sport – football, hockey, baseball, whatever – were called up to the stage, where they accepted their awards, had their photos taken, and returned to their seats without incident.

Because of where we were sitting – near the short stairway that led to the stage – most of the athletes passed us within arm's reach. I didn't recognize a single one of them. No surprise there, given the fact I was embarrassingly clueless about the college sports scene.

As time went on, and nothing happened, I almost started to relax – until I recalled all those security guys.

Jake was a fighter. He was a great fighter, actually. But if things went to crap, this wouldn't be a one-on-one kind of thing. Tonight, most of those security guys had arrived at the same time as Dorian, which meant they were on *his* payroll, not the convention center's.

And they definitely weren't on Jake's, with the possible exception of the stranger sitting at our table. I snuck a quick glance at the guy and felt myself frown. He was still scanning the crowd, as if waiting for trouble that was guaranteed to happen.

Well, that wasn't ominous or anything.

On the far side of the room, the waiters had finally started serving dinner, delivering covered plates while the awards droned on.

By now, I was barely listening. Instead, I was keeping one eye on Jake and the other on Dorian, who was, once again, talking on his cell phone.

"Be ready," he was saying, "we've got like a dozen more of these chicken-shit awards before Ronnie does his thing."

I leaned toward Jake and asked, "What does he mean? What 'thing' will Ronnie be doing? Do you know?"

Jake flashed me a grin. "He means that if Ronnie wins Athlete of the Year, he'll be giving a nice, little speech."

I glanced over at Ronnie, who'd pulled out his own cell phone. His voice rose and carried above the crowd. "Listen, you don't pay my bills. Dorian does. So quit ragging on me, alright?" He paused. "Yeah? Well screw you, too, Mom."

I glanced back to Jake. "About Ronnie," I whispered, "I'm not sure his speech will be all that nice."

Jake turned and gave Ronnie a long, speculative look. "Or maybe, he won't be making that speech at all."

I snuck a quick glance at Trey. He was still clutching his video recorder. He was still smiling. I still hadn't gotten my chicken.

It was kind of a bummer, actually. I hadn't eaten since the waffles. That was how long ago? Twelve hours? Probably, I should've had a sandwich or something. But between my new job and getting ready for tonight, I'd been seriously short on time.

I'd been rushing around all day – first at work, and then to come here. Now, after all that, I wasn't terribly thrilled with the idea of rushing for the exit, assuming I'd even need to.

I tried to look on the bright side. Maybe Jake was just messing with me. He did that sometimes. He had a wicked sense of humor, and always kept me guessing.

In spite of my nerves, I felt a reluctant smile tug at my lips.

Last night, he'd kept me guessing too – not in the funny way, but in the hot, naked way. At the memory, I shifted in my seat and reminded myself that we weren't exactly alone. Still, I felt that familiar warmth creep up my face, and then, by some medical miracle, settle somewhere between my thighs.

A dreamy sigh escaped my lips. Forget the chicken. I wanted Jake.

Next to me, Trey said something too low for me to make out.

I leaned toward him and whispered, "What?"

He gave me a smug smile. "Who's moaning now?"

Horrified, I drew back. "I wasn't moaning," I told him. "It was a sigh."

But Trey was shaking his head. "It sounded like a moan to me."

My cheeks were burning now. I gave a nervous glance around the table. Was anyone staring? No. They weren't. Thank God.

Trey *had* to be exaggerating. And besides, if he thought *that* was a moan, he should've heard me last night – and this morning.

And there it was, that warmth again, creeping downward at the memory of Jake's lips grazing my navel, just before drifting lower. Damn it. I gave a little shake of my head. This was *so* not the time or place.

Deliberately, I turned my attention to the stage, where the regular awards were finally winding down.

"And now," the emcee was saying, "it's time for the one we've all been waiting for." Dramatically, his voice boomed out, "College Athlete of the Year."

I looked to Dorian's table, where the brunettes were laughing at some secret joke. Dorian ended his latest phone call, shoved the phone into his pants pocket, and turned to glare at the girls. "Shut your pie-holes," he said, glancing toward the stage. "Can't you see the guy's talking?"

The girls stopped laughing and frowned. The nearest one made a pouty face and said, "But you told us it didn't matter."

Dorian gave her a withering look. "It matters now, so shut it." He looked toward his brother and called out across the table, "This is it, bro. Be ready."

Ronnie shoved his own cell phone back into his pocket, and then, with a self-satisfied smile, turned his chair toward the stage and waited.

The lights in the audience section grew dim, while the lights on the stage grew just a shade brighter. From some unseen source, dramatic music – the theme to *Rocky*, maybe? – swelled out of the shadows.

Two tables over, the waiters were delivering covered plates. Next to me, Jake looked easy and relaxed. On my other side, Trey gave something like a laugh.

I turned toward him and asked, "What's so funny?"

"Nothing." He gave an evil chuckle. "Yet."

Up on stage, the emcee was still talking. "And, as we all know, it's an honor just to be nominated."

Dorian gave a loud snort. He called out toward his brother, "Even better to win." He roared with laughter. "Right, Ronnie-boy?"

Faltering only slightly, the emcee announced the name of each athlete who'd been nominated. Other than Ronnie North, I recognized none of the names. But then again, I hadn't expected to.

Finally, the emcee reached into his jacket pocket. With a flourish, he whipped out a silver envelope, tore it open, and pulled out a small slip of paper. He looked down at the thing and froze. A slow, confused frown settled over his features. Near the back of the banquet hall, someone coughed.

Into the silence, Dorian bellowed out, "Go on, read it!" He gave a bark of laughter. "Food's gettin' cold, man!" Everyone at his table laughed. Other than a few nervous chuckles, they were the only ones.

On stage, the emcee cleared his throat and gave the paper another nervous glance.

At Dorian's table, Ronnie North pushed back his chair and leaned forward, obviously getting ready to head up on stage.

God, what a dumb-ass. Rigged or not, couldn't he at least *pretend* to be surprised?

The emcee took a deep breath and leaned closer to the microphone. "And the winner is..." He gave a stiff smile. "Becky Summers of Tri-State University."

CHAPTER 3

At the announcement of Becky's name, the place broke into wild applause.

Peering through the shadows, I looked over at Dorian's table. No one *there* was clapping. Dorian was glaring, thunderstruck, up at the emcee, who was looking more uncomfortable with each passing second. Across from Dorian, Ronnie looked too stunned to move while the rest of his companions shared nervous glances.

Near the back of the conference center, a petite brunette was making her way toward the stage.

She wound her way through the maze of tables and passed me within arm's reach. College student or not, she looked around twelve-years-old, with long brown hair and an eager, bouncing step.

When she smiled, *I* smiled. I didn't even know her, but I liked her. She was so darn cute, I wanted to adopt her, like a kitten.

When she bounded up the steps and reached the emcee, he handed her a giant silver trophy, and then stepped aside, giving her access to the podium. Becky moved forward and reached up to lower the microphone before saying, "Wow, I sure wasn't expecting this."

From the shadows, Dorian's voice rang out, "You ain't the only one!" His companions roared with laughter, oblivious to the angry murmurs of those around them. Near us, a table of football-player types looked distinctly annoyed.

Becky froze for a long moment before recovering her composure to say, "I want to thank my parents and my coach, and my big sister, who pushed me into my first somersault." With a small laugh, she lifted the award and added, "Even if you *did* roll me into Mom's gardenias."

The crowd laughed, and Becky smiled, looking more relaxed now. "And I want to thank my team for all their support." Her voice grew more earnest. "When it comes to team sports, I know that gymnastics isn't the first thing that people think of—"

"Got that right!" Dorian bellowed.

From the crowd, I heard louder murmurs of irritation. A deep male voice from somewhere in the back hollered out, "Hey, Dickweed! Shut up, and let her speak!"

The crowd responded with cheers and applause, leaving Dorian obviously stunned. He glared toward the voice and hollered back, "Who said that?"

There was a smattering of laughter, followed by silence until a friendly female voice called out toward the stage, "Go on, Becky! We're listening!"

Becky gave a shaky smile and continued. "But that doesn't mean teamwork isn't really important." Again, she lifted the trophy. "Because this award isn't just for me. It's for—" A loud crash made her stop in mid-sentence.

The crash had come from Dorian, who had leapt to his feet, sending his chair tumbling backward into a nearby waiter, who, in turn, had dropped his tray. I squinted through the shadows and saw breaded chicken, along with thick noodles, strewn in saucy piles across the fancy tile floor.

Yup, it was Chicken Florentine, alright.

My Chicken Florentine? Probably not. A good thing, too, because I sure as heck wasn't going to be slurping it off the slippery tile, even as hungry as I was.

Next to me, I heard Jake say under his breath, "What a pussy."

I looked up and saw what he saw. Dorian had thrown down his napkin and was heading in our direction, making his way toward the same side exit that Jake had pointed to earlier.

I had to agree. It *was* a pussy-move, storming out, just because things didn't go as planned. As for the rest of Dorian's table, they were staying put. Was that a good thing? Or a bad thing? I honestly had no idea.

Just above me, a small clattering noise broke my concentration. I looked up and saw a waiter with a huge serving tray looming over my shoulder. He smiled. "Chicken?"

Without waiting for my response, he set a covered plate in front of me and lifted its shiny silver lid. And there it was, Chicken Florentine, looking all saucy and delicious. The dish was steaming. The chicken was breaded. The noodles looked extra-buttery.

My mouth watered. Things were definitely looking up. And once Dorian was gone, the odds of trouble would go down considerably.

I gave Trey a quick glance, wondering if he'd be disappointed.

Apparently not. Grinning like a crazy person, he had his recorder trained on Dorian, who was still barreling toward us. Funny, he should've passed us by now, but for some weird reason, he kept running into obstacles – a waiter with a tray of food, a big guy in a suit who moved his chair at exactly the wrong moment, a bartender with a drink-cart.

With a string of profanity, Dorian shoved aside the cart and plowed forward.

I glanced toward the podium. Becky was still there, watching Dorian in obvious confusion. I could see why. The whole thing was beyond strange. What about the rest of his companions? Was Dorian just going to ditch them and run off?

And what about his brother?

I glanced over at Ronnie and froze. He was staring straight at our table. His face was red. His nostrils were flaring. I'm pretty sure he might've growled.

Or maybe that was just my stomach.

I leaned toward Jake and whispered, "What's up with Ronnie?"

Jake smiled like he knew something I didn't.

I felt my gaze narrow. Had Jake *known* that Ronnie wasn't going to win tonight? Was *that* why we were here? To capture the fallout?

It made sense in a Jake sort of way. If Ronnie, who already had a reputation for being a sore loser, threw a huge hissy-fit, Jake's fans would absolutely love it. And they'd love it even more if Jake messed with him along the way – throwing some Jake-flavored gasoline on the proverbial fire.

And then, there was the matter of Ronnie's action-star brother, who had just stopped in mid-stride. He looked toward the stage, and his eyes narrowed to slits. A slow, mean smile darkened his features.

Oh, crap.

What was Dorian planning to do, anyway? Rip the trophy out of Becky's hands? And then what? Award it to his little brother? From the look on Dorian's face, the idea wasn't so far-fetched.

Frantically, I glanced around. Where was security, anyway? Shouldn't they be jumping in to stop this? And then I remembered, most of the security belonged to Dorian.

So that left who, exactly?

Without thinking, I started to rise. My butt had barely left the chair when an iron grip yanked me back down. I turned to see Jake flash me a grin. "Don't even think about it." He leaned around me and told Trey, "You ready?"

Trey gave a happy nod.

I looked from Trey to Jake. "Ready for what?" I asked.

Jake flicked his head toward Dorian, who was once again heading toward us – or toward the stage, depending on what, exactly, he had in mind. I didn't really know, and from the look in Dorian's eyes, I probably didn't *want* to know.

My heart was hammering, and I gave Jake a quick, nervous glance. Looking easy and relaxed, he snagged a noodle off my plate and popped it into his mouth. He gave me a smile, the cocky one that made just a little bit nervous.

Again, I looked toward Dorian, who passed me in a sudden blur. And then, with a loud thud, he was gone. I mean, *really* gone. From somewhere near the floor, I heard a muffled groan, followed by the roar of laughter all around us.

I leaned around Jake's chair to look. And there Dorian was, lying on the tile floor amidst buttery noodles and bits of breaded chicken.

What the heck?

Across the room, someone yelled out, "Mother-fucker!"

I turned toward the sound and saw Ronnie North jump to his feet and glare more daggers in our direction.

I froze. The way it looked, he'd been hollering at Jake. But why? Before I could give it too much thought, Ronnie was barreling and weaving his way toward us – or, as a best-case scenario – toward his brother.

With growing panic, I looked to the floor, where Dorian was now struggling to rise. Halfway up, he lost his footing and, once again, hit the floor, hard, landing on his ass.

From somewhere near the back, a male voice called out, "Suck on that, Jones!"

The whole place exploded in laughter.

Dorian tried again, and this time, managed to struggle to his feet. He turned and glared toward the voice. Again, he bellowed, "Who said that?"

The only answer was more laughter, along with a smattering of applause.

From her spot behind the podium, Becky tentatively called out, "Mister North, are you okay?"

"Shut up!" Dorian hollered as he whirled toward the stage, giving me a clear view of his backside. On his ass, I saw soggy noodles stuck to the seat of his fancy dress pants.

At the sight of them, I felt my brow wrinkle. The noodles looked familiar. *Too* familiar. I looked to my plate. It was still there. But the chicken wasn't. And neither were the noodles.

I gave Jake a sideways glance. But this time, he wasn't watching me. He was watching Ronnie, who was still plowing toward us – until he was suddenly tackled by one of the football players who'd been glaring at him earlier.

Somewhere over my shoulder, an unfamiliar male voice said, "Time to go."

I looked up. "What?"

It was the stranger. He flicked his chin toward the nearby exit. "C'mon."

I whirled to my right, looking to catch Jake's eye. Instead, I almost caught a fist to the face as Dorian took a wild swing somewhere near Jake's head.

I heard another thud as Dorian lost his footing once more and slipped sideways onto the tile floor. "Son-of-a-bitch!" he hollered.

Jake stood and turned in my direction. "Go."

Sitting too stunned to move, I stared up at him. "What?"

Behind him, Dorian was struggling to his feet, looking even more unhinged. And yet, for some insane reason, I still wasn't moving.

Looking at Dorian, I couldn't help but think, he looked a lot nicer on the movie screen – friendly, in a jovial sort of way.

But he wasn't looking friendly now. With a guttural roar, he lunged forward, making me flinch backward in my seat.

Jake whirled toward him and caught a fist to the jaw. I heard myself say, "Oh, my God!"

Jake stepped toward him, sending his chair clattering to the tile floor. When Dorian swung again, Jake was ready. He ducked to the left, leaving Dorian stumbling forward. He lost his footing, tripped over Jake's chair, and landed in a messy heap on the floor just behind me.

I felt a hand on my elbow. The hand belonged to the stranger. "Come on," he urged.

I was having a hard time thinking. Around us, the place had erupted into pure pandemonium. The guys at Dorian's table, along with his security team, had waded into the mix, only to be tackled down by other audience members the moment they tried to cause more trouble.

A few table-lengths away, I spotted Ronnie, staggering sideways as a perky redhead with a gymnast's body clung to his back like she'd just jumped him from behind.

Well, that's something you don't see every day.

Jake's voice broke my concentration. "What the hell am I paying you for?" Through clenched teeth, he added, "Get her outta here. Now."

The guy's grip on my elbow tightened. "Come on. Please?"

Reluctantly, I stumbled to my feet and let the guy hustle me toward the side exit. Just before we ducked out the side door, I took one last look. Through the commotion, I zoomed in on Jake.

He was absolutely surrounded by flailing bodies and flying fists. Dorian was nowhere in sight, leaving me to wonder if he'd slipped again.

I spotted Trey, now standing on the table, recording the chaos as it raged around him.

He was grinning. And somehow, I knew that this time, a nipple-sighting wasn't the cause. It was the spectacle – and the millions of views it would generate before the night ended.

Jake was rich. Stuff like this was the reason why. But every once in a while, like now, I couldn't help but wonder, how long things could go on like this?

How long could he take such crazy chances? How long could he wreak havoc all around him, and walk away unscathed? How long before the insanity caught up with him, and took him down, whether physical, financially, or both?

And through all this, one other thought kept nagging at the back of my mind. How long before I lost him, one way or another?

.□

CHAPTER 4

Jake gave me a cocky smile. "Hey, I wasn't arrested."

"Yeah," I said, "but I didn't know that, did I?"

Three hours – that's how long I'd been waiting at his penthouse. Three *long* hours, wondering if he was okay, wondering if he'd been dragged off to jail, wondering if this time, his luck had finally run out.

I'd spent most of those hours glued to my computer, where someone had been live-streaming the commotion outside the convention center. In my mind, I could still picture it – the red and blue flashing of police lights; the crowd, dazed and confused, pouring out of the building; random paramedics treating people on the scene for various cuts and bruises.

In front of me, Jake was saying, "I tried to call."

"Yeah, but I didn't have my phone."

That was another thing. In all the commotion, I'd forgotten my purse, which meant I was missing not only my cell phone, but my wallet and everything in it.

I considered all the things I'd lost – my driver's license, my one credit card, and even my paper punch-card thingy for my favorite coffee shop. Bad timing, too. I'd been just one punch away from a free latte.

I gave a little shake of my head. Who cared about the latte? I wasn't worried about some stupid drink. I was worried about Jake.

I looked over at him, standing just inside the door to his penthouse. He looked surprisingly fine, all things considered.

Into his silence, I tried to explain. "So if you *did* call, I had no way of answering."

His eyebrows lifted. "*If* I called you?"

"I'm not saying you lied or anything."

"You sure about that?"

"Of course I'm sure." I made a sound of frustration. "It's just that I forgot my purse."

Jake removed his jacket and tossed it onto a side chair. "I know."

"Really? How?" I paused as I noticed something new. "Wait a minute..." I gave Jake a good, long look. He was wearing different clothes. At the convention center, he'd been wearing dress slacks and one of his designer shirts. Now, he was wearing jeans and a plain T-shirt.

The shirt wasn't what surprised me. By now, I was used to that. Jake carried spares with him wherever he went, mostly because his shirts had a funny way of getting torn, bloodied, or otherwise destroyed as he fought his way from one crazy scene to another.

But normally, his pants stayed on. I looked down at his jeans. "You changed your pants."

"Yeah. So?"

"So why?" I asked. "What happened?"

He gave a casual shrug. "The usual."

Except it wasn't usual. That was my whole point. "Did they get dirty or something? And since when do you carry around spare pants?"

"I don't," he said. "I had some in the office."

His office was right here in this building, one floor down. "So you've been here? In the building? For how long?"

Part of me realized that I was giving him the third-degree. But I really wanted to know. In fact, I *deserved* to know. I'd been going crazy with concern.

If he hadn't paid some stranger to drag me off, I could've seen for myself hours ago that Jake was perfectly okay. Who knows? Maybe in some small way, I could've helped.

Hey, it could happen.

When Jake said nothing, I pushed the issue. "Seriously, how long have you been back?"

"Not long."

"What does *that* mean?" I asked. "Minutes? Or hours?"

"Why?" He flashed me a sudden grin. "Were you worried?"

In spite of everything, I almost smiled back. "I might've been a little worried," I admitted.

I hadn't been terribly concerned during the first hour or so. But afterward, when I still hadn't heard from him, I'd been imagining all kinds of disturbing scenarios – everything from Jake getting dragged off to jail, to him getting seriously hurt in all that commotion.

In front of me, Jake said, "Don't."

"Don't what?"

"Don't think about it." He spread his arms and said, "Look. I'm fine."

He *was* fine, probably too fine for his own good, and definitely too fine for mine. But there was something he wasn't telling me. I just knew it. I don't know how I knew, but I did.

Trying to figure it out, I said, "Did you know that was going to happen? The riot, I mean?"

He gave a small laugh. "A riot, huh?"

"Well, it was."

Jake crossed his arms and leaned sideways against the entryway wall. For the briefest moment, I felt almost silly for worrying in the first place. He was tall and broad-shouldered, with muscle-bound arms and a chiseled chest. He oozed a maddening level of confidence, and from what I'd seen firsthand, none of that confidence was unjustified.

He was fast. He was tough. He never backed down, no matter how crazy things got. And by some weird miracle, he always came out mostly unscathed.

Either he was the luckiest guy on the planet, or he was living some sort of charmed life.

But that couldn't go on forever. Could it?

When he said nothing, I persisted. "So did you? Know that was going to happen, I mean?"

Why was I even asking?

Of course, Jake knew.

That's why he'd brought Trey along to record it. And that's why he'd hired some guy to drag me away if things got too crazy. And that's why right now, somewhere on the internet, his rabid fans were probably already devouring his latest video.

But in front of me, Jake gave a slow shake of his head. "That's what you think? That I *knew* a 'riot' was gonna break out? And I *still* brought you?"

"So you're admitting it was a riot?"

He gave me a look. "You ever see a real riot?"

"No," I admitted.

"If you did, you wouldn't be asking."

"You're changing the subject," I said. "Did you know?"

"Let me get this straight." He pushed away from the wall and said, "You think if I *knew* that was gonna happen, I'd have brought you within one mile of that place?"

I saw his point. I'd been with Jake for a few weeks. During that time, I'd learned a few things. For one, he was scarily overprotective. For another, he was stubborn as hell.

I lifted my chin. Well, so was I. And I wasn't going to let this drop so easily. "Then why *did* you bring me?" I asked.

"Is that a complaint?"

"No. I'm just wondering, that's all."

"I brought you because you said you wanted to see him."

"Who? Dorian?" At the mention of his name, I felt the first twinge of guilt. I wasn't a fan or anything. But I had been curious. After all, it wasn't every day that a movie star made their way to a place like Detroit.

Jake's gaze probed mine. "You remember what you said?"

Not wanting to answer, I gave a small shrug.

In front of me, Jake waited.

"Oh, alright," I muttered. "I said that if you didn't bring me, I'd show up anyway." I tried to laugh. "But it was just a joke." I glanced away. "Mostly."

"Right." Jake prowled toward me and said, "So you were joking, huh?"

I felt myself swallow. He looked so good, so dangerous, and so damned tempting that I almost forgot why I'd been frustrated in the first place.

Looking at him now, moving toward me in that slow, deliberate way of his, I felt my stomach flutter and my breath catch.

In front of me now, he leaned over me and asked, "You still wanna fight?"

No. Mostly, I wanted to rip off his clothes and show him how very, *very* happy I was that he'd made it out of there alive.

I felt the corners of my mouth give a traitorous lift. "I wasn't fighting."

He moved only slightly closer. Deliberately, he reached out and wound a strand of my hair around his index finger. He lowered his head until our lips were almost touching. "Uh-huh."

My lips parted, and my knees grew weak. I wanted him to kiss me. I wanted to know for sure that he was real. I wanted to prove to myself that he was okay. And yeah, I wanted a few other things, naked things that I'd be embarrassed to tell my mother.

Wait. Scratch that. My mother was a unique case. Nothing embarrassed *her.* Unfortunately.

Shaking off the distraction, I lifted my face a fraction closer, waiting for Jake's lips to close the distance.

But he made no move, and the moment stretched out. The air around us became charged with sin and sex and the hint of danger. When he spoke, his voice was low and seductive. "Tell me. You want a nice, safe guy?"

Again, I felt myself swallow. My voice, when I found it, came out more than a little breathless. "What?"

"Admit it. You love it."

If I were coy, I'd ask him what he meant. But I knew exactly what he was getting at. He knew me, maybe better than I knew myself. If given the choice between Jake or a nice, safe guy with a nice, safe life, I'd choose Jake a million times over.

I couldn't help but smile. "Oh, shut up."

His lips were maddeningly close now. "So let me ask you again. You still wanna fight?"

It was long past midnight, and I had to work in the morning. I still hadn't eaten *or* gotten any of the answers I'd been hoping for. But suddenly, none of that mattered.

I didn't want to fight. I wanted Jake.

And like the bastard he was, he damn well knew it.

I gazed up at him. "What if I want to fight after?"

He gave me a slow, sexy smile. "After what?"

Five minutes later, I was showing him what – first on the nearby sofa, and later in the king-size bed. As for Jake, he showed me plenty of things in return, wonderful things that made me forget everything – the strain of waiting for him, the doubts I had about his long-term safety, and the fact that my life wasn't exactly going the way I planned.

A couple hours later, just before I drifted off to sleep, I felt happy and sated in spite of everything.

Probably, I should've made the most of it, because the next day brought plenty of reasons to *not* smile – and too many of those reasons involved the guy cradling me in his arms.

CHAPTER 5

I glanced down at the drink order. "What's this?"

Melanie shrugged. "Don't ask me. Never heard of it. But hey, you're the bartender, right?"

It was true. I *was* the bartender. Today, this wasn't exactly a good thing. The restaurant's computer system was down, which meant the serving staff was writing all of their drink-orders by hand. Some of them were doing a pretty good job of it. Others, not so much.

I looked down at the scribbled slip of paper. Unless it was written in another language, it wasn't exactly legible. I looked up. "But I can't even read it."

Melanie gave the paper an annoyed look. "What? You want me write it bigger?"

"Not *bigger*," I told her. "Just *better.*"

She groaned in obvious frustration. "God, I hate this hand-writing stuff." She shook out her hand, like her wrist had grown sore and floppy. "I'm like a super-fast texter, you know? But the whole pencil-and-paper thing? It blows, seriously."

She was right. It did blow. We were at the peak of lunch hour, and the place was packed. Usually, lunch wasn't a big time for drinks, but between the computer problems and a table of rowdies on the far side of the restaurant, I was having a hard time keeping up.

I didn't bother reminding Melanie that her texting speed wasn't exactly relevant, since the steakhouse used computers, not phones, to place all of the orders. Besides, I knew what she meant. Take myself, for example. I was so used to texting that on some days, I could barely sign my own name.

"Alright, then just tell me," I said, glancing at the slip of paper. "What drink is this, exactly?"

"Not just *one* drink. Two." She pointed at a messy scribble on the paper's edge. "See?"

I studied the thing. What *I* saw was a potato. I squinted at it and cocked my head to the side. I guess it *could* be a two if I squinted hard enough. "Uh, yeah," I said. "*Two* drinks. But what kind?"

Again, she pointed at the paper. "Moon Pies. Just like it says."

"Oh." I was still looking at the slip of paper. "Yeah. I *guess* that could be an 'M.'" Suddenly, I looked up. "Wait. Did you say Moon Pies?"

Melanie nodded.

I felt my gaze narrow. That wasn't a drink. It was a sign of trouble. I stood on my tiptoes and looked around the crowded restaurant. "Alright, where are they?"

Melanie shook her head. "The drinks? You haven't made them yet."

"Not the drinks," I said. "The goobers who ordered these."

She gave me an odd look. "Goobers?"

From the other side of the bar, Rosalie called out, "Hey, you got my daiquiris?"

I didn't, in fact.

Damn it.

I'd been distracted by that stupid potato. "Sorry," I called back. "Not yet. But I'm making them now." I turned back to Melanie. "I'll have the Moon Pies in a minute, okay?"

She smiled. "Great. I can't wait to see 'em."

"Yeah." Now, I was smiling too, but in a totally different way. "Me neither."

Five minutes later, Melanie was staring down at the two tall glasses. "Wow." She frowned. "Those are so *not* what I expected."

I choked back a malicious giggle. "Yeah. I know. But trust me. They'll love 'em."

But Melanie was shaking her head. "Honestly? I don't think so.

Sorry, but they look all..." She gave a little flutter of her hand. "Um, wrong, I guess."

I looked down at the so-called drinks. They did look wrong, but that was the whole point. Melanie might not understand, but she would after delivering them. And we'd all have a good laugh about it afterwards.

Or, at least that's what I thought. Unfortunately, it didn't play out that way, not even close. They didn't love them, and in the end, no one was laughing – not me, not Melanie, not the customers, and most certainly not my boss. ☐

CHAPTER 6

With a groan, I flopped back onto the camper's lower bunk and shared the unhappy news with my brothers. "I think I was fired today."

"You *think*?" Anthony said. "Like what? You're not sure?"

"Long story," I said. "But the way it's looking now, I'll probably be needing a new job."

Sitting across from Anthony, Steve gave a bark of laughter. "Again?"

"Oh, shut up," I said. "It doesn't happen *that* often."

Now, Anthony was laughing, too. "Sorry, but, actually it does."

I reached out and hugged the nearest pillow to my chest. It had no pillow case and smelled vaguely of stale pizza and even staler beer. Probably, I should've cared. But I couldn't. Not today.

I closed my eyes and sighed. "Yeah. I know."

After the scene at the restaurant, I'd been too embarrassed to head back to Jake's place. So instead, I'd barged in on my two brothers, who were in town for another huge construction project. Luckily, I'd caught them at lunch, eating pepperoni pizza at the small booth inside the camper.

Technically, the camper was a job-trailer, except it wasn't anything like the other job-trailers I'd seen over the years. Most looked like rectangular metal offices on wheels. But this one? It was a vintage, bubble-shaped camper that might've slept four sometime in the 1950s.

This month, it was sleeping zero. My brothers' latest construction job had come with a rare perk – free rooms at a huge, full-service hotel, located just a few blocks away.

In fact, it was the same hotel that was attached to the steakhouse where I'd been bartending for the last couple of weeks. I might've called the arrangement a lucky coincidence, except for the fact that my brothers were the ones who, earlier in the month, had told me the place was hiring – and now, firing, the way things looked.

At the table, Anthony was saying, "Look on the bright side. You won't need to dress like a cowgirl no more."

I lifted my head to look down at my work uniform – a thin, frilly white blouse and Daisy Duke shorts that were a tad *too* short.

On this, Anthony had a point. The way it looked, I wasn't a regular cowgirl. I was a slutty cowgirl with a poor fashion sense.

The uniforms were brand new and universally hated – well, by everyone except for the male customers. In fact, the uniforms were *so* hated that Rosalie had started a petition to get rid of them.

I let my head flop back onto the mattress. I hadn't even signed the petition, mostly because I hadn't wanted to get fired, not so soon, anyway.

So much for *that* plan.

At the table, Steve was saying, "Hey, I like the uniforms." He paused. "Well, except for when *she* wears them. I mean, you can see too much of your sister, you know?"

"No kidding," Anthony said. "If I want a trashy cowgirl, I'll buy a farm, get my own."

From the bunk, I was tempted to point out the obvious. Farms didn't have cowgirls. Hell, most of them didn't even have cows anymore. Did they?

Why was I even thinking of this?

With another sigh, I pushed myself up and looked around, taking in the discarded pizza boxes, crushed soda cans, and empty bottles of beer. "You guys really are slobs. You know that, right?"

Steve gave the mess a quick once-over. "You wanna clean it? Be my guest."

"Yeah," Anthony said. "We're busy."

I gave them a dubious look. They looked the same as always, like two lean, twenty-something guys who could probably change a spark plug, but wouldn't be caught dead at the opera.

Steve resembled our mom, with blond hair and blue eyes, while Anthony looked more like our dad, with olive-skin and dark hair. Right now, neither one of them looked remotely busy.

In fact, it suddenly hit me that it was nearly two o'clock in the afternoon. It wasn't exactly lunchtime anymore.

The trailer had a few tiny windows, covered in faded blue checkered curtains. I stood and shoved aside the nearest curtain. Outside the trailer, a dump truck rumbled past, while behind it, dozens of men in hard hats worked diligently under the hot, summer sun. Everywhere I looked, the site was buzzing with activity.

But my brothers? Not so much.

I turned toward them and asked, "Why aren't you working?"

"We *are* working," Steve said.

"Yeah," Anthony said. "We're waiting on an inspection." He leaned back in the booth and gave a long, leisurely stretch. "If we're lucky, the guy won't show 'til tomorrow."

Tomorrow. At the thought, I wanted to dive back onto that bottom bunk and burrow deep under the covers. I gave it a wistful look and felt my enthusiasm fade. The covers looked lumpy, and I couldn't help but wonder, what would I find if I burrowed deep enough?

I shuddered to think.

Steve's voice cut into my thoughts. "So what'd you get fired for this time?"

I turned to look at him. "Technically, I'm not *sure* I'm fired. I mean, they're gonna think about it and let me know." I winced. "But to be honest, it's not looking so good."

"What happened?" Anthony asked.

"Well, that's the thing." I gave them a no-nonsense look. "In a way, it's kind of your fault."

Steve and Anthony exchanged a glance. It was Anthony who asked, "Mine? Or Steve's?"

"Both of you," I said.

Steve reached for a new slice of pizza and took a huge bite. With a full mouth, he said, "Nah. It was Anthony's."

I made a sound of frustration. "You don't even know what I'm talking about."

"Don't matter," Steve said. "Because I didn't do it."

"Hey!" Anthony said. "I didn't do it neither."

Watching them eat reminded me of something. I'd skipped breakfast and, come to think of it, lunch, too. I edged closer to the table and looked down at the pizza. There were three slices left. One for each of us?

"Is that a new pizza?" I asked. "Or an old pizza?"

Anthony made a waffling gesture with his hand. "Eh. Depends."

"On what?" I asked.

He grabbed one of the remaining slices and said, "On what you consider old."

I gave the final two slices a closer look. They didn't look *that* old. "So it's from today?"

Anthony gave it some thought. "If you count early this morning as today, then yeah."

"*How* early this morning?" I asked.

"One-thirty."

"You mean from last night?" My shoulders sagged. That meant the pizza was over twelve hours old. I didn't bother asking if they'd refrigerated it. I knew my brothers. They weren't big into food-safety, and besides, the camper's fridge was a beer-only zone.

Steve grabbed the second-to-last piece, leaving just the one. It sat there, looking surprisingly tempting in spite of its advanced age. I drew back. No. The last thing I needed was botulism, or whatever you got from eating old food.

Steve looked to Anthony and said, "Ten bucks she eats it."

I gave him a look. "Save your money. I'm not gonna eat it. It's probably spoiled by now."

"Dude," Steve said, "pizza *never* spoils."

"Yeah?" I said. "Well, I have a night in college that says otherwise." Thinking of that awful, toilet-hugging adventure, my stomach churned. That night, it might've been the pizza. Or it might've been the vodka shooters. Either way, I wasn't taking any chances.

At the table, Anthony was grinning again. "Wuss."

Maybe I was. But I'd rather be a wuss than a human barfing machine.

Steve reached into a side cooler and grabbed a Pepsi. Popping open the can, he said, "So what happened at work? You gonna tell us or what?"

Just thinking about it made me tired, too tired to keeping standing there, anyway. I looked to Anthony and said, "Hey, scooch over, will ya?"

When Anthony slid deeper into the small booth, I squeezed in beside him and paused, wondering where to begin. Across from me, Steve nudged the pizza box a couple of inches forward.

I gave the final slice a quick glance. "Nice try, ass-wipe." I pushed the box away and started talking. "So you know how you've been coming in for lunch lately?"

"At the steak house?" Steve said. "Yeah. Why?"

"Well, I thought it was you guys."

Anthony gave me a confused look. "You thought *who* was us?"

"Lemme start from the beginning," I said. "So I'm working there today, and I get this drink order for a couple of Moon Pies."

Anthony was grinning now. "No shit? Is that really a thing?"

"Apparently," I said. "Not that I knew that at the time."

"Yeah?" Anthony said. "So, what's in it?"

I gave a dismissive wave of my hand. "Kahlua, Bailey's, something else – I forget. That's not important. But the thing is, when I get this drink-order, I think it's you guys, ordering something stupid again."

Across from me, Steve chuckled. "Us? Nah."

"Yeah, right." I gave him a long look. "Ass-blasters? Fuzzy berries? Stink eyes? Any of this ringing a bell?"

Now, both of my brothers were laughing.

I wasn't.

For the last couple of weeks, they'd been coming into the steakhouse, ordering outrageous drinks just to get a rise out of me. Usually, I spotted Steve and Anthony in the dining room and did the same thing I always did, poured a couple of beers on draft and called it good.

Today, I *hadn't* seen them. But I'd *known* it was them. I mean, the order was for Moon Pies, the exact same thing that Steve had been calling me for years.

At the table, they were still laughing.

The dipshits.

I made a sound of frustration. "And stop laughing. It's not funny."

To my infinite surprise, Steve actually listened. He put on a serious face and said, "You're right."

Just when I'd decided to *not* beat him over the head with that last slice of pizza, he grinned. "It's freaking hilarious."

"It is not," I told him. "Do I need to remind you? I'm probably fired."

Steve made a scoffing sound. "For what? Serving the wrong drinks? If they're gonna be like that, screw 'em. Who needs a job like that?"

I did. That's who.

But that wasn't the point. I tried to explain. "It wasn't *just* that I served the wrong drinks. It was that I served drinks that were really, *really* wrong."

"How wrong?" Anthony asked.

I let out a long breath. "You don't wanna know."

Steve leaned forward. "You didn't shit in them or anything? Did you?"

Through clenched teeth, I said, "No. I didn't 'shit' in them. God, what kind of person do you think I am?"

"Hey," Steve said, "Chill. I was just askin'."

Anthony spoke up. "So what *did* you do?" He gave another bark of laughter. "Pee in them?"

"Oh shut up," I said. "I just mushed up a couple snacks from the vending machine, stuffed them into a couple of glasses, and topped them off with seltzer-water."

"What kind of snack?" Anthony asked, his eyes brightening. "Like a *real* Moon Pies?"

Moon Pies were a type of snack cake, made with graham cracker cookies and marshmallow filling. According to my sister who'd been living in Alabama, you could find Moon Pies in practically every vending machine down South.

But here in Michigan, they weren't exactly a common thing. Today, I'd been willing to improvise. As it turned out, that wasn't exactly a good thing.

"No," I said. "I used this other snack cake thingy. It might've been a Ding Dong, but I'm not sure"

Steve snorted. "And you got fired for *that*? Damn, your boss sounds like a real hard-ass."

"Actually, he's not," I said. "It wasn't just the drinks. It was the other stuff."

Anthony gave me a puzzled look. "What other stuff?"

Where to begin? I let out another long sigh. "Well, because I thought it was you guys, I didn't 'act professional' when the customers complained."

"Oh yeah?" Steve said, leaning forward again. "What'd you do?"

Just thinking of it, I sank lower in my seat. "I wrote this stupid 'note' and asked the waitress to deliver it. Told her it was an apology and promised her that the customers would totally love it."

Next to me, Anthony asked, "Did they?"

Reluctantly, I reached into my pocket and pulled out the so-called apology. It was crumpled and sticky from spilled beer and whatever else had been slopped across on the bar at the time. I flung the wadded paper at Steve and watched as he smoothed it out and took a look.

A second later, he burst out laughing.

As for me, I wanted to cry. "Well, I'm glad someone's amused," I said, "because the customers sure as heck weren't."

CHAPTER 7

Steve was still looking at the wrinkled slip paper. And, he was still laughing. "This was supposed to be for us?"

"Yeah," I said. "As a joke. And obviously, you think it's funny, so…" I didn't bother finishing the sentence. Just because my brothers would've found it amusing, it didn't mean that a nice, dignified couple would've been nearly as entertained.

Steve tossed the crumpled paper to Anthony, who picked it up and looked. Now, he was laughing, too. "No way," he said. "You sent this to a customer?"

"Not just one customer," I said. "*Two* customers. Unfortunately."

Anthony set the paper, face-up, on the table, next to the open pizza box. It wasn't really a note so much as a doodle. Some might call it a cartoon. I called it sheer stupidity. Bare-butted stupidity, to be exact.

Anthony pointed down at the drawing. "So, whose butts are those supposed to be? Ours?"

"I guess," I said. "Honestly, I didn't give it a whole lot of thought. I was just playing off the whole 'moon' thing, you know?"

Steve gave a slow nod. "Oh, I know. And I totally approve."

"You would," I muttered.

"So how'd they take it?" Anthony asked.

"The customers?" I winced. "Not so good."

"So they complained, huh?"

"They did more than complain." I hesitated. "Well, actually, the guy was a pretty good sport about it, but his date – a *first* date, by the way – threw a giant hissy-fit."

I reached up to rub the back of my neck. It felt all stiff and funny, like I'd slept on it wrong. "I apologized like crazy and tried to explain, but..." I shrugged. "Well, anyway, the lady wasn't really listening at that point. And my manager? He's actually a pretty cool guy, but the drawing? Well, let's just say, he didn't find it nearly as funny as you guys did."

Steve grinned over at Anthony. "Next time we're in there," he said, "let's order a Cock and Balls, see if ol' Moon Pie can draw *that*."

"Oh shut up," I said. "I'm not drawing anything. And besides, I probably won't even be there." At the thought of finding a new job, I wanted to cry. I'd been at *that* job for only a couple of weeks. I was just starting to settle in.

"Aw c'mon," Steve said. "Lighten up. If you lose the job, so what? It's not like you need the money."

"I do, too," I said. "Why wouldn't I need it?"

"Because Jake's loaded," Steve said. "And you live with him. What do you need money for?"

In a way, Steve had a point. Jake *was* loaded, and like clockwork, the money kept flowing in, buckets of it, even while he slept.

And with every video he put out, the bigger those buckets got – more money, more fans – I sighed. More drama. More girls chasing him. More reasons to wonder why, exactly, he'd settle down with one girl, me specifically.

But the way it sounded, that's what he wanted.

Supposedly.

I mean, it's not like he'd made it official or anything. And for the tenth time today, I couldn't help but wonder, why was that? Why would he hint at something more permanent, but then do nothing about it?

Damn it. I needed to stop thinking like that. We'd been together less than two months. I was putting the cart way ahead of the horse, as my grandma might've said.

Steve's voice interrupted my thoughts. "If you want a job so bad, you should work for Jake."

That was another sore subject. For weeks, Jake had been suggesting the exact same thing. And for weeks, I'd been resisting. Lately, he'd been pushing harder. And for whatever reason, I'd been pushing back just as hard.

It wasn't that I didn't want to work for him. It was just more complicated than the way Steve made it sound.

"I can't work for him," I explained. "What happens if we break up?"

At the thought, something in my heart twisted. Forget the job. A life without Jake? It pained me just to think about it. But it would pain me even more if I was without Jake *and* out on my ass with no way of supporting myself.

"What do you mean?" Anthony said. "You think he'd fire you?"

"I don't know," I said. "But either way, I'd have to leave."

I'd seen this dynamic play out before. The job he'd been offering me had to do with my degree in Hospitality Management. He wanted me to handle the same stuff that Bianca, his previous event planner, used to handle.

There was only one problem. I'd seen firsthand how that arrangement had worked out for Bianca. Technically, Jake had been her client, not her employer. But in the big scheme of things, that distinction hadn't really mattered.

Things between them had gotten friendly – too friendly, the way it sounded. And then, when their relationship – if you could call it that – had ended, she'd gone more than a little crazy.

I didn't know what she was doing now. But if I knew Bianca, she was dying to get her old position back. And who knows? If I kept turning Jake down, maybe she'd even get it.

The whole thing was giving me a headache. Or maybe it was just a hunger headache. I glanced at the pizza box. That last slice of pizza was still there, looking surprisingly delicious all things considered.

Steve gave the box another nudge in my direction.

I gave him an irritated look. "Stop that."

He grinned. "Stop what?"

"You *know* what. Besides," I lied, "I'm not even hungry."

Steve looked to Anthony. "So, you want the bet or not?" He pulled out his wallet, dug out a ten-dollar bill, and slapped it onto the table. "I still say she eats it."

Anthony turned to give me a long, speculative look. "I dunno, she looks kinda tempted."

Suddenly, I felt like an animal in a zoo – at feeding time, no less. "Look," I said, "I'll save you both some trouble. I'm not eating that thing. Bet on something else, okay?"

Ignoring me, Anthony reached for his own wallet and pulled out a ten of his own. He tossed it onto the table and told Steve, "You're on."

Smiling like he'd just won the lottery, Steve said, "Sucker."

I didn't know whether to laugh or cry. I'd come here for a distraction. And yeah, they were providing it and all, but somehow, I'd envisioned something a little more comforting.

Like pie. Pie would be good.

My happy thoughts of pie were interrupted by Steve saying, "So, tell us. How mad *were* you last night?"

I gave a little shake of my head. "Huh?"

"We saw Jake's new video," he said. "That was some crazy shit."

"You mean at the convention center?" I said. "Yeah, no kidding." I still hadn't seen the video, but if I knew Jake, it *would* be crazy, because they were all crazy – sometimes violent, sometimes funny as hell, always entertaining, assuming you weren't the squeamish type.

Anthony's voice interrupted my thoughts. "So, who was the girl? You know her?"

I felt my eyebrows furrow. "What girl?"

"The one in the video."

I stared blankly at him. I had no idea what he was talking about. "There was a girl?"

Anthony glanced toward Steve, but said nothing.

"What's going on?" I said.

Anthony turned back to me and said, "You haven't seen it?"

I gave him an exasperated look. "Seen what?"

With obvious reluctance, Anthony reached up into an overhead bin. He pulled his small, tablet computer and fired it up. I braced myself, wondering if it was something I'd even want to see.

Five minutes later, I had my answer. And that answer was a definite no.

CHAPTER 8

The first part of the video was pretty much what I'd expected. I saw footage of Dorian, sliding around on the floor before getting up and plowing into Jake, who knocked Dorian on his ass with surprisingly little effort.

A moment later, Ronnie entered the frame, taking a flying leap that missed Jake by at least two feet. Ronnie slid, face-first, across the table, exactly where I'd been sitting, just before that stranger had hustled me out of there.

The camera shook wildly as the angle suddenly changed. It was easy to guess why. When I'd left that place, Trey, holding his video recorder, had been standing on our table. The way it looked now, he'd just jumped off. But why? To avoid Ronnie?

I kept on watching.

No. It was to zoom in on Jake, who was bobbing and weaving as Dorian took wild swings that never quite connected.

Around them, the place was pure chaos, with half of the people running for the exits while the other half added to the mayhem, by either fighting amongst themselves or cheering on those who were.

The camera did a quick pan of the crowd, and I tried to make sense of it all. In all the commotion, I could hardly tell who was fighting who. But then, I realized something. Mostly, it was the security guys – meaning those who had arrived with Dorian.

I watched as a huge guy in a leisure suit sucker-punched a tall, clean-cut guy who looked around twenty years old. A college athlete? Probably.

Watching this now, I was wishing that I'd paid more attention to the news this morning, or heck, even late last night. With as bad as this looked, there was no way this hadn't morphed into a major news story by now.

I mean, how often did a basic awards ceremony turn into a full-blown riot?

When the camera panned back to Jake, he was squaring off against Dorian, who'd stumbled to his feet yet again.

I focused all my attention on Jake. He was facing away from the camera, so I could only see his back. When I'd left the convention center, he'd been wearing dark slacks and a matching jacket, along with a dark dress shirt – no tie. Now, the jacket was gone, whether flung onto the floor or lying somewhere in shreds.

But even without the clothes, and even from this angle, I'd have recognized Jake anywhere – with that thick, dark hair, those broad shoulders, and something predatory about the way he moved.

Watching, I felt that familiar mix of excitement and shame – excitement because even when Jake horrified me, he thrilled me in ways that just weren't normal – and, shame, because I *knew* that those butterflies in my stomach would soon flutter downward, making me want to rip off the rest of his clothes and remind him that his amazing body wasn't only fit for fighting.

At the thought, my pulse quickened, and I bit my lip. If I left now, I could make it to Jake's place in a half-hour. He might even be home. And if he wasn't, he was probably at his office, located just one floor down. Technically, he was the boss. He could take a break any time, right?

Suddenly, the screen in front of me froze, jolting me out of my X-rated thoughts. I looked to Anthony and asked, "What happened?"

He gave me an annoyed look. "I paused it."

"Yeah. But why?"

"Because you were looking all—" Anthony shook his head. "—I dunno, stoned or something." He studied my face. "Are you?"

"No." Talk about insulting. "I was thinking of Jake."

Across from me, Steve made a sound of disgust. "That's even worse." He practically shuddered. "We don't wanna see that."

I rolled my eyes. "There's nothing to see. Jeez."

It was true. It wasn't like I was going to start masturbating or anything.

On instinct, I glanced toward the nearby bunk and couldn't help but wonder something. If my brothers weren't here, *would* I be getting hot and heavy with thoughts of Jake?

No. Definitely not. If shame didn't stop me, the smell of old beer would definitely do the trick.

Of course, I *could* plug my nose…

Damn it. I *was* stoned. And my drug was Jake. I couldn't help it. The effect he had on me, well, it just wasn't natural.

Across from me, Steve's tone grew sarcastic. "You wanna sext him? We'll wait."

My face grew warm. Sexting wasn't the thing I wanted. What I wanted was the real deal, not that Steve needed to know that. "Oh shut up." I turned back to Anthony and said, "Go on. Hit play, will ya?"

Looking less than enthused, Anthony reached out and tapped the small screen. Once again, the image sprang to life.

As I watched, Dorian swung again, missed Jake by a mile, and slipped onto the floor. It belatedly dawned on me that Dorian must be drunk off his ass. He *had* to be, because there was no way on Earth he'd be having such a hard time staying upright if he weren't.

And where was Ronnie in all this? Unless he'd slid off the other side of the table, it seemed surprising that he hadn't jumped back in. I was still wondering when a new person stumbled into the frame.

It was Nipple Girl – the blonde who'd been sitting at Dorian's table. She lunged forward, but not toward Dorian – I tensed – toward Jake.

What the hell? Was she planning to fight him?

A split-second later, I had my answer.

Obviously, it wasn't a fight she was looking for. It was something else. And the way it looked, it was the same thing that *I'd* been fantasizing about just a few seconds earlier.

Watching her on the small screen, I felt myself frown. Her eyes were glazed, and her smile was sloppy. She staggered into Jake and wrapped her arms loosely around his neck. She shimmied against him, and her silver halter dress slipped to the side.

And there it was – the nipple – except I couldn't technically see it, thanks to some sort of digital blurring effect. But no amount of blurring could hide the fact that it was out there on the loose, surrounded by more bouncing flesh than her sparkling dress could reasonably be expected to contain.

Somewhere behind the camera, Trey *had* to be drooling all over himself.

But what about Jake? With my heart racing, I leaned closer to the screen and studied his face. He wasn't drooling. But he wasn't exactly fighting her off either. When she shimmied again, he turned and grinned straight into the camera, looking like he was having the time of his life.

What the hell?

A few feet behind Jake, Dorian was struggling again to push himself up. When he spotted Jake with the blonde, his nostrils flared, and his eyes narrowed. He lunged forward, as if looking to score a tackle.

Jake – with the girl still latched onto him like a monkey on a tree – twisted sideways just in time. The sudden twist made the girl's legs fly upward, giving me the briefest glimpse of skimpy red panties. She gave a squeal, followed by a giggle that abruptly ended when Dorian plowed into them, sending all three of them tumbling to the floor.

The camera panned down, and I saw a tangle of arms, legs, and blonde hair, thrashing amidst the saucy remnants of yup, *my* Chicken Florentine.

Damn it.

My jaw clenched. Forget the chicken. *My* Jake. And my temper – it was rising with every second.

On the small screen, Jake rolled to the side, taking the girl with him. A few feet away, Dorian wallowed in the same spot, looking like a giant fish, flopping around in too little water, until his forehead flopped suddenly to the floor, and he stopped moving entirely.

I sucked in a breath. Was he dead? No. He couldn't be dead. If he had died, I definitely would've heard about it. Hell, it would've been national news.

I shifted my focus back to Jake. On the floor, she was on top of him now. They were pelvis-to-pelvis, face-to-face – my gaze narrowed– nipple to shirt.

Okay, so I couldn't *see* the nipple, but I knew it was out there, causing all kinds of trouble. I frowned. For all I knew there were *two* nipples on the loose.

I stared down at the screen. Was Jake planning to just lie there? Holding some other girl, while Trey – the jackass that he was – filmed the whole thing?

No. Apparently, he wasn't. As I watched, Jake freed himself from the girl's embrace. Flashing another grin at the camera, he got to his feet and extended a hand to help her up.

But the girl didn't take it. Instead, she lunged forward and grabbed sloppily at his knees. Clutching at his pants, she started to claw her way up, stopping only when her face reached crotch level.

I felt the color drain from my face. What the hell was she doing?

Her lips were dangerously close to his groin. No. Scratch that. They were right there, *on* his groin. I felt my teeth clench, and my fists grow tight. Either that chick was using Jake's crotch as a napkin, or she'd forgotten that it wasn't quite possible to give a guy oral through his pants.

And what about Jake? Why wasn't he stopping her?

But the way it looked, he wasn't even *watching* her. Sometime in the last couple of seconds, he'd turned his head away from the camera, as if eyeballing something in the distance. But what?

And why, for God's sake, wasn't he doing something about the girl? Like for starters, detaching her face from his crotch.

A split-second later, I had my answer. From the direction Jake had been looking, Ronnie North barreled into camera-range. He plowed into Jake, sending the girl tumbling off to the side.

The camera gave a little jump, and it was easy to see why. The girl's boobs had exploded out of the dress in a jiggly mass of bouncing pandemonium. Most of the nakedness was digitally blurred, but no amount of editing could hide the truth. A mostly topless girl was flopping around within arm's reach of *my* guy.

The only good news – if you could call it that – was that Jake was focused on Ronnie, who suddenly struck out with a right hook. Jake turned, and the fist glanced off his jaw and kept on going, sending Ronnie stumbling forward until he tripped over the semi-topless girl and fell face-first onto the tile floor.

And that was it. He didn't move.

I squinted at the screen. Was I seeing things right? Dorian and Ronnie had been defeated not by Jake, but by the tile floor and their own drunken clumsiness?

Well, that was a first.

The camera zoomed in on Ronnie's face. His eyes were open, but vaguely unfocused. He blinked a couple of times before lifting his head to look around. When his gaze met the camera, his eyes widened. He lifted his head higher and slurred out, "Hey, asshole! No pictures!"

And then, his eyes slammed shut, just before his face hit the floor. The camera lingered on him for a long moment and then panned back to Jake.

Watching, I heard myself gasp. He was striding toward the exit with Nipple Girl in his arms. She was cradled tight against his chest, smiling as he carried her away from all the commotion.

And then, they were gone.

I heard myself say, "You've *got* to be kidding me."

The way I saw it, Jake had some explaining to do. Some *major* explaining.

CHAPTER 9

Trey was grinning. "Five million."

He looked absolutely thrilled. I wasn't. Still, trying to be civil, I made myself ask, "Five million what?"

"Views," he said. "On the video we shot last night."

My jaw felt almost too tight to speak. "Shot, huh?"

That word – not to mention related words, like stabbed, mangled, or throttled – well, those were dangerous concepts, considering my mood.

Screw the niceties. My mood wouldn't get any better by making small-talk with Mister Film-a-Nipple. "Where's Jake?" I asked.

Almost immediately after watching that video, I'd left my brothers in the job-trailer and high-tailed it straight back to Jake's penthouse. Unfortunately, he hadn't been there, so here I was, one floor down, looking for him at his office.

I glanced around, but saw no sign of him, or of anyone else, other than Trey. And it wasn't like there were a lot of places to hide.

Jake's office was different than the standard business setup. Instead of rows of cubicles and desks, it was mostly windows and wide open spaces, with marble floors and upscale furniture arranged in stylish clusters.

At the far end of the space was a small graphics studio, a few work stations, and then, Jake's personal office, surrounded by glass walls that hid almost nothing. I could see why he'd gone that route. Normal walls would've blocked his personal view of the urban cityscape, including the

Detroit River, which looked surprisingly nice from this vantage point.

Unfortunately, I was in no mood to appreciate it.

In front of me, Trey gave a dramatic groan. "Aw, c'mon, don't you think that's a lot?"

I was too distracted to think. "A lot of what?"

"Views. I mean, I knew when I shot it that we had something special, but..." He chuckled. "Man, that whole scene was a major goldmine, you know?" He leaned forward, and his eyes brightened. "Did you see the nipple?"

Oh, yeah.

I'd seen the nipple, alright. Multiple times. And I'd seen the girl it belonged to. I bit my lip. Worse, I'd seen Jake carry her away to who-knows-where.

Now, I was having a hard time ignoring the fact that last night, Jake had been missing for a couple of hours, right after carrying her away. It also hadn't escaped my attention that for some unknown reason, he'd changed his pants before returning home.

And when I'd mentioned it last night, what had Jake done? He'd distracted me with sexiness. Was I *that* easy?

Who was I kidding?

Of course, I was, well, when it came to Jake, anyway.

A couple of feet away, Trey was still talking. "Bummer I had to blur it out, but I still think people got the idea, right?"

My stomach clenched. "Oh, they got it, alright."

Trey hesitated. "You feeling okay?" He leaned closer to study my face. "You look kind of like you're gonna throw up."

I *did* feel like throwing up, mostly because of that video. I paused. Of course, that slice of pizza hadn't helped.

Yes, I *had* eaten the stupid thing, but mostly because I'd been so distracted that I'd munched it down without hardly noticing, well, not until Steve, laughing his ass off, had lunged for the bet money, telling Anthony. "Told you she'd eat it."

As for Anthony, he'd been less than thrilled, acting like I'd done it on purpose, just to deprive him of ten lousy dollars, no less.

But it wasn't my fault. It was the video. It had turned my brain to mush.

Trying to forget all that, I looked to Trey and said, "I'm fine."

He gave my face a closer look. "So, are you mad or something then?"

Of course I was mad. What normal girl wouldn't be? But I didn't feel like explaining it, not to him anyway, so all I said was, "I just need to see Jake, that's all."

"Why?" He glanced down at my work uniform, which, come to think of it, he hadn't seen before. "Are you going to a costume party or something?"

Yeah. As Sally the Slutty Cowgirl.

But out loud, I said, "No. It's my work uniform." At his blank look, I added, "You know, from the steakhouse."

Trey gave a slow, approving nod. "I like it." He grinned. "So, uh, does everyone dress like that?"

"Yeah. Unfortunately." I hesitated. "Well, not the guys. Or the cooks." I waved away the distraction. "But back to Jake, do you know where he is?"

"Shopping, I think."

"Shopping? For what?"

I couldn't help but recall something. On my first official date with Jake, he'd taken *me* shopping.

At the memory, I didn't know whether to laugh or cry. He'd been wildly extravagant and such a great sport. Also, he'd been far too generous, no matter how hard I'd protested.

At the time, I'd already been more than a little in love with him. But even if that weren't the case, what girl would be able to resist a guy like that? He had it all – looks, money, fame – and he was generous to a fault.

But for me, his appeal had nothing to do with the fame or money. Even when he'd been poor, I'd been totally crazy about him.

I let that word roll around in my head. Crazy.

I was feeling a little crazy right now, but not in a good way. I pulled out my cell phone and hit the speed-dial. For the tenth time in the last half-hour, the call went straight to Jake's voicemail.

Well, this was just great. I didn't bother leaving a message, because I didn't know what to say, or how to say it without sounding like a paranoid harpy.

Trey's voice cut into my thoughts. "Did you hear what I just said?"

I looked up. "Uh, sorry. What?"

"I said, I think he's shopping for a car."

I gave a little shake of my head. "A car? Really?" Jake had a bunch of cars already. I knew, because they took up a huge section of the basement parking garage. Why he needed another was anyone's guess.

Still, I felt some of the tension in my shoulders ease. A car – that sounded harmless enough.

What was wrong with me, anyway?

I'd never been the jealous type, but with Jake, it was sometimes hard not to be. I blew out a long, unsteady breath. It was especially hard when he carried off strange women and came home wearing different pants.

I thanked Trey for the info and turned away, heading back toward the elevator. Under my breath, I muttered, "I'm sure I'll find him eventually."

But as it turned out, eventually was a lot sooner than I anticipated, because when the elevator doors slid open, there he was, Jake, looking like he'd just gotten lucky ten times over.□

CHAPTER 10

Behind me, I heard Trey call out, "Hey Jake! We're up to five million." He paused. "Wait. Scratch that. *Six* million. Man, this thing's on fire." He laughed. "It must've been the nipple."

I whirled around. "Will you just stop already?"

Trey, who'd been heading toward us, stopped in mid-stride. Sometime in the last minute, he'd pulled out his cell phone, probably to check his video stats. He shoved the phone back into his pocket and said, "Stop what?"

Through gritted teeth, I said, "Stop talking about that stupid nipple." I threw up my hands. "We've all got 'em. What's the big deal?"

Trey's eyebrows furrowed. "Uh, is that a for-real question?"

Was it? I didn't know. What I *did* know was that I was like five seconds away from making a total fool of myself. I couldn't let that happen, because, let's face it, I'd done that plenty already, especially where Jake was concerned.

It was a habit I was trying to break, like checking my daily horoscope, which by the way, had told me that I was going to have a really crappy day today. Surprise, surprise. So far, that darn thing had been right.

I was still facing Trey. Behind me, I felt strong arms wrap themselves around my torso. Jake's arms. Those wonderful, tattooed arms of splendor. The arms that not too long ago, had held me all night long and cradled me tight against his naked chest.

I heard his voice, soft in my ear. "Baby, what's wrong?"

I didn't know what to say. I was confused and angry, but pathetically unsure if any of that anger was justified. And his embrace felt good. So good. So perfect. So exactly what I needed.

Suddenly, I couldn't help it. I turned around and sagged against him. When his arms closed tighter, I heard myself sigh. "I think I was fired today."

He chuckled. "Again?"

I pulled back to look up at him. "It's not funny."

Behind me, I heard Trey say, "Actually, it is. Kind of a bummer though, because I've got this bet with your brothers."

I turned around. "What?"

"Yeah." Trey moved closer, and was now standing within arm's reach. "If you'd kept that job like two weeks longer, I'd have won forty bucks."

I stared at him. What on Earth was he talking about? A bet? With my brothers? And what the hell? Were they betting *for* me? Or against me?

Trey once again pulled out his cell phone. He swiped a finger across its screen. When he found what he was looking for, he frowned. "Aw man, that sucks."

I gave a confused shake of my head. "What sucks?"

Trey was still frowning. "Jake's got tomorrow. Damn, what are the odds?"

I froze. What did *that* mean? My own boyfriend was betting that I'd get fired? Tomorrow? Well, that was nice.

Trey, looking past me, told Jake, "Guess you win."

I was vaguely aware that Jake's arms were still around me, holding me from behind. But suddenly, his arms didn't feel comforting. They felt like a giant, mocking prison. Was everyone laughing at me?

I yanked myself out of his embrace and turned around to face him. "What does he mean?" I asked. "You bet on me to fail?"

On top of everything else, it felt like just another kick to the teeth. I was one of four kids. All my life, I'd been the carefree one, the fun one, the one who didn't worry about tomorrow, because good times today were far more important.

But that kind of attitude had been a total disaster, especially on the job front. So, for the last few months, I'd been trying like crazy to turn over a new leaf.

Unfortunately, my timing stunk, because this happened to fall around the same time that Jake had roared back into my life.

His life was crazy, so my life was crazy. And then, there were my brothers, crazy times two. And Trey? Well, he wasn't quite crazy, but he wasn't exactly grounded either.

All of a sudden, I was feeling like the only sane person around. The sensation was oddly foreign and in truth, kind of scary.

In front of me, Jake remained silent. So I asked the question again, quieter this time. "Did you? Bet against me, I mean?"

But it was Trey who answered. "He sure did. Picked almost the exact date too." He chuckled. "Talk about lucky."

I said nothing. My gaze was still on Jake. Coming out of the elevator, he'd looked obnoxiously happy. Now, he was frowning, looking almost pissed off. At who? Me?

I squared my shoulders. If that was the case, so what? He could get mad all he wanted. I still deserved an answer.

So I waited.

When no answer came, I felt my shoulders sag. "You did, didn't you? You seriously bet on me to get fired."

His voice was quiet. "It wasn't like that."

"Oh yeah?" I said. "Then why'd you do it? Is that what you wanted? Or did you just think I was too incompetent to keep a job more than two weeks?"

Jake's gaze shifted past me, looking toward Trey. "Trey," Jake said. "You wanna head out?"

"Nah, that's okay," Trey said. "I'm good."

Jake's jaw tightened. "You sure about that?"

After a long, awkward moment, Trey cleared his throat. "Oh. Um, yeah, I've gotta check on that thing. So, uh, see you in about an hour?"

Feeling suddenly guilty for driving the poor guy off, I made myself say, "No, that's alright." I turned around and told Trey, "Don't go on my account. Jake and I can talk upstairs." I turned back to Jake and said, "Right?"

But Jake was shaking his head. He looked to Trey and said, "Let's call it a day. See you tomorrow, alright?"

I watched, confused, as Trey, with obvious reluctance, gathered his stuff and trudged toward the elevator. I couldn't help but stare. In my whole life, I'd never seen anyone so disappointed to leave work. The guy seriously needed a social life.

After the elevator carried him away, I turned to Jake and asked, "Why didn't you want to talk upstairs?"

He gave a casual shrug. "I didn't think we needed to."

Like everything else, this made no sense. Why would he choose to kick out his assistant instead of hopping on that same elevator and going up just one floor? Or hell, we could've taken the stairs. It was only one flight, after all.

I shook off the distraction. What did it matter now? Trey was gone. Jake was here. And I had some things I desperately wanted to know.

But now that we were actually alone, getting those answers seemed a tricky proposition.

I was still pondering where to begin when I heard myself blurt out, "I saw that video."

CHAPTER 11

Breathlessly, I waited, wondering what Jake would say. Around us, the office felt too big and too quiet. In the cool silence, my statement echoed off the high ceiling in a way that made me feel just a little bit foolish.

It sounded almost like an accusation, although what I was accusing him of, I still wasn't sure.

In front of me, Jake's expression was carefully neutral. "Yeah? What'd you think?"

Where to start? I thought that girl had gotten way too friendly. I thought she should've been wearing a lot more clothes. I thought there was no reason on Earth for Jake to be carrying her anywhere, especially toward an exit, where who-knows-what might happen out of camera-range.

And besides, she had two perfectly fine legs of her own. And they *were* fine. Damn it. I knew, because I'd seen them – a lot of them, considering her skimpy clothes.

Looking at Jake now, I searched for a decent answer to his question. What did I think? "Well, uh, it was pretty exciting." I searched his face for clues. "What'd *you* think?"

His voice was flat. "Five million views. That's what I think."

For some reason, the cold, numerical assessment surprised me. I heard myself mumble, "Actually I think it was *six* million."

"Even better."

I searched his face, wondering what I was missing. Jake loved what he did. Didn't he?

I recalled the Jake I'd known back in our hometown. *That* guy had been dirt-poor and a notorious hell-raiser. He was still a hell-raiser, except that now he was a million times more notorious, and he got paid buckets of money for letting the world witness the action.

But what kind of action was it, exactly?

Thinking of his latest video, a flood of unwanted images slammed into my brain – that stupid nipple, those lips on his crotch, Jake grinning for the camera, him carrying her away – I gave a hard blink – and returning home hours later, in different pants.

I gazed up at him, waiting for him to offer a better explanation. Today, he was dressed in casual clothes – jeans and a basic T-shirt. But as far as the man himself, there was nothing basic about him. His hair was thick, his jaw was square, and his muscles were so defined, they could've made a Greek god weep with envy.

I felt myself swallow. He was pure perfection. And he was all mine, supposedly.

But now, I didn't know what to do. The conversation wasn't going exactly how I'd imagined it. I made a sound of frustration. "Why didn't you tell me?"

His voice was sharper than I expected. "Tell you what?"

"About the video."

He gave me a what-the-hell look. "You think it's a secret?"

"Well, no," I stammered. "Not exactly. But it would've been nice to hear about it firsthand."

"Yeah? Why?"

"What kind of question is that?"

"I dunno."

I tried again. "Did you know that girl?"

Now, he looked almost bored. "What girl?"

"Oh come on. You know which one." My tone grew snotty. "Nipple Girl. Before last night, did you know her?"

"Nope."

I stared up at him. "Nope? Is that all you're gonna say?"

"What do you want me to say?"

Damn it. It was like talking to a brick wall. Whatever I threw at him, it just bounced off without making any impression whatsoever.

I gave him a pleading look. "Jake—"

"Why were you fired?"

I blinked up at him. "What?"

"You said you were fired. What were you fired for?"

I paused, startled by the sudden change of topic. "Technically, I'm not *completely* sure I was fired. I just *think* I was. It's all kind of complicated."

"Right."

Standing there in my stupid work uniform, the room was feeling colder with every passing second. "Gee, thanks for the sympathy."

He gave a half-hearted shrug, but said nothing. His gaze drifted downward, and I was increasingly conscious of my stupid, frilly white blouse and my high-cut shorts. No wonder I was cold. Probably, I should've grabbed a coat or something.

When Jake still said nothing, I asked, "Are you mad at me or something?"

"Nope."

Just great. Another nope. "Is that all you can say?"

A ghost of a smile softened his response. "Nope."

"Oh come on," I said. "Now you're just goading me."

Jake was good at goading people. I'd seen that for myself. From what I'd witnessed firsthand, he could make just about anyone lose it. But why me? And why now? What was I missing?

He glanced toward the elevators. "We done?"

I crossed my arms. "Nope."

This time, he offered no hint a smile. In fact, I saw no real expression at all as he gazed silently down at me, waiting for what, I had no idea.

I waited, too, and as the seconds passed, all of my frustrations – my crappy day, the uncertainty of my job, the fact that he was acting like a giant asshat – it all bubbled to the surface, and I couldn't help but say, "God, what's your problem?"

"Luna," he said in an obscenely calm voice, "you don't wanna know."

"You're wrong," I told him. "I do want to know."

"No. You don't, because it's nothing new, and I don't want to fight about it. Not today."

I made a scoffing sound. "Yeah, right."

"Meaning?"

"Meaning that you're always up for a fight. Why should today be any different?"

Over the years, I'd seen Jake in countless fights. Some I'd seen in real-life. Others, I'd seen on-line. Some of them were so brutal, I could hardly watch. But I knew one thing. Jake didn't shy away from anything, especially a good fight.

But in front of me, he remained obscenely calm. "Is that so?"

With a look of defiance, I nodded.

"You sure you don't want rethink that?"

"Oh, I'm sure."

Again, he grew silent, and I started to feel slightly uncomfortable, because I knew exactly what he was getting at. When it came to me, he wasn't exactly the fighting type.

It wasn't that he was a pushover – far from it – but he didn't like to argue any more than I did.

And I *hated* it.

"Alright, fine," I finally said, "I know you don't pick fights with me, but come on. Let's discuss this like adults, okay?"

"Sure." His voice hardened. "Go ahead."

"What?"

"Yeah. You wanna talk?" He made a forwarding motion with his hand. "Let's hear it."

"That's not what I mean. If something's bothering you, I want to know."

"Yeah? Well, it looks to me like you're the one who's bothered."

Why deny it? "You're right. I *am* bothered. And you're not helping."

Again, I thought of that girl, cradled against his chest as he carried her away from all the commotion. I thought of the hours that I'd spent waiting at his penthouse, alone, wondering if he was okay. I thought of her lips on his crotch and his smile for camera.

I didn't want to ask. But I had to, because if I wondered one more minute, I'd go insane. In a very soft voice, I said, "That girl, do you like her?"

And then, there were the questions I didn't ask.

Do you want her?

Did you have her?

I felt myself swallow. *Is she going to be my replacement?*

CHAPTER 12

Standing in the quiet space, Jake looked at me like I'd lost my mind. Who knows? Maybe I had.

Finally, he said, "What girl? The one from last night?"

I felt myself nod.

"You serious?"

Of course, I was serious. And honestly, I was a little surprised that he didn't know exactly what I was talking about. Or was this all some sort of act?

Looking up at him, I said, "Well, you're being kind of secretive, so you know, I just thought I should ask."

He made a sound of disbelief. "Secretive?"

"Well, yeah."

"Let me get this straight," he said. "You think that I'm so fucking stupid that I'd be messing around on you, putting the moves on some other girl…" He made air-quotes. "In secret, in front of six million other people?"

I heard myself mutter, "Probably seven million by now."

"Screw the numbers," he said. "Why would you think that?"

I gave him a pleading look. "Do I even need to explain this?"

"Yeah. You do."

"Well, you were carrying her–"

"Not my idea."

"Oh, please," I said. "What'd she do? Force you?"

"No. What she *did* was sprain her ankle." He gave a half-shrug. "Or so she said."

"So she said?" I hesitated. "So she might've been lying?"

"Don't know, didn't ask."

"Why not?"

"Because I didn't care."

"You cared enough to carry her."

"As opposed to what?" he said. "Taking off, and letting her deal with Dorian on her own?"

I was glaring at him now. "Well maybe Dorian wouldn't have been so mad if she wasn't using *your* crotch as a napkin." At the image, I felt that sick feeling grow in my stomach. "And the way it looked, you weren't doing a whole lot to stop her either."

"Sorry, I was kind of busy."

I gave him a good, long look. He didn't sound very sorry. My voice was shaking now. "And you were smiling. You smiled straight into the camera like you were loving every minute of it."

"Yeah?" His jaw clenched. "Well, I wasn't."

"Could've fooled me."

"It wasn't meant to fool you. But fooling those other people?" His tone grew mocking. "My fans? Yeah, I'll fool 'em all day long and sleep easy doing it."

"That doesn't make any sense," I said. "I don't even know what you're talking about."

"No? Then pretend you're me, and try again."

"I can't," I said, "because I don't have girls throwing themselves at me."

His voice grew quiet. "You think I liked that?"

I recalled the look on his face, that shit-eating grin, straight into the camera. "No. I think you *loved* it." When he said nothing, I added, "At least, you sure looked like you loved it."

"Yeah? Well, lemme ask you something. Let's say I didn't love it. What then?"

"What do you mean, 'What then?'"

"Let's say I was disgusted, you think I'm gonna show it?"

I blinked. "Were you? Disgusted, I mean?"

"Hell yeah, I was disgusted. That chick was a mess. Sloppy as hell. Godawful perfume." He practically shuddered. "And you wanna hear something else? Chick almost barfed on me."

I stared up at him. His description was at such odds with what I'd seen on that video, I didn't know what to say.

"So yeah," Jake continued, "I was disgusted. You feel better now?"

Yes.

I paused.

And no.

Yes, because I'd rather have him disgusted than fawning over some other girl. And no, because even though I desperately wanted to, I couldn't quite believe what he was saying.

I gave him a dubious look. "You didn't look disgusted."

"Yeah," he said. "And thus, the six million views."

I tried to think. What was he telling me? That the whole thing was just an act?

I shook my head. That couldn't be true. I knew Jake. He'd always been a hell-raiser. And his personality hadn't changed, not really. The only thing that was different now was the number of people who got to watch him.

Thinking aloud, I spoke slowly, trying to work it out in my own mind. "So with that girl, you just pretended to like it? Is that what you're saying?"

"Yeah. That's what I'm saying."

It felt like a lie – a pretty lie, designed to make me feel better. Still, I made myself ask, "But why?"

"You know why."

I made a sound of frustration. "Honestly, I don't."

"Alright. I'll spell it out. You know my fans. You think they're gonna line up to watch some guy who *doesn't* smile when a hot girl plants her face against his cock?"

I drew back, disturbed at the image. And I couldn't help but notice that he'd called the girl hot. Maybe it shouldn't have mattered, but I still didn't like it.

I looked away, gazing out toward the tall windows of his luxurious office suite. The day had been sunny when I'd arrived. But now, dark storm clouds were rolling in.

Good.

It matched my mood.

Jake's voice cut through the silence. "What was I supposed to do? Shriek and run away?"

I turned toward him and said, "Well, you didn't have to look so happy about it."

"Hey, you play the hand you're dealt."

"What's that supposed to mean?"

He shrugged. "I dunno."

I didn't want to, but I had to ask. "And what about your pants?"

"What about them?"

"Why'd you change them?" I hesitated. "Was it because of her?"

"What do you mean?"

Fearful of sounding even more like a jealous harpy, I struggled to find the words. "Well, you were gone a long time, and when you showed up, you were wearing different pants, so I was just wondering how that happened…" I let the words trail off, hoping he'd pick up the thread.

He didn't.

His arms were crossed, and his muscles were bulging. The look on his face was making me just a little bit nervous. I couldn't quite read his expression, but I'd be a fool to think it was a happy one.

Lamely, I continued. "So I was just wondering, you know, what happened?"

His voice was cold. "To my pants?"

"Well, uh, yeah, actually."

"Like I told you last night, I changed them."

"But why?"

"Is that a serious question?"

I felt myself nod.

As an answer, he turned away and stalked across the open space, heading toward his private office. I watched, silently, as he opened the glass door and headed to the area behind his desk. Across the distance, I saw him reached down and grab a wadded bundle off the floor.

I recognized the bundle immediately. It was his pants from last night. He left the glass-enclosed space and stalked back until he was, once again, standing across from me.

He shook out the pants and held them up between us. "What do you think? Nice, huh?"

I stared at the pants. Nice? Not really.

Jake continued. "Let's say I came home wearing these, would've you liked it?"

I was still staring. All across the crotch were smeared streaks of pink – *bright* pink, lipstick obviously. Right there. At ground zero.

Jake made a scoffing sound. "Yeah, you'd have loved that, right? Me, showing up, in these?" He tossed the pants onto the floor and waited in stony silence until I looked up to meet his gaze.

His eyes were dark, and his expression was stormy. There was something vaguely accusatory about the way he was looking at me.

I didn't like it, because for one thing, I'd done nothing wrong. But of course, he could probably say the same. Couldn't he?

I felt myself swallow. "Jake—"

"And what kind of dick would *I* be?" He gave a slow shake of his head. "To show up, wearing those fucking things in front of you?"

"Well maybe, it wouldn't have been a problem if you hadn't let that chick use you as a human napkin."

Even to my own ears, the analogy sounded woefully inadequate. It wasn't like that girl had wiped a mouthful of chicken grease on his sleeve. It was so much worse. She'd been pressing her lips onto his groin.

She'd wanted him. They all wanted him. I recalled how I'd felt when Jake *hadn't* been mine. I'd wanted him with every fiber of my being. I *still* wanted him that way.

But now, gazing up at him, I was feeling more uncertain with every passing second.

Again, Jake glanced toward the elevator. For the second time, he said, "We done?"

The coldness in his voice hurt to hear. Desperately, I tried again.

"No. We're not done. Because I have a question."

He gazed down at me in stony silence.

Taking that for a yes, I struggled to find the words, words that might make him understand exactly how I was feeling. Deliberately, I softened my tone. "If that were me, if our positions were reversed, if some guy planted his face in *my* crotch, what would *you* do?"

His jaw clenched. "You *know* what I'd do."

He was wrong. I didn't. But I *did* know that he wouldn't like it, and that was my whole point.

But before I could drive the point home, Jake leaned closer and spoke again. "I'd fuckin' kill him. That's what I'd do."

CHAPTER 13

Standing there, I craned my neck to look up at him. All the prior coldness – in Jake's eyes, in the office, on my skin – it was gone in a flash, replaced by heat so searing, I wanted to fan myself.

I was horrified. And thrilled. And just a little bit scared. Looking to tone everything down a notch, I said, "You mean rhetorically, right?"

He gave a shrug.

"That's no kind of answer," I said.

"Yeah? Well too bad. Because that's all you're getting."

I drew back. "Why?"

"Because there are some things you don't need to know. That's why."

Well, that wasn't ominous or anything.

I reminded myself that normal people – normal guys – they didn't think that way. And they sure as heck didn't *act* that way.

Over the years, I'd dated a lot, especially in college. Those others guys? None of them would do this. None of them would hint at dark and deadly things, and then refuse to discuss it afterward.

And what, exactly, was he saying, anyway?

Wanting a better view of him, I took a step backward. "Let me get this straight. Some chick can practically molest you in public, and that's okay, but–"

"I never said that."

Ignoring his lame protest, I continued. "But if the situation were reversed, if it were a *guy* doing the same thing to me, that *wouldn't* be okay?"

His voice hardened. "What do *you* think?"

At this point, I didn't know what to think. But I *did* know it wasn't fair. It wasn't even logical.

Jake was smart. He might not always show it, but he was. Back in our hometown, I'd always suspected as much. But over the past few weeks, I'd seen a lot more of his business operations. I'd also seen a lot more of *him*.

He was sharp and had a real knack for numbers. Yeah, he spent a lot of money, but he invested a whole lot more. I wasn't a big numbers person myself, but I knew enough to realize that he could stop working at any time and still live like a king for the rest of his life.

I pushed those thoughts aside and focused on the present. "What do I think?" I said. "I think it's a double-standard. That's what."

"No," he said in a voice that grew annoyingly calm, "because it's *not* the same thing."

"It is, too." I glared up at him. "What are you gonna tell me next? That you're allowed to cheat or something? And I'm not?"

Probably, it was a stupid point. I didn't want to cheat. And the thought of him cheating? Well, it hurt. It hurt a lot. But if that was his attitude, I needed to know. "Well?" I said. "Is that the way it is?"

He gave me a look that I couldn't quite make out. "You think I'd cheat on you?"

Did I? I didn't *want* to think that. But how I could not wonder, especially after seeing him smile while another girl crawled all over him?

I closed my eyes and tried to think. That scene from the video – he'd explained that. And stupid or not, I believed him, even if I still didn't like it.

I opened my eyes and struggled to find the words. "It just sounds like there's one set of rules for you, and another set for me. You know?"

"That's not it."

"Well it sure sounds like it." I gave him a pleading look. "Come on, Jake. Look at it from my point-of-view. Some girl jumps you, and that's okay? But some guy jumps me, it's not?"

His expression darkened. "You really wanna go there?"

"Go where?" I said. "Truth-land? Yeah. I do." My voice rose. "Because for once, I just want a straight answer. Why is that so hard?"

Slowly, he moved closer until we were once again, almost touching. Towering over me, he said in a very quiet voice. "I'll tell you why. It's because you're not me."

"What does *that* mean?"

He lowered his head the barest fraction. "It means that if I want to stop somebody from doing something, it's a hell of a lot easier for me than it is for you."

I knew what he was getting at. Yeah, he was bigger than me. And stronger than me. By a lot.

And yeah, he was something else, a lot more brutal than I could ever be on my worst day. From watching some of his videos, I knew how quickly his easy demeanor could morph into something different, something just shy of deadly. Or worse.

I wanted to say something, but I didn't know what.

In front of me, Jake lowered his head another fraction. "You wanna compare?" he said. "Take me and that girl. If she were a threat to me – which she wasn't – I could've handled her in a heartbeat."

I wasn't following. "How?"

"I'm not gonna go there, because she wasn't." His voice grew a shade darker. "But if I see some guy, with you, giving you the kind of attention you don't want…" His jaw clenched. "…touching you when you don't want to be touched, putting his lips or his hands, or anything else on you, when he doesn't have your okay." His voice dropped to a whisper. "I'm not gonna let that stand."

At something in his voice, I felt a shiver go straight through me. I didn't know what to say. Should I argue? Part of me felt like I should. But that would be like arguing for the wind not to blow or the sun not to shine, because Jake was Jake. And I knew, just by looking at him, that he meant every word.

Still, I couldn't let it go, not completely.

I'd never been a fan of possessive guys. In college, I'd had this roommate whose boyfriend was practically a stalker. He checked her phone and read her texts. He followed her in secret and threatened her friends. And if she so much as smiled at another guy, he found some reason to start a fight, sometimes with her, sometimes with the guy.

It was sad, really. It was even sadder when, after months of creepy craziness, she caught him in bed with her best friend – twice. And even afterwards, long after they'd broken up, the guy still wouldn't leave her alone.

But that wasn't Jake. Was it? I didn't want to ask, but suddenly, I felt like I had to. In a halting voice, I said, "So let's say for whatever reason, we break up—"

"We're not going to."

I prayed he was right. Life without Jake? I didn't even want to think about it. "I know," I said, "but just for the sake of argument—"

"What are you asking?" he said. "If I see you with some other guy, am I gonna kick his ass?"

"Well, I wouldn't have put it quite *that* way."

"Uh-huh." He gave me a hard look. "In this scenario of yours, are we together? Or apart?" He leaned a fraction closer, and I swear, I could feel the heat of his emotions radiating off him.

Or maybe that was just me.

And yet, I gave another shiver. My neck felt stiff, and my mouth went dry. Still, I managed to croak out, "Um, apart?"

Abruptly, he pulled away. "If we're apart, you do what you want. There. We good now?" Before I could answer, he turned away and started striding toward the elevator.

"Hey!" I called after him. "Where are you going?"

He didn't answer. He just kept on going, and he wasn't looking back.

"Jake!" I called. "Seriously. Stop."

Finally, he stopped and slowly turned around. "Why?"

"Because we're not done. That's why."

"We're done enough."

Frustrated, I strode toward him and said, "But where are you going? Upstairs?"

"I dunno."

Well, this was just great. He wasn't going anywhere, not really. He was just leaving to get away from me. It was the same thing he always did whenever our discussions got too heated.

Well, not this time.

I glared up at him. "You can't leave."

"Yeah? Why not?"

On impulse, I said, "Because I am." And with that, I elbowed my way past him and stalked to the elevator. I smacked the down button and waited, while my heart hammered, for the doors to slide open.

While waiting, I refused to turn around, but I could feel his brooding presence in the space behind me, probably exactly where I'd left him.

Good.

Sort of.

Part of me was glad he was staying, but the other part – the stupid part – was desperately wishing he'd plunge forward and beg me to stay.

Or at least ask me nicely.

He didn't.

And so when the doors slid open, I strode forward into the empty elevator. The emptiness wasn't a surprise. The building had four elevators total, but only one of them serviced the two top floors, which made the arrangement surprisingly private.

A security measure? Probably, not that I'd ever asked about it. And I was in no mood to ask now.

Instead, I turned around and slapped the button that would take me down to the lobby. A moment later, the elevator doors began sliding shut, leaving me with only the briefest glimpse of Jake, standing in the same spot as before, watching me with an expression that I couldn't quite decipher.

But I did know one thing. It definitely wasn't happiness.

CHAPTER 14

When the elevator reached the lobby, I strode out, only to feel my steps falter as reality slammed into me. Where the hell was I going? And how would I get there?

I glanced toward the rear of the lobby, where a pair of wide steel doors led to the parking garage. I'd walked through those same doors less than hour earlier, after driving here using one of Jake's cars.

I heard myself sigh. I didn't have a car of my own, thanks to my slime-ball of an ex-boyfriend and my own stubbornness in refusing to let Jake buy me a replacement car. So in the meantime, I'd been borrowing one of Jake's vehicles – a sleek luxury sedan that was well beyond my price range.

Funny, the car was almost starting to feel like my own. But it wasn't, which made me feel all the more ridiculous now.

I mean, I couldn't really drive off in one of Jake's cars, when the whole point of walking out of Jake's office was to assert some sort of independence.

And now, here I was, stranded and feeling like an idiot.

Talk about pathetic.

I stepped away from the elevators and looked around. The building's lobby was ornate, with high ceilings and clusters of expensive furniture, artfully arranged into semi-private seating areas. The first time I'd been here, just a few weeks earlier, I'd been blown away by how posh it was.

But for the past couple of weeks, I'd walked through this same lobby every day, so frequently, in fact, that I almost took its opulence for granted.

My shoulders slumped. These days, I was taking a lot of things for granted. I no longer paid rent. I no longer paid utility bills. I barely paid for food.

Sure, I had no car. But I also had no car payment and a nearly new vehicle to drive whenever I wanted.

There was a time, not too long ago, when I would've gladly wallowed in all these free luxuries, not caring that they might evaporate tomorrow.

Who knows? Maybe they were already gone, along with Jake, thanks to our recent fight.

At the thought, I blinked hard, hoping to stem the tide of unshed tears. The luxuries, I could do without. But Jake? Losing him? The thought was almost too painful to bear. And yet, I knew that if I slunk back upstairs now, I'd look like just another girl who didn't have the self-respect to challenge him on anything.

I was mulling all of this over, when the sound of a male voice, just a few feet away, made me jump almost out of my skin. "Miss? Is everything alright?"

I turned and saw Pete, the doorman, eyeing me with obvious concern.

I gave him what I hoped was a normal smile. "Um, yeah. Everything's fine. Thanks." I glanced toward the glass double-doors that led to the street outside. "I'm just, uh, going for a walk. That's all."

He frowned. "Alone?"

Oh for Pete's sake. Literally.

Sure, I realized that Detroit wasn't known for being the safest city on the planet, but this particular area was really nice. And besides, it was only five o'clock, hours yet from nightfall. My last apartment was in a neighborhood ten times worse than this, and that never stopped me going where I wanted, well, not during the daylight hours, anyway.

I gave Pete a pathetic wave and began striding toward the doors. "It'll be fine."

He hustled forward to pull open the nearest door. But even as he held it wide, he said, "It looks like rain. You sure you don't want to drive instead?" He glanced out toward the city street. "Or, I could call you a cab?"

I didn't feel like debating it. I felt like crying. But breaking down in front of anyone, especially someone who'd surely tell Jake, wasn't what I had in mind, so I tried for a friendly laugh. "It wouldn't be much of a walk if I were in a car." Trying to soften the words, I added, "But thanks, seriously."

Pete was still frowning when I walked through the open door and onto the sidewalk. The air was humid, and I could smell the promise of a summer storm. I looked up to the sky. Sure enough, the clouds were still dark, just like my mood.

But it wasn't raining yet, and there was no guarantee that it would. But I *could* guarantee that if I stood around here another moment, I'd probably lose it right here, in front of Jake's building.

So on auto-pilot, I started walking, hoping against hope that the activity would somehow clear my mind.

After a few blocks, I wasn't so sure. With my thoughts in a jumble, I passed high stone buildings with upscale awnings, along with other buildings that weren't so nice. Some showed signs of recent renovations, while others showed only lingering decay, with crumbling bricks and empty spaces where windows must've been, back in the city's glory days.

But there were plenty of people out walking, business-people mostly, probably headed to their cars. It was, after all, quitting time on a Friday afternoon.

Trudging along the city sidewalk, I let myself get lost in my thoughts – of Jake, of my uncertain future, and of every stupid thing I'd done to get to this point.

There was the hotel internship that I'd turned down my senior year of college, because I'd wanted to tend bar at the beach. There was that extra loan I'd taken out after college graduation, to pay for furniture that had gotten destroyed by unseen vandals only a few months later. There was Rango, my last boyfriend, who'd crushed my car for fun and refused to pay for it – well, until Jake forced him to, that is.

And what had I done with the money? I'd played catch-up with my student loans, too embarrassed to tell Jake how insanely delinquent I'd been on all my bills.

I heard myself sigh. Jake. Lately, he'd been riding in to solve all of my problems. A crazy ex-boyfriend? Solved by Jake. No place to live? Solved by Jake. No car to drive? Solved by Jake.

What, exactly, was I bringing to this relationship, anyway? I blinked long and hard. Nothing – that's what, or at least nothing that Jake couldn't get from a million others girls who'd kill to take my place.

Walking block after block, I became so lost in my thoughts that I barely noticed when the first raindrops started to fall. But then, coming to my senses, I stopped walking and looked around. At least it wasn't a downpour, not yet anyway.

For now, the raindrops were few and far-between. But they were big, the kind that plopped onto the sidewalk and left a distinct circle showing where they'd fallen.

That was definitely a bad sign. I looked up. Any minute now, the sky would surely open up and drench anyone stupid enough to be caught outside – me, apparently.

Damn it.

I looked around. I was on a narrow side street between two rows of tall, brick buildings. It slowly dawned on me that I'd strayed farther from Jake's place than I'd planned. There was absolutely no one around, whether because I'd wandered so far from the business district, or more likely, because the rain was keeping smarter people inside.

How long had I been walking, anyway? A half-hour? An hour? Longer? At this point, I had no idea.

I turned around and picked up the pace, heading back the way I'd come. Or at least, that was my intention.

Surrounded by tall buildings, it was hard for me to tell for sure. It's not like I'd been walking along a single street or anything. Instead, I'd wandered along the side streets, looking to avoid the sights and sounds of rush-hour traffic.

Now, that felt like a giant mistake. Around me, there were still no signs of life. No people. No occupied office buildings. No stores with open signs.

It was actually kind of surreal, making me feel like the lone survivor of a zombie apocalypse. I made a scoffing sound. Yeah, well in that case, I'd be fine too, because the way it looked, I was seriously lacking in the brain department.

What zombie would want me?

I was walking faster now, conscious of the fact that I didn't even have my phone. Stupidly, I'd left it at Jake's penthouse, along with everything else in my purse.

My purse – that was another thing. As it turned out, Jake had snagged it last night from the convention center, and returned it to me with nothing missing. Well, nothing except my sanity, as it turned out.

Had I even thanked him? I meant to. But had I?

I was almost running now, and not only because the raindrops were falling in faster intervals. It was the desolation. It was creeping me out more than I wanted to admit.

It wasn't until I turned the next corner that I saw the first signs of life. Up ahead, maybe five or six blocks, cars were zipping along the city street – Jake's street, if I wasn't mistaken.

I breathed a sigh of relief. Civilization. Thank God.

I plowed forward, determined to make it back before I found myself in serious trouble.

Unfortunately, I didn't quite make it.

☐

CHAPTER 15

I was only a couple of blocks away from Jake's street when a big gold SUV, with dark tinted windows, squealed around the nearest corner and popped the curb right in front of me.

I'd barely jumped out of the way when the passenger's side window slid down, and a frizzy haired woman in a gold halter top leaned out the open window to call out, "How much, honey?"

I drew back. "What?"

She spoke again, slower this time. "I *said*, 'How much?'" She grimaced. "Honey."

I tried to look past her. That obnoxious vehicle was *on* the sidewalk, blocking my path. But just beyond it, only two blocks away, was Jake's street, with regular cars and regular people, going about their regular business, supposedly.

I felt myself swallow. "How much for what?"

The woman's gaze travelled rudely down the length of me. "You know."

I glanced down and felt my face go suddenly hot in spite of the ever-increasing rain. Like an idiot, I was still dressed in my work getup – those ridiculous Daisy Duke shorts and that low-cut frilly white blouse.

At work, where I wasn't the only person dressed this way, the uniform was bad enough, but out here, it didn't exactly blend. Probably, I looked like a working girl alright, just not of the bartending variety.

What the hell had I been thinking?

But I knew the answer. I *hadn't* been thinking. I'd been too upset to think. What else was new?

The woman spoke again. "Well?" Her tone grew snippy. "How much?"

Okay, dressed like a slutty cowgirl or not, I was feeling more than a little insulted. "It's not what you think," I told her. "I'm on my way home."

"Why?" She gave a brittle laugh. "The party's just starting."

I glanced ahead, toward Jake's street. It was right there, within sprinting distance – assuming I could leap over that stupid vehicle – except I couldn't.

But I *could* go around it. Muttering, "I've gotta go," I turned away. Walking quickly, I crossed the narrow street, making for the opposite sidewalk.

It was raining even harder now. I wanted to run, but somehow, I knew that would be a mistake. So instead, I strode forward, keeping my eyes ahead and my senses on high alert.

I'd barely made it to the end of the block when I heard the roar of a nearby engine. On instinct, I leapt out of the way just in time to avoid getting squashed as that same vehicle, just like before, plowed onto the sidewalk and stopped just inches away from the nearest brick building, effectively blocking my path.

I whirled around, intending go back the way I'd come, but I didn't have the chance, because a new obstacle was in my way. It was a huge, slick-looking guy, dressed in all black, with a big, diamond earring that glittered even in the gloom.

Where on Earth had *he* come from? The vehicle? Had he been the one driving?

If so, he wasn't anymore. Obviously.

And didn't he care about the rain?

Next to me, the SUV's window slid down yet again, and the same woman leaned out, this time from the driver's side. She gave me a mean, little smile. "Hi. Remember me?"

My heart was pounding, and the rain was falling in buckets now. I looked from the woman to the man. It occurred to me that the guy's clothes looked awfully pricey – way too nice to be getting soaked like this.

Then again, I was dressed stupidly too.

Just great.

We had something in common. Somehow, the thought was less than comforting.

Slowly, I backed up until I felt my ass hit the side of the SUV.

In front of me, the guy smiled and moved deliberately toward me. I didn't know what he had in mind, but the possibilities weren't looking too great.

He leaned close and spoke in a low, deep voice. "You working here?"

I gulped. "What?"

He made a show of looking around. "Here. You working this place?"

"What? No," I stammered. "I'm just on a walk, that's all."

He laughed long and loud, like a crazed killer wielding a machete. Lightning flashed, followed by the quick clap of thunder.

Whatever this was, it couldn't be happening. I was like one zombie away from a real-life horror movie.

When the guy finally stopped laughing, he looked over to the woman and said in a loud sarcastic voice, "You hear that, Violet? She's just out on a walk." He looked back to me and said, "Nice day for a stroll, right?"

I swallowed hard and pushed a clump of soggy hair out of my eyes. Desperately, I blurted out, "I'm, uh, meeting someone, so I've gotta go."

He leaned closer. "Is that right?"

The woman, oblivious to the rain, was hanging halfway out of the vehicle now. She called over to the guy. "We should make her pay."

I glared over at her. "For what?"

She flicked her head toward the guy. "For walking on *his* street. Dumb-ass."

I whirled toward the guy and said, "You don't own the street. Nobody does."

He gave me a wide grin that sent chills down my damp spine. "Sorry, but you're wrong, baby-doll."

I sucked in a deep breath and tried not to let my panic show. His vehicle, the way he was dressed, the things he was saying, it was pretty obvious what he was getting at. Somehow, I'd infringed on his territory, or at least, that's what he *thought* I was doing.

But I wasn't. I had to make him see that. I held up my hands. "Look, I was just heading home, honest. I live around here, okay?"

Again, he laughed. "No one like you lives around here."

No one like me? What did that mean?

The guy's gaze drifted down to my breasts. He nodded like he saw something he liked. "Yeah, you're the good stuff, aren't you?"

I didn't bother looking down. It didn't take a genius to understand what had captured his attention. My white blouse, skimpy as it was, was now soaked and clinging to me like a second skin.

Stupid work uniform.

Maybe I *should* have signed that petition. Who knows? Maybe I still would. But first, I needed a ride out of here, and fast. Without thinking, I blurted out, "Hey, can I borrow your phone?"

The guy laughed like I'd said something funny. "Why? Who you gonna call?"

"My boyfriend."

"Boyfriend, huh?"

Unsure what to do now, I started blathering like an idiot. "He lives around here. I mean, I live with him. And with it raining and all, I figure I should call and get a ride, you know?"

From the SUV, the woman called out, "You want a ride? He'll give you a ride, honey."

Oh, for God's sake. Tired of this whole twisted scene, I snapped, "I'll stick with Jake. Thanks."

At this, her expression froze. Her eyes shifted toward the guy, who'd just muttered a low curse. When I turned to look, he said, "Jake who?" He wasn't laughing anymore. "Bishop?"

Why lie? I nodded.

The guy shook his head. "Fuck."

I didn't bother asking if he knew Jake. From the look on his face, it was pretty obvious that he did. But was that a good thing? Or a bad thing?

I was still wondering when the guy turned and splashed his way back to the SUV.

He yanked open the driver's side door and claimed the driver's seat, leaving the woman to scramble into the passenger's side.

A moment later, the vehicle roared out of sight, leaving me standing alone in the pouring rain – not that I was complaining.

Above me, I heard the crack of thunder, and the skies opened up, delivering a torrential downpour that made it hard to breathe. Or who knows? Maybe my ragged breathing had nothing to do with the weather. Whatever had just happened, I was insanely glad it was over.

Or, at least, I sure hoped it was over.

Unable to stop myself, I started running as fast as I could. I didn't pause until I reached Jake's street, still packed with rush-hour traffic, in spite of the downpour.

Looking down the street, I stifled a curse. I was still a long way from Jake's place, ten or twelve blocks at least.

Unsure what to do, I started running again, ignoring the weather and the strange looks I got from random people, scurrying forward under their nice, safe umbrellas.

The air was cooler now, but my lungs were burning, making me gasp and sputter as I splashed my way forward, desperate now to reach Jake's condo.

Ignoring everything – the rain, the looks, the traffic – I kept on going, until I heard a familiar male voice, calling out my name.

Confused, I stopped and turned to look. Unfortunately, the voice didn't belong to Jake. It belonged to my least favorite sports agent, Vince Hammond.□

CHAPTER 16

I squinted through the rain and sure enough, spotted Vince, calling out from the open driver's side window of a black sedan, idling at the curb across the street.

When our gazes met, he called out again. "You need a ride?"

I glanced around and hesitated for only a split-second before sloshing forward, dodging traffic as I crossed the street and circled around to his car's passenger's side, only to discover that it wasn't exactly empty.

In the passenger's seat, sat Bianca, Jake's former event planner and one of my least-favorite people.

Oh great. A twofer.

But even as I thought it, I reminded myself that I was incredibly lucky they were stopping at all. My gratitude was reduced only a fraction when Bianca opened her car-window barely a crack and said, "You're gonna have to sit in the back, you know."

Well, obviously. It's not like I was planning to sit on her lap or anything.

She pursed her lips. "And grab a towel or something, will you? These are leather seats."

I looked around. Where on Earth was I supposed to find a towel? And besides, weren't leather seats *more* water-resistant than cloth? I hesitated, wondering what I should do now.

But from the driver's seat, Vince called out, "She's not serious. Now, c'mon, get in, before you drown out there."

That was all the prompting I needed. I yanked open the rear passenger's side door and dove inside, feeling an embarrassing surge of relief when I slammed the door shut behind me.

It wasn't even the rain, as uncomfortable as it was. It was that scary-ass guy, and the frizzy-haired woman with him, along with the fact that my clothes were plastered to me like a cold, second skin.

Stifling a shiver, I sat up and looked out toward the street ahead. From here, we were only five or six blocks away from Jake's place – not a long distance, but longer than I wanted to walk now, all things considered.

I reached up and shoved back that same annoying clump of wet hair. As thankful as I was to be huddled here in the backseat, I had to admit that I would be even more thankful if I could somehow make myself invisible.

I'd gotten only a quick glimpse of Bianca before diving into the car, but I'd caught enough to catalogue the basics. As usual, she looked like a million bucks. Her sleek, dark hair was perfectly styled. Her dress was a tailored, sleeveless number, in peach no less – a color that I could never pull off, even on my best day.

And today, was most certainly *not* my best day. My hair was dripping, my clothes were soaked, and I felt like I had goldfish swimming in my shoes. Still, I tried to sound normal as I said, "Thanks for the ride."

Bianca snorted. "You can thank *him*. It wasn't *my* idea to stop."

From the driver's seat, Vince spoke in a tone was half playful, half serious. "Now Bianca, be nice."

Nice? Bianca? It was *my* turn to snort.

Bianca whirled around to face me. "What's that supposed to mean?"

I gave her my clueless face. "I didn't say anything."

She glowered at me. "Well, maybe not with words, but I know perfectly well what you meant."

Yeah? Well, I knew a few things too. Bianca was in love with my boyfriend. She blamed me for the fact that he wasn't her client anymore. And, if I wasn't careful, she'd trick me to making a fool of myself – not that I needed any help in *that* department.

Bianca and I had a history, and it wasn't a good one. Determined that this time, she wouldn't get the best of me, I summoned up a cheery smile and said, "Sorry. Should we hug it out?"

She drew back like I'd just offered her sex with a corpse. "What?"

"You know," I said. "Hug and make up." I spread my arms wide. "Aw c'mon, I'm willing if you are."

In truth, I wasn't all that willing, and given the fact that she was in the front seat, and I was in the back, it probably wasn't even possible. But none of that mattered, because I knew for a fact that Bianca wouldn't be caught dead hugging anyone as soggy as me, even if we were friends, which we definitely weren't.

Her lips curled in obvious disgust. "I'm not going to *hug* you."

"Oh well," I said, dropping my arms. "At least I tried."

Somewhere in the back of my mind, I was vaguely aware that the attitude I was giving Bianca was my last defense against totally losing it.

Inside, my heart was still racing, and my thoughts were a disjointed, jumbled mess. My legs were trembling, and I had a sneaky suspicion that it wasn't because of the run, or because I was cold and wet. It was because of everything else that had happened within the last hour.

So in a twisted way, I was almost glad that Bianca was here, sneering at me like she always did. If she wasn't, I might have to think about what could've happened to me a few minutes earlier if things had gone down differently.

I might also have to think about the fact that soon, I'd be skulking through the lobby of Jake's building, looking like a drowned rat, and giving Pete the opportunity to say, "I told you so." Not that he would. He was far too professional for that.

But he'd definitely be thinking it.

Vince's voice broke into my thoughts. "I think there's a hoodie in that duffle bag. You want it? It's yours."

I glanced around and spotted a red gym bag sitting on the floor mat, just behind Vince's seat. Gratefully, I started reaching for it, only to be interrupted by Bianca, whining, "But she's gonna get it all wet."

I hesitated. She did have a point. And I'd learned from experience that accepting favors from Vince was a dangerous proposition. He didn't do anything just to be nice. I'd learned *that* myself, the hard way.

Still, through the shivers, a little voice in my head whispered, "*Yeah. But so what?*"

I'd already crossed *that* bridge by getting into his car. There was no going back now – and probably, I wouldn't, even if I could. The street suddenly seemed far too dangerous, and not only because of the storm.

So I ignored Bianca and leaned down to unzip the bag. Sure enough, I found a navy hoodie nestled atop some workout clothes. No towel. Unfortunately.

Buy hey, I was in no position to complain.

From the driver's seat, Vince said, "Don't worry. I don't need it back."

Beside him, Bianca made a sniffing sound. "Eauw." She sniffed again. "Something smells like a wet dog." She peered around her seat and wrinkled her nose at me. "Is that *you?*"

Oh, for God's sake. I didn't smell like a wet dog, even if I did feel like one.

Still, I made myself smile. "Woof, woof."

Her gaze narrowed. "You are *so* immature. You *do* realize that?"

Yeah, and she was a turd. But since I wasn't thrilled with the idea of walking, that sentiment was better left unsaid, especially because the car hadn't yet moved. If they were going to kick me out, now would be the perfect time.

Vince leaned around his seat and said, "You're heading to Jake's, right?"

"Uh, yeah," I said. "Actually, I was walking back there when I got caught in the rain."

Vince nodded. "Good timing. We're headed there, too."

They were? For what? The last I'd heard, Jake and Bianca weren't quite on speaking terms, and as far as Vince, he and Jake were practically arch-enemies.

From the passenger's seat, Bianca added, "So you can thank your lucky stars that we were in the neighborhood."

I resisted the urge to snort again. I'd seen my horoscope. My stars weren't lucky. Not today, anyway.

And, as I soon learned, my luck wasn't about to improve any time soon.

CHAPTER 17

Vince pulled his car up to Jake's building and stopped in the turnaround, under the building's wide, protective awning. Graciously, he offered me and Bianca the chance to exit the car without getting drenched.

Bianca, lovely person that she was, actually protested, although not in any way that would do her credit. "You can let *me* off," she told Vince, "but why Luna?"

She turned around to sneer at me, still shivering in the back seat. "Look at her. She's soaked already. What difference does it make *now*?"

She gave a mean little giggle. "What you should do," she told him, "is let *her* park the car, so you don't ruin your suit." She flashed me an overly sweet smile. "You don't mind, do you? Because let's all be reasonable here. If it weren't for us, you'd still be out there walking."

Silently, I looked to Vince. If it were just Bianca, I'd tell her to shove it. But Vince was the one who'd actually given me a ride, in spite of Bianca's protests, apparently.

I didn't like the guy, but I didn't want to be ungrateful either. And rude or not, Bianca did have a point. It's not like I could get much wetter.

But Vince was shaking his head. "I wouldn't dream of it. Now, go on. I'll park the car and see you both inside."

Ignoring more snide commentary from Bianca, I pushed open the car-door and began stepping out of the vehicle, only to see Pete, the doorman, bolt out of the building and yank my door open even wider – so wide, in fact, that I was half-worried it would fly off its hinges.

His eyes were frantic as he told me, "Am I ever glad to see you."

It was so unlike him that I paused in mid-step. "Why? Is something wrong?"

As if remembering himself, he straightened and said in a much calmer voice. "No. Everything's fine. I'll just inform Jake that you're back."

"That's okay," I told him, hoping to soothe away whatever was wrong. "I'm heading upstairs now." I tried for a reassuring smile. "So I'll just tell Jake myself. You know, in person."

Pete froze, as if unsure how to respond. I waited, wondering why that might be a problem. And the longer he stood there, not saying anything at all, the more uncertain I became.

Before I'd left for that ill-fated walk, Jake and I had been fighting. I'd stormed out, and he hadn't tried to stop me. And now, Pete was acting all funny. What did that mean? Had Jake changed the key-codes while I'd been away? Was I not allowed in his condo anymore?

No, I told myself. Jake wouldn't do that. He wouldn't kick me out over one stupid fight. And even if he *were* kicking me out, he wouldn't do it like this.

Would he?

Jake was the guy I loved, and I knew he loved me. But I'd seen him act in ways that were beyond cold when it came to other girls. When he was done with them, for whatever reason, he didn't mess around with the normal niceties.

The sound of throat-clearing jolted me back to reality. It was Bianca, leaning her head out of her open car window. She was glaring at Pete. "Excuse me," she called in a tone of obvious annoyance, "Aren't you planning to get *my* door?"

Before Pete could answer, *I* did. "Oh for God's sake, get it yourself, will you?"

Her lips pursed. "In case you haven't noticed, the car is wet."

"Really?" I said, letting the sarcasm drip from my voice, much like the water that was still dripping from my hair. "I had no idea."

She ignored my comment and kept on talking. "And why should I *have* to get it, when there's a perfectly good doorman, right there?" She gave a toss of her long, dark – and yes, perfectly dry – hair. "I know *you're* not used to such things, but trust me, there's a protocol to this."

She turned back to Pete and said, "Well? I'm waiting."

"Of course," he stammered, hustling forward to open her car door. "I apologize. It won't happen again."

"See that it doesn't," Bianca snapped. And then, while he waited, she took her sweet time getting out of the vehicle, showing off her long, tan legs and jaunty peach heels that, of course, perfectly matched her designer dress.

When Pete closed the car door behind her, she waltzed away, giving him zero thanks.

I felt my blood pressure rise. I'd been in Pete's shoes countless times, maybe not as a doorman. But I'd had my share of service jobs. Most people were great. But others – people like Bianca – seemed to get a real kick out of pushing someone around, just because they could.

As Vince's car pulled away, I watched Bianca stroll casually across the ornate outdoor rug that led to the building's glass double-doors. My gaze narrowed, and my fingers clenched. Maybe she could use a good push, and I didn't mean verbally.

In spite of everything, the thought was *almost* enough to make me smile.

I turned back to Pete. "Sorry about that." I wasn't even sure why I was apologizing. Obviously, Bianca's rudeness wasn't my fault, but that didn't change the fact that I was really sorry to see it.

But Pete wasn't even listening. He'd pulled out a cell phone and had it pressed against his ear, as if waiting for someone to answer on the other end. A second later, he said, "She's back." Pausing, he glanced briefly in my direction. "Here. In front of the building."

He waited a beat, and then said, "Yes, sir. Will do." He disconnected the call and shoved the phone into his pocket. He turned to me and said, "Let's get you inside, shall we?"

My eyebrows furrowed. "Was that Jake you were talking to?" I knew the question was kind of nosy, but since his conversation had obviously been about me, I figured a little nosiness was perfectly justified.

But before he could answer, we were interrupted, once again, by the sounds of loud throat-clearing. We both turned to look, and there she was, Bianca, standing just outside the building's glass double-doors.

Her eyebrows lifted as she eyed Pete with obvious impatience – waiting, apparently, for him to get one of those doors, too.

Oh, for crying out loud. The building's lobby wasn't even locked, not at this hour. And unless her arms had mysteriously broken within the last minute, she was perfectly capable of pulling open at least one of those doors all by herself.

But apparently, she had something else in mind. She was still glaring at Pete. "I'm waiting," she told him.

I made a sound of annoyance. "For what?" I called. "For him to carry you inside?"

Her eyes flashed in my direction. "I wasn't talking to *you*." She lifted a long finger and pointed it at Pete. "I was talking to *him*." She gave Pete a stiff smile. "You do realize that I'm friends with the owner of this building, right? One call, and I'll have your job."

That made me pause. Who *did* own the building? Honestly, I had no idea. But based on Bianca's confident demeanor, it seemed a mistake to goad her further – not for my sake, but for Pete's.

The building was nice. It had twenty floors of high-end apartments, along with a few condos and a fitness center.

As far as premium space, Jake had claimed a good chunk of it. He owned the penthouse on the top floor, and rented – or owned, I still wasn't quite sure – the floor just beneath it. No doubt, that meant he had a lot of pull as far as building-politics were concerned.

But if the building's owner wanted to get rid of Pete, I wasn't a hundred-percent sure that Jake would be able to save him, assuming he'd even want to.

Suddenly, I was drowning in a sea of uncertainty. Was Jake on his way down, right now, to kick me out? And if he did kick me out, where would I go? More importantly, how would I ever live without him?

And then, there was the other thing, something that I didn't want to think about. What, exactly, had almost happened to me today?

Considering the worst-case scenario, I stifled another shiver.

I'd been so incredibly stupid. And I'd almost paid for it, too. Bigtime.

And, on top of everything else, there was Pete. I had a sad suspicion that somehow, I'd already gotten him into trouble for reasons unrelated to Bianca.

I wrapped my arms tight around my torso and tried not to shiver. It was almost July, smack-dab in the middle of summer, but I was freezing cold and not feeling so great.

It would be nice to blame it on the pizza, but somehow, I knew that wasn't it. It was everything else – the fight with Jake, the stress of that weird encounter, and now, the sudden cold.

Sometime between the time I'd left Jake's office and now, the temperature had dropped at least twenty degrees. Or maybe, it just felt that way, because I was soaked to skin and weighted down with cold, damp clothes, as skimpy as they were.

I started to shake, harder now, whether because of the chill, or because of everything else. When my teeth started to chatter, I couldn't seem to make them stop.

Pete reached for my elbow. "Are you alright?"

Before I could answer, Bianca's voice rang out yet again. "Hey, Doorman! Do you want to keep your job, or what?"

That was the jolt I needed. A rush of anger flashed hot and hard against my skin. I stalked forward, heading toward those stupid doors. Once I reached them, I grabbed the nearest door handle, and yanked hard, flinging the door wide open.

And then, I laughed like a crazy person when Bianca had to leap out of the way to avoid getting smacked in the face. She made a show of stumbling backward and dropped her purse in the process. Still moving, she tripped over the fallen thing, fell backward, and landed hard on her ass.

She was shrieking now. "You did that on purpose!"

"Did what?" I hollered back. "Opened the stupid door? Wasn't that what you wanted?"

She was still sprawled across the ornate, outdoor rug. Glaring up at me, she yelled, "I didn't want *you* to open it. I wanted *him* to open it!"

Oh, crap. Him. Pete. Reluctantly, I looked over at him and felt my cheeks grow hotter still. Standing, dumb-struck, near the curb, his gaze was darting from me to Bianca. Obviously, he had no idea what to say.

Well, that made two of us.

Silently, Pete hustled over and extended a hand to help Bianca up.

She slapped his hand away and screeched out, "I'll have your job for this!"

Double crap.

His job. My shoulders sagged, and I belatedly realized that I was still holding the door handle. I let go, and the door swung slowly shut, leaving all of us standing outside. Correction – two of us were standing. As for Bianca, she was still on the ground, with her legs splayed and one of her jaunty high-heels lying a few feet away.

Looking at her now, a horrible thought occurred to me. What if she was hurt? Was that my fault? Probably. And even worse, what if Pete was the one who'd end up getting blamed for all this?

I shook my head. No. I wouldn't let that happen. I *couldn't* let that happen, not if I wanted to live with myself.

My mouth opened, but all that came out was a muttered curse. Oddly enough, no one heard it, because Bianca was still screeching, insulting both of us, up, down, and sideways. Finally, she flopped back onto the rug and announced, "You'd better call an ambulance, because I'm pretty sure I broke something."

And this is when a flashy red sports car roared into the turnaround. Jake's car. And, sure enough, there was Jake behind the wheel, but not for long. □

CHAPTER 18

Jake cut the engine and jumped out of the driver's seat, not bothering to shut the car door behind him.

Bianca, still sprawled on the rug, called out, "Jake! Thank God you're here. You won't believe what just happened to me."

Whether he heard her or not, I had no idea, because he didn't even pause. Instead, he strode forward, heading toward both of us — Bianca on the ground, and me, standing just a few feet beyond her.

As I watched, he literally stepped over Bianca and made his way to my side. His gaze searched my face. "Are you okay?" His voice hardened. "Where the hell were you?"

Startled, I drew back. "Out walking. Why?"

His jaw tightened. "Alone? You're joking, right?"

Obviously, I wasn't joking. And from the look on his face, he darn well knew it. But his reaction, well, I didn't know what to make of it.

From a few feet away, Bianca called out, "Didn't anyone hear me?" Her voice rose. "I *said* I need an ambulance!"

Jake turned, letting his cool gaze travel the length of her. "No, you don't."

With a sound of frustration, she pushed herself up into a sitting position. "Why doesn't anyone care? I think I broke my foot."

Jake's eyebrows lifted. He looked slowly and deliberately toward her feet. She was wearing only one shoe. The other still lay on its side a few feet away.

With obvious indifference, Jake said, "Yeah? Which one?"

She hesitated. "I'm not sure. Uh, the right one, I think."

I made a scoffing sound. "You don't even know?"

"Hey!" she said. "I've had a hard day, alright? So excuse me if I'm a little confused." Plaintively, she looked to Jake and reached out with both arms. "Forget the ambulance. Just carry me inside, okay?"

I gave Jake a sideways glance. It suddenly struck me that this sounded an awful lot like what had happened last night with Nipple Girl. She'd supposedly hurt her foot, too. Had she been faking it just like Bianca was now?

I mean, I wasn't a medical expert or anything, but it was pretty obvious that Bianca was fine in spite of her claims otherwise.

I felt my gaze narrow. "You saw that video. Didn't you?"

She blinked up at me. "What video?"

"The one where Jake carried that girl." I turned to Jake and asked, "Does this sort of thing happen to you a lot?"

"Forget that." He reached toward me and touched the side of my face. He frowned. "You're freezing."

I tried for a laugh, but only shivered. "Really? How'd you know?"

He moved closer and wrapped me in his arms. He was warm and dry, and I gave a happy sigh against his chest. Guiltily, I murmured, "I'm getting you all wet."

He lowered his head and spoke into my still-dripping hair. "Nah."

It was a lie, and we both knew it. I could feel his warmth seeping into me, which meant that my cold dampness was seeping into him. Sure, it was great for me, but what about him? What was *he* getting from all this?

I pulled away and gazed up into his eyes. What I saw there took my breath away. He might've been angry. But he still loved me. I could see it, as clear as day, all over his face. Apparently, I *wasn't* getting kicked to the curb, not today, anyway.

I breathed a sigh of relief, and not because of my living situation. I was so obnoxiously in love with him, and suddenly, I was beyond eager to put our fight behind us, or at least, take a break from all that.

A truce – there was nothing wrong with that, right?

My clothes were soaked, and I was still freezing. And yet, I couldn't help but smile. I knew just the thing to warm me up – and Jake, too, while I was at it.

Make-up sex.

Jake's voice, harder again, chased my smile away. "What the hell were you thinking?"

"What?" Talk about verbal whiplash. "What do you mean?"

Before he could answer, I heard that dreaded sound – *more* throat-clearing. I turned to look, and sure enough, there she was, Bianca, standing almost within arm's reach.

Yup. Standing.

So much for her broken foot.

I looked around and became painfully aware that sometime within the last couple of minutes, we had attracted a small audience – a dozen-or-so people, who were clustered around us, under the wide, protective awning.

I recognized a few of them as tenants who lived in the building. About the others, I had no idea. Probably, they were random gawkers, who'd been walking by and stopped because of all the commotion. Or who knows? Maybe, they were just normal people, trying to get in out of the rain.

Either way, they were all staring, mostly at Jake, not that I could blame them, all things considered.

Next to us, Bianca cleared her throat yet again. By now, it was like fingernails on a chalkboard. I decided that if I never heard that sound again, it would be way too soon.

I turned to her and said, "Just so you know, if you do that much more, I'm pretty sure you're gonna hack up an esophagus or something."

She gave me an annoyed look. "I was *trying* to get Jake's attention."

"Yeah? Well, it's *your* esophagus, not mine."

"Exactly," she said. "It *is* mine. So don't worry about it."

I wasn't worried. Mostly, I wanted to rip that thing out and use it as a muzzle.

But that was probably better left unsaid, so I looked to Jake. As far as I could tell, no amount of throat-clearing would be snagging his attention now. He was scanning the crowd as if searching for someone in particular. Finally, he turned to Bianca and asked, "Where's Vince?"

"Parking the car." She gave me a dismissive glance. "Because someone else wouldn't do it."

Yeah. That someone was me, obviously. Score one for Bianca, not that I was keeping track…much.

Jake frowned. "He's late."

That made me pause. Late for what? I turned to Jake and said, "You knew they were coming?"

"I knew Vince was." He flicked his gaze toward Bianca. "This one's a surprise."

The way it looked, it was a day full of surprises. Vince and Jake weren't exactly friends. Vince was a hot-shot sports agent who represented some of the world's most famous athletes. And Jake? Well, he had a real knack for making those athletes look like total morons.

I knew for a fact that Jake's antics – all caught on video, by the way – had cost Vince and his clients a ton of money in lost endorsement deals and who-knows what else.

"I don't get it," I said. "Why are you meeting with Vince?"

Next to us, Bianca said, "It's not just Vince. He's meeting with me, too. Remember?"

As if I could forget.

Seeking a shred of privacy, I leaned closer to Jake and asked, "But why? What's going on?"

For a few crazy weeks, I'd actually worked for Vince. During that short, tumultuous time, I'd learned a few things, and most of them were unpleasant.

For starters, Vince wasn't nearly as nice as he pretended to be. And even if he were, Jake had plenty of reasons to loathe him. Some of those reasons involved me.

"Ask me later," Jake said. "For now, wait here, okay? I'm gonna give Pete a message. And then, we'll get you upstairs."

Silently, I nodded. The way I saw it, the sooner we were inside, the better.

Jake gave me a serious look. "I mean it. Don't go anywhere, okay? Because if I have to find you again–" He paused. "Just don't make me, alright?"

That didn't make any sense. Jake hadn't found me. I'd shown up here mostly on my own, right here, where we both lived. Finding me couldn't have been *that* hard.

I might have argued, but Jake was already making his way toward Pete. As he did, Bianca sidled closer to me and said, "In case you were still wondering, the answer is 'no'."

I gave her a perplexed look. "No to what?"

"To your question."

I blinked. "There was a question?"

"The video from last night," she said. "No. I didn't see it. I didn't have to." She smiled. "Because unlike some people, I was there."

At this, I almost laughed in her face. "Where? At the convention center?" I rolled my eyes. "Yeah, right."

"You don't believe me?"

"Hell no, I don't believe you." I straightened. "*I* was there last night. *You* weren't."

"That's what *you* think." She smirked. "And unlike you, I was there for the whole thing."

"Like I'm gonna believe that. You're like the biggest liar on the planet."

At this, she had the nerve to look insulted. "I am not!"

"Oh yeah?" I glanced down. "How's your broken foot?"

"Much better." She pursed her lips. "Thanks *ever so much* for asking."

I gave her a snotty smile. "You're so *very* welcome."

With that, I turned away, hoping she'd take the hint. I was already cold and soggy. A double-dose of Bianca wouldn't improve anything.

But apparently, she wasn't done yet. "If you don't believe me," she said, "ask Jake. *He* was the one who invited me."

"Uh-huh," I said, not bothering to look at her. "Sure he did."

Just then, Jake returned to my side. He wrapped an arm around my waist and said, "Come on. Let's get you upstairs."

I glanced out toward his car, still parked in the turnaround. The driver's side door was still open. "What about your car?" I asked. "Don't you want to move it or something?"

"No. What I *want* is to get you inside."

I gave his car a worried look. "Yeah, but—"

"Don't worry about it," Jake said. "It's handled."

Next to us, Bianca spoke up. "What about me? I'm not 'handled.' Aren't you taking *me* upstairs, too?"

Jake spared her half a glance. "Nope."

"Why not?" Bianca demanded.

As an answer, Jake started steering me away. Over his shoulder, he told Bianca, "When Vince shows up, have him meet me in my office."

A minute later, Jake and I were finally alone inside the elevator. His arm was wrapped tight around my waist, and I couldn't resist leaning into him. I heard myself sigh. "Talk about a crazy day."

And it *had* been crazy. Unfortunately, none of it was the good kind of crazy.

But, in happier news, the day wasn't over yet. Next to me, Jake felt so amazingly good. All I wanted to do now was forget everything, at least for a little while, and get lost in the nearness of him.

Unfortunately, it didn't work out that way.

Inside the elevator, Jake pulled away and turned to face me. His gaze grew dark, and an unfamiliar edge crept into his voice, "You wanna know what's crazy?"

From the look on his face, I wasn't so sure. Still, I managed to say, "What?"

He gave a slow shake of his head. "You."

My mouth fell open. Here I was, standing next to a guy who took insane chances every day, and he was calling *me* crazy?

"Me?" I tried to laugh. "*I'm* the crazy one?"

"Yeah. You are." His voice held no hint of humor. "And wanna know what else?"

At the tone of his voice, my own humor was rapidly evaporating. "I dunno. Do I?"

"You keep it up, you're gonna make *me* crazy."

I stared up at him, wondering what on Earth he was talking about. It was true that before I'd left for that stupid walk, we'd been arguing, and probably, that argument wasn't quite over. But there was no way on Earth that Jake's craziness could be pinned on me.

I thought of all the wild stunts he'd pulled off, long before I'd been part of the picture. By any measure, he was a million times more crazy than I could ever be on my craziest day.

"I hate to tell you this," I said, "but you were crazy long before I showed up."

"Yeah? You think?" Suddenly, he slammed the back of his fist onto the elevator's emergency-stop button. Almost immediately, we came to an abrupt stop.

Startled, I looked up. According to the display, we were somewhere between the fourteenth and fifteenth floors. I looked to Jake and asked, "What'd you do that for?"

He reached into his pocket and pulled out his cell phone. He scrolled across the screen until he found whatever it was he was looking for. He shoved the phone in front of my face and said, "You wanna explain *this*?"

I felt myself frown.

Actually, I didn't.

CHAPTER 19

Looking at the image on his phone, I felt a surge of heat flash across my face. Maybe that was a good thing. If nothing else, I wasn't cold anymore.

Think positive, right?

I was looking at an image of me, rushing along that deserted city-street sometime within the last half-hour. In the picture, my hair was already soaked, and worse, so were my clothes.

Embarrassed by how I looked, I wanted to look away. But I didn't. Instead, I gave the picture a good, long look, taking in every detail – correction, every *sordid* detail.

My low-cut, frilly white blouse was plastered to my skin in a way that was shockingly obscene. Through the thin, soaked fabric, I could see the clear outline of my lacy white bra, and worse, the faint pink circles of my nipples, embarrassingly erect, thanks to the cold – because let's face it, there had been nothing arousing about *that* whole experience.

My gaze dipped to the shorts. Obviously, the denim wasn't see-through – thank God – but the soaked fabric was plastered so tight to my skin that the shorts looked like they might've been painted on.

Overall, the effect was pretty darn disturbing. It's not that I looked bad, exactly. I mean, if I were alone with Jake, that was one thing. But to be out in public looking like that?

I looked like a party-girl of the paid variety.

Yikes.

But it's not like I'd planned it that way.

I was still staring at the picture when Jake abruptly pulled his phone away and said, "You got something you wanna tell me?"

No. I didn't. Not if he was going to ask like that.

And, besides, I had a question of my own. "How'd you get that picture?"

"You wanna know? Answer my question first."

"That's not fair," I said, feeling my own anger bubble to the surface. "I deserve to know how you got that."

In my mind, I saw hidden cameras and spies, lurking around every corner. Was Jake having me followed? And if so, why? Didn't he trust me?

Jake spoke again. "Are you gonna tell me or not?"

"I don't know." I crossed my arms and tossed his own words right back at him. "Are you gonna tell *me* or not?"

Silently, he stared down at me, looking like he wanted to hit something. I wasn't worried, not about that. But if I were someone else, like a guy for example, the look on Jake's face would be ringing all kinds of alarm bells.

I paused. Alarm bells – that made me realize something. Jake had just hit the elevator's stop button. Probably, somewhere downstairs, alarm bells were ringing for real.

I glanced toward the elevator's control panel. "You wanna talk? Fine. But let's talk at your place, okay?"

"No."

"Why not?"

"Because I don't know who the fuck's there. That's why."

I drew back, startled by his language. Sure, I'd heard that word before, plenty of times – from Jake *and* from my own lips. But if he thought that cursing at me now was going to get him the answers he wanted, he had another thing coming.

I gave him my snottiest smile. "So we have company? Who the fuck is it?"

He wasn't amused. "What do you want? An apology?" His tone grew sarcastic. "Does my language offend you?"

Did it? Not really, except when he sounded so mad.

I didn't know what to say, so I shrugged and left it at that. Let *him* figure it out. And if he did, maybe he could tell me, because I was so confused I could hardly think.

He was still looking at me. "Get offended all you want. But you're gonna tell me." His voice grew a shade darker. "Here. *Now*."

What the hell?

"This isn't a conversation," I told him. "It's an interrogation." I dropped my arms and stiffened my spine. "And I don't like it."

"You don't like it, huh?" His jaw tightened. "I bet there's a lot of things you wouldn't like."

Something about the way he said it sent a cold shiver down my spine. There was a nasty edge that I couldn't quite decipher. What, exactly, was going on?

With an effort, I shook off the chill and demanded, "What's that supposed to mean?"

"Just answer the question. Is there something you wanna tell me?"

"Yeah," I said. "You're being a jerk. How's that?"

I waited for him to argue the point. But he didn't. Instead, he just stood there, looking like he'd be willing to wait all day, if that's what it took.

I didn't want to wait all day. I was cold and tired, and Vince's hoodie wasn't nearly as dry as when I'd put it on. Suddenly, all I wanted was a hot bath and a glass of wine. Or hell, how about the whole bottle? The day had been *that* craptastic.

Again, I thought of that picture on Jake's phone. How, exactly, did he get that?

"What's going on?" I demanded. "Are you having someone spy on me? You think I'd cheat on you or something? Is that it?"

It seemed far-fetched, but what other explanation was there? Everything about him – his demeanor, his words, the way he was looking at me – it felt like one giant accusation, which totally sucked, because I'd done nothing wrong.

When he made no response, I took a deep breath and kept on going. "Because it seems to me, you have a lot more opportunities to cheat than I do. Maybe I should have someone follow *you* around. See how *you'd* like it."

Somewhere in the back of my mind, I realized that I *had* to be missing something. If Jake really were having someone follow me around, they probably would've stopped to help me when those two losers had cornered me on the street.

I paused.

Oh.

Already, Jake had shoved his phone back into his pocket. But in my mind, I could still see the picture, not just of me, but of my surroundings. And suddenly, I knew exactly where that photo had come from. And I also knew why Jake was so pissed off.

He knew those people.

Crap.

And worse, the way it looked, those psychos had told on me.

CHAPTER 20

Inside the elevator, I held out my hand, palm up. "Alright, lemme see it."

"My phone?" Jake gave me a hard look. "Where's yours?"

I made a sound of frustration. "What does *that* have to do with anything?"

"Just tell me. Where is it?"

I knew exactly where my phone was. It was up in Jake's penthouse, inside my purse, on the small table near the entryway. But that was hardly the point.

I wanted to scream in frustration. But instead, I took a deep, steadying breath and said in a voice that was far calmer than I felt, "I'm not looking to make a phone call. I want—"

"Why'd you leave it?"

The questions were coming so hard and so fast that I was having a hard time keeping track. "Why'd I leave what? My phone?"

As an answer, Jake reached into his back pocket and pulled out a cell phone. Not *his* cell phone. *My* cell phone. Silently, he held it out vaguely in my direction, as if to say, *"You want it? Well, there ya go."*

Well, that was rich. So all along, he'd known exactly where my phone was? If so, why the third-degree?

I stared down at the thing, still in Jake's possession. "You took my phone?"

Given where I'd left it, it felt like a huge invasion of privacy. What was he doing, anyway? Going through my things? And why?

Feeling ready to explode, I snatched the phone out of his hand and shoved it into the front pocket of my borrowed hoodie. I glared up at him and waited for some sort of explanation.

Jake looked down at the hoodie and frowned, as if noticing it for the first time. From the look on his face, he'd also noticed that the hoodie was a few sizes too big and obviously not my own.

But he said nothing about the hoodie. Instead, he lifted his gaze to my eyes and said, "You gonna answer my question?"

At this point, I didn't even know what question he meant. But I did know one thing. I'd had just about enough of this.

"No," I told him. "You answer my question first." To drive the point home, I spoke very slowly and clearly. "What were you doing with my phone?"

"Screw your phone."

"Oh yeah?" Suddenly, I felt like crying. "Well, screw you, too, Jake."

He had no reaction, not even a flinch. That shouldn't have been surprising. Jake had a long, public track-record of pissing people off. A basic "screw-you" would be nothing to him. And pathetic or not, I wasn't willing to go any further.

As a kid, I'd seen my own parents go through the whole name-calling thing. That wasn't going to be me, not if I could help it.

So I took a deep breath and tried again. "What were you doing? Checking my text messages? Reading my email? Because I have nothing to hide, and even if I did…" I threw up my hands. "Well, I don't, okay?"

At this, he gave a small laugh. "Right."

"God, what is your deal today?"

But part of me *knew* what the deal was. And it had to do with that stupid picture. For the second time, I held out my hand. "Your phone. I need to see it."

When he made no move, I added, "What's the big deal? You had *my* phone. So fair is fair, right?"

After a long, tense moment, he finally reached into his front pocket and pulled out his own phone. Silently, he dropped it into my open palm.

I went to work immediately, sliding my finger across the smooth screen. As usual, I was greeted with the password-prompt. Assuming he hadn't changed it, the password was my name.

I paused. But what if he *had* changed it? How humiliating would *that* be, to try my own name and have it fail?

Trying not to sound pathetic, I said, "Is the password the same as before, or…?" Stupid or not, I couldn't bring myself to finish the sentence. I looked up and was startled to find Jake staring, not at the phone, but at me.

His eyes were dark, and his mouth was tight. "You *know* what the password is."

When I answered, my voice came out embarrassingly small. "Do I?"

"It hasn't changed." His own voice grew softer now. "It's not gonna change."

At this, I felt a pitiful surge of relief. "Really?"

"What do you think? That I'm gonna grab my phone and change the password – or shit, change how I feel about you – just because you pissed me off?"

"I pissed you off?" I tried to smile. "Funny, I hadn't noticed."

Jake swallowed, and his face, all hard angles and shadows, softened into something that melted my heart. "I was so fucking worried."

The look in his eyes hurt to see. "You were?"

He glanced down at his cell phone, still cradled in my hands. His voice grew raw. "You have no idea."

He was right. I didn't. But I was desperate to know more, so I looked down at his phone and tapped in the password. The answers had to be in there somewhere. I was sure of it.

And, as it turned out, I was right.☐

CHAPTER 21

Holding Jake's cell phone, I scrolled until I found it, that awful photo of me. Trying not to cringe, I gave it a quick glance, but noticed nothing new.

I kept on scrolling, not through his pictures, but through the other screens. I knew exactly what I was looking for, and I wasn't planning to stop until I found it.

By now, I had a theory. The scary duo had taken that picture from the window of that gold SUV. And then, trouble-makers that they were, they'd texted that stupid picture to Jake, along with some sort of message.

Finally, I found it – the series of texts that accompanied the photo. Turns out, I'd been right.

Score one for me.

Hey, I needed the point. Today, I was so far behind, I needed all the help I could get.

I squinted down at the sender's name. "Who's Moe?" I recalled the two losers who'd given me such a hard time. "The guy or the girl?"

"If there was a girl," Jake said, "it's first I've heard of it."

I looked up. "So, that guy, Moe, you know him?"

It was a stupid question. Of course, Jake knew him. Not only had Moe practically fled at the mention of Jake's name, he was a personal-contact on Jake's cell phone. And to top it all off, the way it looked, he and Jake were on texting terms.

What were they? Best buddies or something?

Jake gave a shrug. "Yeah, you might say I know him."

"How?" I asked. "Are you friends or something?"

"I wouldn't go that far."

Well, that was a relief. I guess. I looked down to the phone and started scrolling up, looking for the first text in the series.

"If you're gonna read them," Jake said, "read them out loud."

"Why?"

"Just do it."

Well, that wasn't bossy or anything. But fearful of Jake snatching his phone away, I decided not to argue.

Already, I'd found the first text. It was the one that accompanied the photo. It had only four words, from Moe to Jake. Reluctantly, I read those words out loud. "This belong to you?"

The words burned in my throat. *This?* Meaning me? What the hell?

I looked up, meeting Jake's gaze. "So I'm a 'this'? Like a possession?"

"In Moe's world? Yeah. You are." His jaw clenched. "But you're my 'this,' which is why you're standing here, nice and safe, right now."

His words, filled with hints of unspoken danger, sent another cold shiver down my spine. Trying for a bravado that I didn't quite feel, I said, "Yours, huh? As opposed to what? Moe's newest party girl?"

Silently, Jake looked down at me for a long, tense moment. And then, when he finally spoke, his voice was deadly quiet. "That's not a party you'd enjoy."

"Well, obviously." With an effort, I shook off the chill and looked back to his phone, determined to keep on reading. "And then you say, 'Yes. That's mine. *All* mine.'" The "all" was in capital letters. But that wasn't what caught my attention. It was the way Jake had phrased it.

With growing resentment, I said those first words again, this time as a question. "*That's* mine?"

In a sense, it was true. I was his. And he was mine. But the phrasing was off in so many ways.

It felt wrong and foreign. I was so offended I could hardly speak. And yet, I'd be lying if I didn't admit, if only to myself, that it sent an embarrassing thrill straight through my heart and lower, to places covered by the cold denim of my soggy Daisy Dukes.

That was *so* seriously messed up.

Jake's voice interrupted my thoughts. "Get mad all you want, but that's the way Moe talks, which means it's what he understands."

"Oh." I guess that made sense in a weird, twisted sort of way.

"And," Jake continued, "I sure as hell wasn't gonna waste time looking for a nicer way to tell him hands-off." He gestured toward his phone, still cradled in my hands. "Now, go on. Finish the rest."

I scrolled down and winced. This text was from Jake to Moe. Reluctantly, I said, "And you say, 'Where the fuck is she?'"

I looked up, meeting Jake's gaze. His eyes looked haunted for reasons that I was only beginning to understand.

Lamely, I mumbled, "I just went for a walk."

"Yeah. So you said."

"You think I'm lying?"

He closed his eyes for a long, painful moment. "I thought you were upstairs."

Something in his voice caught me off-guard. "What?"

"When you left my office, I thought you were going upstairs."

"To your penthouse?"

He shook his head. "Not my penthouse. *Our* penthouse."

"Oh come on, Jake. That's really nice and all, but you don't have to put it like that. I mean, I know it's yours. And that's okay. Really. I'm just glad you let me stay there. Honest."

It was true. The place was a palace. I'd arrived as a house guest, and hadn't quite left. Part of me was thinking I might never have to leave – the penthouse *or* more importantly, Jake. But it seemed a supreme arrogance to simply assume so.

Inside the elevator, Jake was looking at me like I'd lost my mind. "*Let* you stay there?"

"Well, you know…"

"No. I don't." He made a scoffing sound. "But forget that. We'll talk about it later." Again, he gestured to the phone. "Keep reading."

I scrolled lower. The next text was from Moe. Looking at it, I felt myself frown.

"What?" Jake said. "You want *me* to read it?"

"No." I squared my shoulders. "That's fine. I'll do it." Trying to sound casual, I read the message out loud. "Bitch gonna get herself killed."

In truth, I wasn't sure what bothered me more – that he'd called me a bitch, or that he had such low expectations for my survival. After all, I'd made it back to Jake's place just fine, a little soggy maybe, but thankfully unharmed.

I looked up, wondering what Jake would say now.

He said nothing, and the silence stretched out.

Trying to make a joke of it, I said, "Well, he seems nice."

"You think it's funny?"

"No. That's not it." In a softer voice, I added, "I know you were worried, but everything was fine." I tried to smile. "See? Here I am. All in one piece."

Jake's gaze slid down my borrowed hoodie, and then lower, as if recalling how I'd looked in that stupid picture. Even now, I wasn't quite decent. Vince's hoodie, as large as it was, fell nearly to the bottom of my shorts, which to be honest, were a little too short for my own good.

Probably, I looked half-naked, even now. I shifted uncomfortably, wondering what Jake was thinking. From the look on his face, it couldn't be good.

He was no prude, and he didn't mind me dressing sexy. I knew that firsthand.

But he *was* protective. And I didn't need a crystal ball to tell me that everything would've been fine if only that guy – Moe – had just minded his own damn business.

Desperate to put all of this behind us, I tried again. "Oh come on, Jake. That guy was totally wrong. He got you worked up for nothing."

Okay, that wasn't quite true. In reality, I had a sneaky suspicion that my poorly timed walk could've ended a lot differently. But saying so wouldn't make Jake feel any better now, and if nothing else, I owed him a certain peace-of-mind.

Going for a distraction, I said, "And a little rain isn't gonna kill me. Right?"

But Jake was frowning again. "You think it's the rain I was worried about?"

"No. But I'm just saying—"

"Wanna know why I had your phone?"

Startled by the change of subject, I managed to say, "Um, yeah. That would be really nice, actually."

"I had your phone, because as soon as I got that message – the first one – I called you. You didn't answer."

"Well, yeah, because—"

"So I ran the hell upstairs to grab my car-keys."

I blinked. "Ran?"

"You think I'm gonna wait for the damn elevator?"

"Oh. Sorry." I wasn't sure why I was apologizing. The building did have that emergency stairway, but no one actually used it, except, apparently for Jake, especially when psychos in gold SUVs got him worked up for no good reason.

"And the whole time," Jake continued, "I'm calling you, thinking, 'Please, fuck, answer.' But you don't." His voice grew ragged on the edges. "And so I'm grabbing the keys, and I heard this ringing. I recognize the ringtone. It's your phone. And I find the damn thing in your purse, where it's not gonna do you a damn bit of good."

He sounded so worked up that I didn't know what to say. Finally, I mumbled, "Yeah. I know. I forgot it."

"You forgot it," he repeated.

"Oh, come on. You don't take *your* phone everywhere."

"Yeah? Well, you're not me."

And there it was again. That same double-standard. Probably, I should be angry. In principle, I guess I was. But looking at him now, so worked up on my behalf, lofty principles seemed kind of unimportant in the big scheme of things.

And, as much as I hated to admit it, Jake did have a point.

It wasn't his fault that I'd ended up on the wrong street at the wrong time. And it wasn't his fault that some psycho had sent him that stupid text. And it sure as heck wasn't his fault that I'd forgotten my phone at a time when he'd been so desperate to get ahold of me.

And he *had* been desperate. Even now, I could see it in his eyes. I could hear it in his voice. And a few minutes earlier, after he'd practically jumped out of his car to get to me, I could feel it in the intensity of his embrace.

I looked down and stared at my soggy shoes. Never in my whole life had anyone cared so much for my wellbeing. Even when I'd been a kid, my parents had been too wrapped up in their own things to obsess over where we were, or what we were doing.

For most of that time, I'd been doing a lot of things that I shouldn't have been, not that my parents realized half of it. But unlike my parents, Jake was street-smart in ways they could never be. He saw it all and didn't look away when things got bad.

I felt myself frown. Of course, it didn't help that he literally had people telling on me.

Jake's voice interrupted my thoughts. "What is it?"

I looked up. "I dunno. I guess I'm feeling overwhelmed." I gave him a pleading look. "It's been such a crappy day, and then that guy..." I let the words trail off, fearful of igniting yet another argument.

His voice sharpened. "Which guy?"

"You know, Moe, sending you that stupid text. I mean, if he hadn't said anything, you wouldn't be all mad at me now." I gave him a weak smile. "I would've come home just fine, and everything would've normal."

"So you think the text was the problem?"

"No. Not really. But I'm just saying, if he hadn't contacted you, everything would've been okay."

His eyebrows lifted. "Is that so?"

"Isn't it?"

"That picture," he said, "you get a good look at it?"

Once again, I felt my cheeks grow warm. "I *know* how I looked. But in my defense, I didn't know my shirt would get all see-through at the first drop of rain."

About the weather, this was a slight exaggeration. It hadn't been a few drops. It had been a raging downpour. But hey, I was trying to make a point.

Unfortunately, the point looked totally lost on Jake. Again, his gaze dipped to the hoodie, and then lower still.

I watched, feeling my blush deepen, as he eyed the ragged edges of my skimpy shorts and then, my bare thighs. His gaze kept on going and didn't stop until he reached the pink laces of my white tennis shoes.

Well, at least *those* were decent.

I lifted my chin. "But hey, it could happen to anyone, right?"

"But you're not anyone." He looked up, meeting my gaze. "You're mine."

CHAPTER 22

Jake's words hung in the cool, quiet air. *You're mine.*

The words were simple. And true.

Still, something about the way he said it made my breath catch and my knees go wobbly. I tried to speak, but couldn't find the words.

"And," Jake continued, "you were on Moe's street." Slowly, he reached out and gripped the zipper of my borrowed hoodie. He nudged it down barely an inch, and I felt the cool air tickle my throat.

Suddenly distracted, I felt myself swallow. "You mean like where he lives?"

Jake's fingers were still on the zipper. "Guess again."

I didn't want to guess again. I wanted Jake to give that zipper another tug.

I don't know why or what I expected. From the look on his face, our argument wasn't quite over. And, as for myself, I was cold and damp and overly conscious of what I was wearing.

True, Jake had seen me in a lot fewer clothes, but as far as this particular outfit? It was obviously an issue, even now.

In front of me, Jake stood very still, waiting, apparently, for me to answer.

I tried to think. There was a question. What was it? Oh, that's right. It was about Moe. If Moe didn't *live* on that street, how could it be considered his?

I tried to find the words. "Is it, uh, where he does business?"

Jake gave the zipper another tug. "You might say that."

My shorts were still cold, but the parts they covered were growing warmer with every tug of that zipper.

I glanced around, suddenly curious whether or not the elevator had security cameras. I didn't see any, but that didn't mean they weren't there.

Jake had lived in this building a lot longer than I had. Would he know the answer?

Probably, he would. I was tempted to ask, but was far too embarrassed. Supposedly, we were still fighting, and if I asked about cameras now, Jake would know exactly what I'd been thinking.

I returned my gaze to his and felt a new flush rise to my cheeks. From the look in his eyes, he already knew.

The cocky bastard.

Mortified, I tried to change the subject. "So, uh, that's his territory or something?"

Jake gave a slow nod. "And in case you didn't notice, it's not a nice place."

His hand was still there, poised on that same zipper. Distracted as hell, I murmured, "It isn't?"

Jake gave another slow nod, followed by another yank. "It's not nice. *Or* safe." His dark gaze bored into mine. "Especially for someone as sweet as you."

My lips suddenly felt very dry. I wanted to lick them, but I made myself stop. Somehow, I managed to say, "I'm not *that* sweet."

"Yeah?" He gave the zipper another yank, this one longer and harder. The hoodie fell open down to my navel, exposing a long, narrow gap where the hoodie's dark cotton no longer met. Within that gap was the thin fabric of my soaked, white blouse.

The gap was so narrow that nothing much was exposed, just a long, thin swath of fabric, straight down the center of my chest. Even so, I was starting to feel just a little bit naked.

And heaven help me, I liked it.

Jake's fingers still gripped the zipper. "Later, I want you to look at that picture again."

I didn't care about the picture, not now. The real-life image in front of me was far too compelling. It was the sight of Jake, standing there, close enough to touch.

And I *did* want to touch him.

His hair was dark, and his eyes were darker. His loose, gray T-shirt clung to his broad chest and bulging biceps in a way that defied description.

My gaze dipped lower, skimming his abs. Wordlessly, I drank in the sight of his stomach-muscles, flat and tight, outlined just above the waistband of his faded jeans.

Again, I swallowed, feeling a new kind of wetness, hot and slick, dampen my rain-soaked panties.

I wanted him. I was ready for him, too. And unless I was mistaken, the feeling was mutual.

Looking for confirmation, my gaze drifted lower. And there it was, that delicious bulge, straining against the thick denim fabric. I reached out, wondering if two could play at the zipper game.

But Jake's voice, laced with steel, made me stop in mid-motion. "Promise me."

Startled, I let my hand drop. "What?"

"The picture," he said. "Promise me you'll look. And I mean a good, long look."

I didn't get it. What was he trying to do? Make me even *more* ashamed of what had happened? As if I didn't already feel stupid enough?

This wasn't like him, and I had the distinct feeling that I was missing something.

Struggling to think, I said, "Why? I already saw it. And I'm sorry, okay?"

"Not as sorry as you could've been."

"What does *that* mean?"

His expression darkened. "It means, I want you to know what kind of bullet you dodged, so you don't do that again."

I made a sound of frustration. "I wasn't planning on doing it again. And there were no bullets."

"Uh-huh." His hand was still poised on the zipper. I glanced down, chagrined by the fact that even now, after his maddening interruption, I still wanted him.

And I didn't want to wait.

I recalled his warning that he didn't know who exactly might be at his penthouse. But what about his office? Maybe *that* was empty.

It *was* after business hours, right?

I paused. Who was I kidding? Even if Trey wasn't there, Vince and Bianca would be arriving there soon.

And besides, Jake wasn't going to let everything go so easily. Even now, that much was obvious.

Considering where we were, maybe that was for the best – or at least, that's what I tried to tell myself.

Determined not to make a further fool of myself, I forced a casual shrug. "Okay. Fine."

"Okay what?"

In a monotone, I said, "I promise I'll look at the picture. There. Are you happy now?" I glanced toward the elevator's control panel. "So, can we go?"

The corners of his mouth lifted the barest fraction. "No."

I sighed in frustration. "Why not?"

His gaze dipped to my lips, and when he spoke, his voice became softer, almost a caress. "Is that what you want? To go?"

At something in his look, my pulse quickened. "Uh, yes?"

He flashed me a sudden grin. "Was that a question? Or a statement?"

That grin, sexy as anything, made my stomach flutter and my breath hitch. When I answered, my voice came out nearly too breathless to be heard. "I don't know."

"If you wanna go," he said, flicking his head toward the nearby control panel, "go ahead. Hit the button."

I glanced toward the panel. I wasn't following. Why wouldn't he just hit it? I looked up, meeting his gaze. Almost embarrassed, I asked, "What if I don't?"

At this, he gave the zipper one final yank. The hoodie fell open, and slowly, he lowered his head until his lips tickled my right ear. In a rough whisper, he said, "Then I'll fuck you right here, and show you how 'mine' you are."

I sucked in a breath. Oh, my God. Crude or not, that was sounding really, really good.

Nervously, I glanced around. "But, uh, aren't there cameras in here?"

Jake's mouth slid to my neck. "Yeah."

I pulled back. "What?"

"In the back corner."

"You're kidding." I looked, but didn't see anything. Still, I moved to tug the hoodie shut.

Jake's hand stopped me. "Don't."

I paused. "Don't?"

"Don't worry. No one will see."

"You can't guarantee that."

"That's what *you* think." He reached out with a warm hand and stroked the underside of my breast. Through the thin, damp fabric – of my blouse *and* of my bra – I could feel the heat of his touch, and I whimpered with need.

Somehow, I managed to say, "Seriously Jake."

His hand crept higher. "Who says I'm not serious?"

"But what about the camera?"

"You think I'd share you with anyone?" His fingers found a nipple, and he gave it a tender squeeze. "You think I'd share even the sight of you?"

His fingers squeezed again, rolling the nub gently, persistently, until a soft moan escaped my lips. Breathlessly, I asked, "How can you be sure?"

Slowly, he pulled his hand away, leaving the nipple, cold and wanting, in the cool elevator air. "I'm sure. But if you wanna go..." He glanced toward the control panel. "There's the button."

I gave the button a good, long look. And then, slowly, I reached out, but not toward the control panel, toward Jake.

My eager fingers found the bulge in his jeans, and I ran a soft hand over his swollen hardness, straining, harder now, against the rough denim.

In almost a whisper, I admitted, "I don't wanna go."

A slow smile spread across his lips. "Good."

Deliberately, he reached out with both hands and nudged aside my borrowed hoodie, letting the fabric fall loosely off my shoulders. His gaze dipped to my soaked blouse and everything underneath it. "The next time you wear that," he said, "it had better be for me." His voice grew lower, rougher. "And only me."

Wordlessly, I nodded. I didn't *want* anyone else to see me like this. Not now. Not ever.

His fingers moved to the neckline of my blouse. He gripped the fabric in both hands, and then, with one quick motion, he ripped it open, sending buttons scattering to the elevator floor.

I gave a quick, excited gasp. I loved this, and he damn well knew it.

Deliberately, his hands moved to my lacy bra. His fingers traced the upper outline of the delicate fabric, and then, he shoved aside the tops of the cups, exposing my damp nipples to the cool, elevator air.

He looked down and smiled like he was loving what he saw.

Unable to resist, I looked, too. The filmy lace material was cupped under my breasts, raising them higher, as if they were begging for Jake's attention, which, in a way, they were.

My skin was damp, and my nipples were so erect, they practically ached.

When he reached up to palm my breasts in his large, warm hands, I gave a soft moan and let my eyelids flutter shut. His fingers tightened, squeezing my nipples between them as he lifted my breasts with both hands.

It felt so wonderful and yet, considering our surroundings, so terribly obscene. Probably, I'd be embarrassed tomorrow, but for now, all I could think was *more* – more of this, more of him.

Unable to stop myself, I moaned his name, "Jake."

He silenced me with a kiss, hard and possessive. His tongue found mine, and I sagged against him, molding my body against his. My heart was racing, and I was so wet, I could feel it, dampening my already soaked panties.

Jake's lips slid from mine, and he trailed his mouth slowly to my ear.

In a low, husky voice, he asked, "How do you want it? Slow and easy?" His teeth grazed my earlobe. "Or fast and hard?"

There was nothing easy about the way I felt now. Breathlessly, I said, "Fast. Like, *now* fast."

With a low, chuckle, he said, "That's my girl."

Yes, I was his girl. I liked being his girl. Desperate to prove it, I reached between us and gripped the waistband of his jeans. With fumbling hands, I unfastened the button and then went for the zipper.

As for Jake, he was working on my zipper too, and doing a lot better job than I was.

Before I knew it, my Daisy Dukes were lying somewhere in the corner of the elevator, and his jeans, along with his briefs, were somewhere around his ankles.

I still had on my panties, but that wasn't stopping anything. With one smooth motion, Jake cupped his warm, strong hands around my wet, cold ass and lifted me up against the elevator wall.

Almost panting now, I gripped his length with one hand, and guided him toward my opening, even as I shoved aside the crotch of my panties to give him quick and easy access.

He surged forward, taking me hard and fast, just the way I'd wanted. My lips parted, and I said his name, over and over while he drove into me, harder and faster until I thought I'd die of pure bliss.

And if I did die? Well, this was totally the way to go.

Surging forward yet again, Jake lowered his head and whispered in my ear. "Don't forget."

I could hardly think. Almost beside myself, I breathed, "Forget what?"

"That you're mine." As he said it, he pulled back, and surged forward once more, claiming me with his body as much as his words.

"Yes," I breathed into his shoulder. And then, my breathing became too ragged to speak. I was falling into that sweet oblivion, where nothing else seemed to matter, nothing except for the feel of Jake's body, hard and strong, holding me tight, and taking me straight to heaven, right here on Earth.

And then, I was there, moaning my release into his hard shoulder, even as he drove harder, and came to his own climax, with his hands still cupping my ass, squeezing it as he murmured my name.

When it was all over, I lowered my head, resting it on his strong shoulder. "Jake?"

"Yeah?"

"I love you."

"You'd better."

In spite of everything, I heard myself laugh. "You're supposed to say you love me, too."

"Baby, I do love you. More than life itself."

Like a sponge, I soaked up those words, wanting to drink them up and keep them forever.

And then, there was ringing. Not in my ears, and not from the elevator.

It was a phone. And not mine either. I murmured, "I think that's your phone."

"Screw the phone," he said. "It can wait. What about you?"

"Me?" I gave a happy sigh. "I feel better than I have all day."

He pulled away and leaned his forehead against mine. "Remember your promise, because I'm gonna hold you to it."

I knew which promise he meant, the promise to look at that picture. But right now, I had happier things to consider.

Jake was mine. I was his. And, soon, we'd put all of this drama behind us – or at least, that's what I thought, right until we reached the top floor, and found our next unwelcome surprise. ☐

CHAPTER 23

When the elevator doors slid open, I stifled a gasp. There they were – Vince and Bianca, standing just outside the ornate double doors that led to Jake's penthouse. Unfortunately, they weren't facing those doors. They were facing the elevator, with us inside.

Desperately, I grabbed the bottom of the oversized hoodie and gave it a ferocious tug downward. It did almost no good. The hoodie was big, but not big enough to hide the fact that I was mostly naked underneath it.

Even now, I could feel the cool air wafting across the lower part of my partially exposed ass-cheeks. As for the cheeks on my face, they were burning with raw embarrassment.

I was half-naked and reeked of sex. Like an idiot, I hadn't even put back on my shorts. Instead, I'd wadded them up into a soggy ball and tucked them under my arm, thinking I'd simply make a mad-dash from the elevator to the privacy of Jake's penthouse.

At the time, it had seemed like a perfectly reasonable plan, especially when I learned that Jake knew a special elevator code that would deliver us, non-stop, to the privacy of the top floor.

In hindsight, the plan had been totally stupid, especially considering his comment earlier, about not knowing who might be coming over.

Sex with Jake – it turned my brain to mush. Sure, it was a happy mush, but it wasn't without a downside.

Of all the people on Earth, why did I have to be facing Vince and

Bianca? Weren't they supposed to be in the lobby? Or in his office or something?

Already, Jake had moved in front of me, blocking me from their view. He told Bianca, "I *said* to meet me in the office."

I couldn't see Bianca anymore, but I *could* hear her, loud and clear, as she said in a distinctly annoyed voice, "I know you did. But you weren't there."

There was only one elevator that led to the top two floors. And, as I knew from blissful experience, that elevator had been occupied. So how did they get up here?

I peered around Jake and called out, "What'd you do? Take the stairs?"

"It's none of *your* concern!" Bianca called back. "I was talking to Jake."

I knew Bianca. When it came to Jake, she wanted to do a lot more than talk. She had it bad, as in crazy-stalker bad. If she were a nicer person, I might've felt sorry for her. But she wasn't nice, and any sympathy from me would be a total waste.

My gaze shifted to Vince. He was looking amused more than anything. With a nod in my direction, he said, "If you wanna return that to me, now's a good time."

I blinked. Return what? And then it hit me. Oh, my God. The hoodie. It was his. And if I gave it back now, I might as well be buck-naked. How humiliating was that?

But it was Jake who answered on my behalf. "If you're talking about that hoodie, forget it."

Vince shrugged. "Eh, well, can't blame a guy for trying."

Bianca turned to glare at him. "Do I need to remind you? I'm standing right here."

That made me pause. When it came to Vince and Bianca, I couldn't quite figure them out. Like me, Bianca had spent a few weeks as Vince's employee, and, if the rumors were true, his main-squeeze. But what they were to each other now, I had no idea.

Vince turned to Bianca and told her, "You wanna parade around naked? You won't see *me* complaining." Turning back to Jake, he added,

"You want her to? Just say the word. She'd do it."

Bianca sputtered, "I would not!"

"Right," Vince said. "Keep telling yourself that." His tone grew sarcastic. "We believe you."

Listening, I tried to look on the bright side. If Bianca did, in fact, parade around naked, it would definitely take the focus off me.

But short of that happening, I was stymied on what to do. I ducked my head back behind Jake and tried to think. He stood directly between the open elevator doors, which meant they wouldn't shut as long as he was there. I couldn't decide, was that a good thing? Or a bad thing?

I mean, I'd love for those doors to slide shut and hide me from prying eyes. But then what? I couldn't exactly ride down to the lobby and show my goodies *there*.

Almost too late, I recalled the jean shorts, wadded up, under my arm. If Vince and Bianca would only turn away, I could put them on – I paused – and then what? Waltz forward like Jake and I *hadn't* just been caught been screwing in the elevator?

I reminded myself that they hadn't technically caught us, not in the act or anything. But it wouldn't be hard for anyone to figure it out. I shifted my stance and tried not to think about it.

In front of me, Jake told them, "Turn around."

Bianca called back, "Why should *we* turn around? We were here first."

"Alright," Jake said. "Don't turn around. Just get out."

Bianca made a sound of disbelief. "Well, that's just lovely. There's only one elevator. What? You want us to join you in there?"

"Hell no," Jake said. He jerked his head toward a plain gray door, located a few paces away from the much fancier doors to his penthouse. Above that nondescript door was a classic exit sign. "You can take the stairs."

"But we're twenty floors up," Bianca protested.

"Not my problem," Jake said.

Again, I peered around him. I called out to Bianca, "Oh, stop whining. You took the stairs up here, right? So, just take them back down again."

She glared at me. "Have you forgotten my foot? It really does hurt, in case you didn't know." She gave a dramatic sigh. "But I guess no one cares about that, do they?"

Well, I didn't care, but only because I didn't believe her.

Next to her, Vince gave a small laugh. "You're fine," he told her. "It was two flights, and you survived those, didn't you?"

Two flights? Oh. Of course. They'd done what any smart person would've done. They'd taken the elevator to the eighteenth floor, and then, they'd walked up only the last two. That wasn't so bad.

Next to him, Bianca hissed. "Oh shush, they don't need the details."

Vince chuckled. "Too late now."

"I don't know what's so funny," Bianca muttered. She looked back to Jake and said, "Alright, fine. We'll wait in your office. But I don't know what the big deal is." Her lips twisted into a smirk. "She was, after all, practically naked when we picked her up."

It was my turn to sputter. "I was not!"

"Well, you sure *looked* naked." She gave a fake, tittering laugh. "I'm surprised you weren't arrested for indecent exposure."

In front of me, Jake's body tensed, but he said nothing. From where I stood, I couldn't see the look on his face, but I'm guessing it wasn't friendly, because a moment later, Vince gripped Bianca's elbow and started hustling her toward the stairs.

Already, she was whining. "But I don't like stairs. They're always grubby. And I'm wearing high-heels."

Vince ignored her complaints and paused to give me a boyish grin. "Keep the hoodie," he said. "We'll call it a gift."

That grin, as harmless as it looked, didn't fool me one bit. Not anymore. Underneath all that charm, he was a total snake. But within the last hour, he *had* given me a ride *and* loaned me the hoodie, so I couldn't exactly be rude about it.

But apparently, Jake had no such qualms. "No," he told Vince. "You'll be getting it back."

Vince gave a laugh. "Why?"

"Because she doesn't need 'gifts' from someone like you."

Vince shrugged off the insult. "Suit yourself." Once again, Vince, with Bianca in tow, began walking toward the stairway door. Just before it swung shut behind them, Vince called out over his shoulder, "Hey Jake, if you're more than five minutes, give us a call. We'll come back and join the fun."

Well, that wasn't disturbing or anything.

Peering around Jake, I stared at the door. I lowered my voice and asked, "Did that mean what I think it means?"

"If it does, he can piss off." Jake turned around and reached for my hand. "Now come on, let's get you inside."

Five minutes later, I was alone, soaking in a hot bath. As for Jake, he'd gone downstairs to meet with Vince and Bianca. About what, I still had no idea. In all the commotion, I'd forgotten to ask.

But now that I was alone, I was more curious than ever.

I also couldn't help but wonder why Vince was looking so happy all of a sudden. I'd seen him confront Jake on several occasions. Every single time, Vince had been royally pissed off for reasons that made a lot of sense.

Over the past few months, Jake had cost Vince and his clients a ton of money, mostly by making those clients look like total idiots. They'd lost their tempers. They'd lost fights. And then, they'd lost it, literally.

I recalled one guy – some hotshot basketball player – who'd been caught beating the crap out of a taco stand two days after losing an impromptu fight with Jake.

It didn't help, of course, that until then, the guy had spent most of his free time cultivating a bad-ass, tough-guy image, mostly by bullying people half his size.

Now, his image was toast, along with his endorsement deals – except for, sadly, a regional taco chain that had made a mockery of the whole situation.

Soaking in the tub, I was still trying to make sense of it all when I heard my cell phone ring. I sat up in the tub and looked around.

And then, I sighed.

My phone was still in the pocket of Vince's hoodie, now lying across the bathroom counter. From the tub, I couldn't even begin to reach it. But I definitely needed to.

Ever since leaving work, I'd been waiting for a call from my boss, telling me whether or not I still had a job.

Hoping for good news, I scrambled out of the tub and almost ran, naked and dripping across the tile floor. I dug out the phone and glanced at the display. I didn't recognize the number, but that didn't stop me from answering with a breathless, "Hello?"

A male's voice, low and smooth, responded with a phrase that had become painfully familiar. "Hey Babe."

Oh, crap.

I recognized that voice, and unfortunately, it didn't belong to my boss, or to Jake, for that matter.

CHAPTER 24

I stood, naked and dripping, clutching my cell phone with slippery fingers. I didn't bother to hide my irritation. "What do you want?"

It was Rango, my asshat of an ex-boyfriend. A few months earlier, the guy had caused me all kinds of trouble when our relationship had crashed and burned like the disaster it was.

He'd trashed my apartment. He'd crushed my car. He'd turned up in odd places to give me all kinds of grief. But those days were over. Or at least, I *thought* they were.

A few weeks earlier, Jake had kicked Rango's ass spectacularly – *and* secured a promise from Rango's mobster of a stepdad that Rango would finally leave me alone. In fact, until this phone call, my life since then had been blissfully Rango-free.

On the other end of the phone, Rango gave a low chuckle. "So you're still mad about the car, huh?"

It wasn't just the car, but I didn't want to get into it. So all I said was, "You paid me for the car. Remember?"

"Nah. Sorry. Don't remember *that*."

That made me pause. He *had* paid me, in cash, no less. He'd given the money to Jake, who'd passed it to me in crisp hundred-dollar bills.

Oh, no.

I closed my eyes and let out a sigh. Maybe the money *hadn't* come from Rango. Before I could stop myself, I said, "So you *didn't* pay for that? Are you serious?"

Rango paused. "Wait. You got money for that thing? How much?"

That "thing" was a cute little Ford Focus. It was the only car I'd ever owned. The way *I* heard it, Rango and his friends had crushed it for fun in a night of drunken stupidity.

At the image, I wanted to crush something of Rango's in return. Like his face, for starters. I was still doing a slow burn when Rango spoke again. "You know, come to think of it. I'm pretty sure I did pay you. So, uh, we're good, huh?"

I made a sound of disgust. "Nice try."

His tone became flirty. "Well, how do you know that I *didn't* pay you?"

I *didn't* know, and that was the problem. But I did know one thing. If I wanted the whole story, I was talking to the wrong guy.

To Rango, I said, "I know what I know."

In truth, I didn't know squat. But Jake was just one floor down, and one way or another, I'd find out what had really happened.

"Yeah?" Rango said. "Well, I know something, too."

Against my better judgment, I said, "What?"

His voice became low, with a hint of sex. "You want me back. Am I right?"

Ick.

At the thought, I almost threw up in my mouth. Rango was a hot-shot D.J. with a big local following. He was rich, good-looking, and charming when he wanted to be. Lots of girls wanted him. Me? Not so much.

"Whatever you're smoking," I told him, "you might want to give it up. It's affecting your judgment."

"Aw come on," he said. "I saw Jake with that other girl, so I figured you were like, available again."

The words, as stupid as they were, found their mark. I knew which girl he meant. Nipple Girl, obviously.

I felt myself swallow. He'd *better* be talking about Nipple Girl, because if he meant someone else, I had bigger problems than six million views of Jake with a drunken hussy.

In the calmest voice I could muster I said, "You thought wrong.

Because Jake and I *are* together. And we're staying together."

I bit my lip. At least, I sure hoped we were staying together.

Rango gave a low chuckle. "So you don't mind sharing, huh? You should've mentioned that when *we* were together. I mean, I like to party as much as the next guy."

"Yeah. And I like waffles. So what?"

Ignoring me, Rango launched into some side story about his DJ gig. As he talked, it slowly dawned on me that I was standing there, utterly naked, in Jake's bathroom, listening to a total jackass.

I pulled the phone from my ear and stared down at the thing.

Why had I even answered? But I knew why. Thanks to what was obviously a new phone number, I hadn't known it was Rango calling.

I wouldn't be making *that* mistake again.

When I returned the phone to my ear, Rango was still blabbing, saying something about his new condo. He finished by saying, "So, uh, you wanna get together?"

"No," I said. "Definitely not."

"If you want," he persisted, "we can meet on the sly, talk, have a few laughs, see what happens."

"Nothing's *going* to happen," I told him, "because we're not getting together. Not now. Not ever. And Rango, seriously, don't call me again. I mean it."

And with that, I disconnected the call, tossed the phone onto the folded bath towel that I'd placed by the tub earlier, and crawled back into the steaming water.

I'd barely settled back in when my cell phone rang a second time.

With a muttered curse, I reached down to grab it off the towel. I looked at the display and frowned. Again, I didn't recognize the number, but it was definitely different from the last one.

Was it my boss? Finally?

Unwilling to take the chance of missing him, I answered with a tentative, "Hello?"

"Hey Babe."

"Oh, crap," I muttered.

Rango gave an oily laugh. "What? You're not happy to hear from

HODGKINS PUBLIC LIBRARY

me?"

"No. And I wasn't happy the first time either."

"Eh, you know what they say. If at first you don't succeed—"

"What? Make an ass of yourself?"

"I haven't heard *that* phrasing before," he said, "but hey, you always were the smart one."

Now, I *knew* he was full of crap. I hadn't been smart. About Rango and too many other things to count, I'd been excessively stupid.

It was a real shame, too. It wasn't that I didn't have brains. It was just that I hadn't spent a whole lot of time using them.

But now, I was turning over a new leaf, and Rango's words had me thinking. There had to be more to this story. The first call from Rango made a weird kind of sense. But two calls? Back to back?

I knew the guy. He never tried this hard.

He had to be playing some angle. But what kind of angle, I just didn't know. Determined to cut to the chase, I said, "What do you want?"

"I already told you—"

"Cut the crap," I said, sitting up straighter in the tub. "This isn't about me, and we both know it. You want something. What is it?"

Rango paused. With a smile in his voice, he said, "Hey, are you naked?"

I froze. I was, in fact, naked. But there was no way on Earth that I was going to admit it. "Oh shut up," I said. "Just answer the question."

Still smiling, he said, "You are. Aren't you? Don't lie. I can hear the splashing."

Even more self-conscious now, I held myself very still. "Yeah? Well, maybe I'm doing dishes. You ever think of that?"

"Nah. I don't hear any dishes. Just you." He gave a low chuckle. "Is there room for two?"

"Yeah," I snapped, "and Jake's gonna be here any minute."

"Nope. Sorry. He's still downstairs."

I felt my eyebrows furrow. How did Rango know that? And then it hit me. Bianca, trouble-maker that she was, had to be feeding him information. Of course.

Suddenly, it all made sense. If I hooked up with Rango, Jake would finally be free, and Bianca would move in for the kill.

My jaw clenched. The kill – that was sounding like a fine idea. Envisioning Bianca's neck, I squeezed my phone a little tighter. Too tight, as it turned out. It popped out of my grip and landed with a sickening splash in the soapy water.

"Son-of-a-bitch!" I hollered, diving down for the thing. A split-second later, I plucked it out of the water and tossed it onto the nearby bath towel. I scrambled out of the tub and began frantically drying the phone off.

As I fumbled around, I could hear Rango, on the other end, laughing his ass off.

The sound of him should've been a relief, because it meant that the phone was still working. But I was too far gone to be relieved about anything. Letting my anger get the best of me, I responded with a string of profanity that would've made a sailor blush.

Rango was still laughing, even louder now. "You dropped it, didn't you? Oh man, I wish I were there. I bet you're cute as hell."

My heart was pounding, and my mouth was tight. I wasn't cute. I was homicidal.

"Hey, I know," Rango continued. "Send me a picture, okay? C'mon. Don't even think about it. Just do it."

I was still desperately drying off the phone, not that it probably needed it. I saw no more signs of water – at least not on the outside. Still, I gave the phone a few more swipes with the towel and held it up for a closer inspection.

Surprisingly, it looked okay. And it was still working. So that was good, right?

"I'll tell ya what," Rango was saying. "Come on over. I'll give you a new phone. A nice one, too." He gave another laugh. "You won't believe this, but I've got like a dozen right here. Come on by. You can take your pick."

I could almost see it, Rango sitting there, surrounded by a slew of new phones. He owned a few small businesses, so it actually made sense. For all I knew, he'd acquired a cell phone outlet as part of what he used to call his "diversification plans."

I held up my middle finger. *Diversify this, Jackass.*

Out loud, I told him, "Screw your phones. And while you're at it, screw *you* too, Rango."

"Hey," he said, putting some real sleaze into it, "sounds good to me. I'll be waiting."

With a sound of disgust, I ended the call. And then, not wanting to take any chances, I pulled up the display and blocked this latest phone number, along with the first one while I was at it.

Frowning, I imagined Rango sitting somewhere, surround by a dozen phones. "Only ten more to go," I muttered.

Standing there, naked and dripping all over Jake's fancy tile floor, I looked longingly at the bathtub. Suddenly, it felt sullied by the whole Rango thing, and I was almost tempted to simply get dressed and be done with it. But I still had conditioner in my hair and needed to rinse it off, unless I wanted to embrace the greaser look, which I definitely didn't.

So, reluctantly, I crawled back into the tub and dipped my head backward, under the bath water. It had barely reached my forehead when I heard, once again, the dreaded sound of my cell phone ringing.

Screw it. It could ring all it wanted. I wasn't answering. Or at least, that was the plan, until I recalled that I still hadn't heard from my boss.

With a sigh, I reached for my phone. This time, I held it outside the tub as I checked the display. Once again, the number was unfamiliar.

Reluctantly, I answered with a wary, "Hello?"

"Hey, Babe."

"Shit." I ended the call and returned the phone to the driest part of the towel. Hurrying now, I finished rinsing my hair and practically leapt out of the tub, feeling dirtier, mentally anyway, than when I'd gotten in.

By the time I'd dressed and dried my hair, the phone had rung at least seven more times from seven different numbers. Each time, I forced myself to answer. And each time, the caller had been Rango.

Apparently, he *hadn't* been lying about the phones.

Goodie for him.

As for me, I wanted answers. Not from Rango. From Jake. If he had, in fact, paid for my car, I really needed to know – not only to thank him, but also, to find some way of paying him back.

Soon, I was heading down the building's stairway, figuring it would be quicker than waiting for the elevator. I was halfway down when my cell phone rang yet again.

Damn it. □

CHAPTER 25

Standing in the stairwell, I pulled out my phone and studied the display. Once again, I didn't recognize the number.

Surprise, surprise.

But I *had* to get it. If I were, by some miracle, keeping my job, I was scheduled to work tomorrow. So I couldn't exactly put this off.

With grim resignation, I hit the answer-button and placed the phone next to my ear, not bothering with the usual hello. Instead, I waited, letting the caller speak first.

If it was Rango, I had a plan. It wasn't a great one, but it was the only one I had. I'd just keep blocking all of his numbers until he finally ran out of phones – or until I crushed my own phone in a Rango-induced rage, whichever came first.

Already, I was gripping my phone so tight that my fingers ached. I was still listening, but all I heard was silence, except for the faint sounds of dance music somewhere in the background.

Yup, it was Rango, alright.

With an irritated sigh, I said, "Go ahead. Get it over with."

A male voice, and unfortunately, not Rango's, replied with, "Uh, Luna? Is that you?"

I froze. *Oh, crap.* It was my boss. Still clutching the phone, I wanted to kick myself. It's not like I hadn't been expecting his call. It's just that, well, I'd been expecting it like seven calls ago – from a D.J. who loved dance music.

Stupid Rango.

Stupider me.

On a cheerier note, at least I hadn't answered with a string of profanity.

Trying for a recovery, I managed to say, "Um, yeah. Sorry about that. I was just—"

"Waiting to be fired?"

I hesitated, unsure what to say. In truth, I *was* expecting to be fired, even as I hoped against hope for another chance.

Before I could come up with a decent response, my boss spoke again. "Forget that. Bad joke. Hey, I've got some good news."

Good news? My shoulders sagged in relief. Aside from the mind-blowing elevator sex, most of my day had been a giant crap-fest. Trying not to sound pathetic, I said, "Really? How good?"

"Let me cut to the chase." With a smile in his voice, he continued. "I worked it out with corporate, and they're gonna give you another shot."

I let out a huge sigh of relief. "Oh wow, that *is* good news." I gave a weak laugh. "A lot better than I was expecting, actually."

"You and me, both," he said. "You know corporate."

Actually, I *didn't* know corporate. I'd been to the corporate offices exactly once, and that was for my orientation. It was ironic, really, because I was hoping to work there someday. I just prayed I hadn't ruined my chances.

My boss cleared his throat. "There's just one condition."

"Sure. Anything."

"You'll need to apologize."

"Oh."

Yeah, it was a lame response, but I wasn't quite following. Already, I'd apologized to the customers, several times, in fact, not that it had done much good. The guy had been a decent sport about it, but the woman had gone totally berserk.

And the more I apologized, the crazier she got. In the end, she'd told me to stick my apologies where the sun didn't shine, because in her words, "Apologies were for failures who didn't get it right the first time."

I tried to think. Who else would need an apology? My co-workers? Management? Someone at corporate? I wasn't sure, and I hated the thought of asking.

Into my silence, my boss asked, "Is that a problem?"

"No. Of course not." And then, desperate for more information, I said, "So, I'll be apologizing to...?" I let the sentence trail off, hoping he'd fill in the blank.

"The customer. Who else would it be?"

"Sorry." I winced. "I guess it was a stupid question, huh?"

"Eh, I've had stupider. Don't worry about it."

I bit my lip, not wanting to continue. But I had to, for his sake as well as mine. "So, while I'm at it, can I ask another one?"

At this, he laughed. "Sure, why not?"

I knew I was pushing my luck, but there was something he *had* to know. "Don't take this the wrong way, but are you absolutely sure that's a good idea?"

He was silent for a long moment before saying, "You're right."

Relief washed over me. "I am?"

"Yeah. That *was* a stupid question."

"Oh." I squeezed my eyes shut and tried to think. "I know. I'm doing a horrible job of explaining it." Fearful of losing my nerve, I took a deep breath and continued. "It's just that when I apologized before, it only made things worse. That lady? She kind of flipped out, actually."

"Yeah. I saw. Remember?"

"Right. So, it's not that I'm unwilling to apologize. It's just that, well, I don't know if it will turn out so great. I mean, what if she doesn't *want* any more apologies?"

"Trust me. She does." He hesitated. "Listen, I shouldn't be telling you this, but she's the reason you still have a job."

I blinked. "She is?"

I couldn't imagine how. After my failed apology attempt, she'd stormed out of the restaurant, leaving a trail of insults in her wake. It wasn't exactly a ringing endorsement.

But my boss said, "Yeah. She is. Just between you and me, I went to bat for you, but my boss wasn't having it, which meant that corporate wasn't having it."

Disappointment coursed through me. The primary reason I was so desperate to keep this job was because it was a foot in the door, a way to someday use my college degree.

The steakhouse was a tiny part of a huge company. When I'd interviewed for the job, I'd heard encouraging stories about how they hired from within and made a point to promote people who worked in – as my boss had put it – the service trenches.

The bartending job, I could do without. But the job it might lead to? Well, that was something I desperately wanted.

Had I already burned those bridges?

No. I squared my shoulders. One way or another, I'd make this right.

My boss was still talking. "The way it happened, she came in a couple hours later, said she didn't want you to get fired." He paused. "But she *does* want that apology."

As for me, I was more than willing. Trying to plan ahead, I asked, "What about her date? Does he want another apology, too?"

"No. Just her. It's set for Monday afternoon. You'll be ready?"

This time, I didn't hesitate. "Definitely." And I meant it, too. It would be unpleasant. I had no doubt of that. From what I'd seen so far, the woman had a crazy streak a mile wide.

But maybe, I reminded myself, I wasn't being fair. If she'd taken the trouble to come back in, that was a good sign, right?

My boss said, "Great. Then it's settled. To quote *her*, it'll be a good learning opportunity. And I agree."

At this point, I wasn't going to argue. So I thanked my boss for the second chance, confirmed I was still working tomorrow, and ended the call on a positive note.

In three days, I'd be apologizing. But for now, I had other things to worry about, so I silenced my phone, shoved it back into my pocket, and continued down the stairway, only to pause on the final step.

I heard yelling. The way it sounded, it was coming from Jake's office. And, the yeller was Bianca.

Of course.⬚

CHAPTER 26

From inside the stairwell, I couldn't understand what Bianca was saying, but her tone was unmistakable. She was throwing yet another giant hissy.

Part of me wanted to hunker down and listen undetected, but I'd been down *that* road before, and I was determined to be a better person.

So I took the final step and pushed through the steel gray door that led to the nineteenth floor, where Jake's office suite was located. I spotted Bianca immediately, standing near the elevator with Vince on one side and Jake on the other.

She was facing Jake, who stood, looking bored more than anything, even in the face of Bianca's wrath.

She was screeching, "But I don't care! I insist something be done about it!"

"Insist all you want," Jake said, "it's not gonna happen. And stop yelling. You're gonna break something."

Bianca paused. "Like my voice box?"

"No. Like a window."

Bianca gave a little stomp of her foot. In a slightly quieter voice, she whined, "But he was rude to me."

Jake shrugged. "Not my problem."

"It is, too, your problem," she said. "You own the building. Don't you care?"

This made me pause. Jake owned the building? Why hadn't I known that? I frowned. I should've known that.

Or, if nothing else, I should've guessed. He had the top two floors. He had secret elevator codes. And everyone in the building treated him like royalty.

All along, I'd been assuming it was for the usual reasons. He was rich, obscenely good-looking, and famous in his own kind of way.

But apparently, there was a lot more to this story.

Again, I asked myself, why hadn't I known?

Jake's gaze shifted in my direction, and he flashed me a grin. It was the one I loved best, the cocky one that made my breath hitch and my knees go wobbly.

I ignored my knees and tried to think. What else didn't I know?

But then, my traitorous face took over, and I felt my lips curve into a ridiculous smile, aimed straight at him.

How could I *not* smile? Jake was everything I'd ever wanted. And there he was, smiling at me like I was the only girl on Earth.

Bianca's voice broke the spell. "And *she* was rude to me, too."

I looked to see her pointing straight at me.

Sparing Bianca only half a glance, Jake said, "If she was, you probably had it coming."

"That's not true!" Bianca yelled.

Jake shrugged. "Eh, still don't care."

Bianca glared up at him. "So let me get this straight. She can abuse me all she wants, and you won't do a solitary thing about it?"

Well, that was rich. *Abuse her? Seriously?*

I stalked toward her and said, "Oh, so now I've 'abused' you? How?"

"Outside the building," she said, "you practically smashed that door right into my face."

Technically, this was sort of true. But oddly enough, I felt zero guilt. And I knew exactly why. "Yeah?" I said. "Well, *you* were so anxious to have the door opened that *I* was just helping out." I smiled. "So you're welcome."

She sputtered, "You're welcome? Like I'm supposed to *thank* you?" She whirled back to Jake. "She made me fall. You *saw* that, right? Don't you even care?"

I was tempted to point out the obvious. If he'd cared, he wouldn't have literally stepped over her to get to me. He hadn't even paused. It would be funny if it weren't so cold.

I hesitated. Actually, it was still funny. Or maybe, I just had a twisted sense of humor. Something to think about later.

When Jake said nothing, Bianca whirled to Vince and said, "And what about you? Don't *you* care?"

Vince glanced at his watch and said to Jake, "So we have an agreement?"

Now, Bianca was glaring at *him*. "Are you ignoring me?"

Vince shrugged. "Looks to me like it's a battle you're not gonna win. Might want to cut your losses and move on."

Bianca made a sound of frustration. "How come nobody cares? I twisted my ankle, you know."

Unable to resist, I chirped, "Better than a broken foot."

Bianca turned to me and said, "Will you stop bringing that up? I *thought* it was broken. Obviously, I was mistaken. But it's not like I'm a medical doctor, so stop judging me, okay?"

I glanced down at her ankles. "Neither one looks twisted to me."

She rolled her eyes. "What do you think? It's gonna look like a pretzel or something? Tell me, have *you* ever had a twisted ankle?"

"No," I said, "but I do like pretzels. Does that help?"

She looked at me for a long moment, and I swear, I saw smoke coming out of her ears.

It was Vince who finally broke the silence. "So Jake, we're all set. Right?"

Jake gave him a nod, and Vince turned and walked toward the elevator. He hit the down button and waited.

As for Bianca, she was still standing in the same spot. Worse, she was staring straight at me. As I watched, her cool gaze travelled from the top of my head to the toes of my sneakers.

I could almost hear her thoughts. *What exactly, does Jake see in her?*

It was a good question, and one I didn't like to dwell on. It's not that I didn't see my appeal. I was reasonably good-looking, and unlike Bianca, I wasn't a screaming shrew.

Plus, love-aside, I honestly liked Jake, and cared for him in ways that Bianca would never understand.

Still, I wasn't blind to the fact that Jake was the big leagues, and I was just a girl who happened to grow up in his hometown. Was that my appeal? Our shared history?

Bianca was still staring, and I tried not to wilt under her scrutiny. She might be a shrew, but she had a certain sophistication that I'd never have, no matter how hard I tried.

When the elevator dinged, and the doors slid open, I forced a cheery smile and told her, "Your ride's waiting."

"Yeah, whatever," she muttered, turning away. As I watched, she limped the short distance to the elevator, wincing as she moved.

I knew it had to be an act. After all, she'd tackled at least a few flights of stairs with no problem. And she'd been standing there just fine.

Plus, hadn't there been some foot-stomping? It was hard to stomp with a sprained ankle. Right?

Still, watching her, a little voice in my head whispered, *What if she really is hurt?* To laugh at her pain seemed needlessly cruel.

But Jake, apparently, saw things differently. Next to me, he gave a low chuckle.

Bianca, having limped her way to the deepest part of the elevator, slowly turned around to face us. In a pathetic, choked voice, she said, "What's so funny now?"

"Ask Vince," Jake said. "He'll know."

Bianca looked to Vince and demanded, "Well?"

Vince looked down and gave a slow shake of his head. Just before the elevator doors slid shut, I heard him say, "You were limping with the wrong foot."

CHAPTER 27

I stared at the closed elevator doors. "The wrong foot?"

Next to me, Jake said, "Yeah. Before you came down, she was limping with the other one."

"Oh, my God," I said. "She was faking it the whole time?" I wanted to kick myself. I'd known better, and yet, she'd almost had me feeling sorry for her.

I was such a sucker.

I started to laugh. And once I started, I didn't want to stop. It wasn't even that funny, but the day had been so crazy-awful that I was beyond anxious to put it all behind me.

Still laughing, I told Jake, "Wanna hear what else she told me?"

Jake moved forward and pulled me into his arms. With a smile in his voice, he said, "What?"

"She claimed she was there last night. You know, at the convention center." I laughed against his chest. "Like I wouldn't have seen her."

Jake's arms stiffened, but he said nothing.

My laughter faded, and I pulled back to study his face. "Is something wrong?"

He looked toward the elevator doors, but made no response. His silence hung heavy between us.

"Oh, crap," I groaned. "She *was* there. Wasn't she?"

He was still looking toward the elevator. "Yeah. You didn't see her?"

"No. Was I supposed to?"

"Well, she *did* shush you."

"What?" I sputtered. "That was her?"

"Yeah. I figured you knew."

"How would I know?" I said. "I didn't see her. And if it wasn't a secret, why wasn't she sitting at our table?" Before he could answer either of those questions, I added. "She told me that you invited her. Is that true?"

Jake raised a single eyebrow, but said nothing. On his lips, I saw the hint of a smile.

Confused, I squinted up at him. "Why aren't you saying anything?"

With a grin, he pulled me tighter against him. "Because I was waiting to see if you were done."

I couldn't help but feel vaguely insulted. Either he was teasing me, or he was avoiding my questions. Knowing Jake, it could be both.

Pushing the issue, I said, "So you did invite her?"

"Yeah," he said. "Months ago, when she still worked for me. And she wasn't sitting at our table, because I found her a new one."

"But why?"

"You've gotta ask?"

I was mulling that over when I felt a familiar vibration against my hip. It was my cell phone, tucked into the front pocket of my jeans. Guessing who the caller might be, I hated the idea of answering.

If it was Rango, which it probably was, Jake wouldn't like it. And neither would I. Already, I'd had more than enough of that idiot for one day.

Sooner or later, I'd need to tell Jake about those calls, but I didn't want that time to be now. So I ignored my phone and focused on what really mattered.

The person I *really* wanted to talk to was right here, with his arms still wrapped around my back. Through the thin cotton of his shirt, his chest felt warm and hard, and I had to remind myself that I'd come down here for a reason – to get some answers about my car.

Who, exactly, had paid for it? Sure, Rango had destroyed it, but who had reimbursed me for the destruction? Based on Rango's comments earlier, I was fairly certain that person was Jake.

"Actually," I told Jake when my phone stopped vibrating, "I'm *not* done."

"Yeah?" He ran a hand up into my hair. "Should I grab a pen or something?"

The implication was obvious. I was asking so many questions that soon, he'd be needing to write them down.

I didn't know whether to scream or kiss him. A reluctant smile tugged at my lips. "Oh, don't worry," I teased. "I'm keeping track."

Mostly, I needed to know about the car. If Jake had paid for it, I *had* to know. I hated the thought of taking any more charity, but there was something else I hated more – the idea of Rango getting credit for something nice that Jake had done.

"It's about my car..." I began, only to stop when my phone started vibrating again.

Damn it.

"You need to get that?" Jake asked.

I froze. So he'd felt the vibration? Of course, he had. Our hips were, after all, pressed against each other.

Reluctantly, I pulled away and reached into my pocket. Praying it was my sister or something, I pulled out the phone and checked the display.

Just great – another unknown number.

Rango? Probably.

But there was no way I wanted to confirm it. So I shoved the phone back into my pocket and told Jake, "Nah, it can wait."

I'd barely finished the sentence when Jake reached into his own pocket and pulled out *his* phone. He studied the display for a long moment before swiping his fingers across the screen, as if searching for something else. He paused, and then frowned.

"What is it?" I asked.

He shoved the phone back into his pocket and said, "I've gotta go."

I stared up at him. "What?"

"An appointment," he said. "It can't wait."

I gave him a puzzled look. "Did you just find out?"

"Something like that." He pulled me close and kissed me hard on the lips. "I'll be back in a few hours. Don't go anywhere, okay?"

I pulled back and tried to make a joke of it. "So, you want me to wait right here?" I made a show of looking around. "In the office?"

He gave me a distracted smile. "Nah, go upstairs. I'll see you there."

As much as I hated this, I wasn't blind to the upside. In my pocket, my phone was vibrating yet again. If Jake disappeared for a few hours, I'd have some time to deal with Rango and his stupid phone calls.

Maybe I'd get lucky, and he'd finally run out of phones.

I summoned up a smile and told Jake, "Alright. See you later."

Again, he reached for me, pulling me close yet again. "I mean it," he said. "Don't go anywhere."

Something about his tone was off, and I didn't like it. I pulled away and asked, "Is that a request or a command?"

Abruptly, he asked, "That picture, did you look at it?"

Startled by the change of topic, I gave a shake of my head. "What picture?"

"You know which picture."

Oh. *That* picture. Heat flooded my face, and I couldn't help but glance away.

Just before I'd crawled into the bathtub, Jake had texted me that stupid image, the one of me walking along the street in those wet, embarrassingly obscene clothes. Accompanying the image had been three simple words. *Remember your promise.*

It was the promise to look at that photo, obviously. But I didn't want to look. I wanted to forget. Unfortunately, Jake wasn't helping.

This whole thing was starting to feel like a punishment. I crossed my arms and said, "You know what I'm starting to feel like?"

Jake looked down at me, but said nothing.

Into his silence, I said, "I'm starting to feel like a dog who peed on the carpet."

His voice was flat. "A dog?"

"Yeah. And it's like you're dragging me back there, saying, 'Look at it. Bad dog! Bad!'"

With an effort, I softened my tone. "Look, I know it was a mistake, but you don't have to keep rubbing my nose in it. So can't we just drop it already?" I gave him a pleading look. "Please?"

"You told me you'd look, so just do it, alright?" He glanced toward the elevator. "Now, I've gotta go."

I made a sound of frustration. "That's no kind of response."

"Yeah? Well until you look, it's all you're getting." And with that, he turned away.

I watched in sullen silence as he crossed the short distance to the elevator, hit the down button, waited, and strode inside after the elevator doors opened. The doors slid shut, and then, he was gone.

I stared at those doors, wondering what had just happened.

I was still staring when my phone started buzzing again. With a muttered curse, I pulled it out and looked at the thing. Another unknown number.

Well, this was just great.☐

CHAPTER 28

An hour later, I was down in the lobby, waiting for my brothers. With Jake gone on such a sour note, I couldn't stomach the thought of eating alone. So I'd called for pizza, and for my brothers, hoping for a distraction from my murky thoughts.

Stubbornly, I'd refused to look at the picture. And, after five more calls from Rango, I'd started refusing to answer my phone. But there was one thing I wasn't refusing – and that was to face reality.

The way it looked, Rango had *more* than a dozen phones, which led me to a sad realization. Probably, it would be me – not him – who needed a new phone number.

Tomorrow, in fact, I'd be hitting the cell phone store, looking to make a switch. But in order to do that, I'd need money. Already, I'd gone through my last paycheck, as meager as it was, in order to pay some outstanding bills.

It was true, I *did* have a credit card, but I hated the thought of using it, mostly because I was already pushing the limit.

The pizza, I could afford. A new cell phone contract? Not so much. I paused – unless, maybe I could roll over the old one? Just change the number or something?

I was still pondering this when, through the lobby's front windows, I saw my brothers' truck zoom past the building, heading toward the attached parking garage. In that garage, Jake had a few extra spots, including one where my own car would go, assuming I ever bought one.

That spot was where my brothers parked whenever they visited. Looking to meet them there, I ducked out the side door that led to the garage, only to stop dead in my tracks at the sight of a familiar figure, blocking my path.

It was the same guy who'd hustled me out of the convention center the previous night. Confused, I glanced around. Where on Earth had he come from?

And more to the point, why was he standing in my way?

Surprised, I blurted out, "What are you doing here?" And then, realizing how rude I sounded, I forced a smile and said, "Sorry, you just surprised me. That's all." I tried to remember his name. "Um, Marshall, right?"

He didn't move, and he didn't smile back. In a low monotone, he said, "That's right."

My own smile faltered. Mister Personality strikes again. He'd been like this last night, too – all business, zero charm.

I tried again. "If you're here to see Jake–"

"I'm not."

"Oh." I paused as several possibilities ran through my brain. Did he live here? Doubtful. Was he here to see someone else? Unlikely. Was he a random garage-lurker, hanging out for kicks? That was too ludicrous for words.

That left only one possibility, and it wasn't one I liked. I squinted up at him. "So why *are* you here?"

"Working."

"Right." And it didn't take a genius to figure out his current job-description. *Stop Luna from going anywhere.*

Talk about humiliating.

Looking to test my theory, I sidestepped to go around him. As I moved, he moved. Again, we were standing chest to chest. Or, more accurately, we were standing head to chest, since he was at least a foot taller than I was.

Waiting for some sort of explanation, I crossed my arms and glared up at him.

No explanation came. Instead, he reached into the inside front pocket of his jacket and pulled out a cell phone. He started tapping at the screen. Texting, obviously.

I made a sound of annoyance. "What are you doing?"

"Reporting in."

"With Jake? Well, don't bother. Because there's nothing to report. I'm not going anywhere."

"Uh-huh." He was still tapping. "Except you're heading toward your car."

"I don't *have* a car," I snapped.

Admittedly, it wasn't my finest hour. On some level, I did realize that the guy was just doing his job. But at the moment, I was too irritated to care.

In front of me, Marshall continued tapping at his phone, ignoring what I'd just said.

My temper rose with every tap-tap of his beefy finger. "You should probably include a picture," I said. "Jake just *loves* those. Want me to back up so you can get a good shot?"

He didn't even look up. "No. That won't be necessary."

"Oh, well thank Heaven for *that*."

We were interrupted by the sounds of a vehicle pulling into the parking garage. I looked, and sure enough, it was my brothers' pickup, emblazed with the Moon Construction logo.

"Look," I said, pointing to the truck, which was now pulling into its usual spot. "I'm only down here to meet my brothers, not that it's anyone's business."

No response. And no pause in the texting.

"So, what is it?" I demanded. "You're telling on me? If so, you're wasting your time, because there's nothing to tell."

He finished with the text and tucked the phone back into his pocket. He crossed his arms and continued to block my path.

I gave an epic eye-roll. "Un-freaking-believable."

Halfway across the garage, my brothers were getting out of their truck. At the sight of me, facing off against some big guy in a suit, they both paused.

I cupped my hands around my mouth and hollered out, "Hey! Over here!"

Yeah, it was stupid. Obviously, they knew exactly where I was, but I was looking to make a point.

Together, Steve and Anthony sauntered over. They gave the guy a good, long look.

Turning to me, Steve asked, "Want us to get rid of him?"

If only it were that easy. "How?" I asked.

Steve shrugged. "Eh, we could get the truck, run him over."

In unison, we all turned to look at the guy. He was big, but not nearly as big as the pickup. If I really *were* looking to hurt him, it would be a decent plan, assuming the guy didn't have a gun, which he probably did.

So much for that idea.

Besides, I didn't want to hurt him. I just wanted him to go away.

It was Anthony who said, "We can't run him over. We just got the bumper repaired." He turned to me and said, "Six hundred bucks. Can you believe it?"

I thought of my own vehicle situation. "It could be worse," I told him. "You could have your car flattened by a crazy ex."

Anthony gave a slow nod. "Well, there *is* that."

Through all this, Marshall just stood there, looking so stoic that I wanted to scream.

Inside my front pocket, my cell phone vibrated. Reluctantly, I pulled it out and checked the display.

Well, at least it wasn't Rango.

It was Jake.□

CHAPTER 29

I answered with a terse, "What?"

Jake's voice was annoyingly calm as he said, "Is there something you wanna to tell me?"

I was getting a little tired of that question. "Yeah," I said. "I'm trapped in a parking garage. How's that?"

Next to me, Anthony snickered.

On the phone, Jake asked, "Who's that?"

My tone grew snotty. "Don't you know?"

"If I did, I wouldn't be asking."

"Right. Except it seems to me that you're getting all these updates, so you probably know exactly who that was." I glanced around. "And where we are. And what we're doing. And–"

"Let me talk to Marshall," he said.

"No," I told him. "If you want to talk to Marshall, call him yourself."

"Alright." And then he was gone.

A moment later, a cell phone rang. Marshall reached into his inside front pocket and pulled out his phone. He answered with a no-nonsense, "Marshall here."

It was so ludicrous that I might've laughed, except for the fact that by now, I was far too irritated.

I watched in sullen silence as Marshall and the caller – Jake, obviously – exchanged a few words, mostly along the lines of, "Yeah. She's out here with two guys claiming to be her brothers..."

"Claiming?" I muttered. "Well, that's rich."

A moment later, Marshall ended the call and returned his phone to the same pocket. Immediately, my own cell phone started buzzing again.

Sure enough, it was Jake. I hit the answer button and said, "So, were you happy with what you learned?"

"Happy as I'm gonna be."

"What does *that* mean?"

"It means you promised to stay put. If you're not, I need to know."

"Oh yeah? Why's that?" A sudden popping noise made me pause. The sound hadn't come from my end of the phone. It had come from Jake's. I swallowed. Fireworks? Somehow, I didn't think so. "What was that?"

Jake's response was scarily long in coming. "Eh, normal stuff. Not a big deal."

"Normal stuff? What kind of normal stuff?"

"It's nothing," he said. "So you're not going anywhere, right?"

"Quit trying to change the subject. That wasn't 'nothing.' I could tell."

I heard fumbling like he was looking out a window or something. "Eh, nothing that involves me." In his voice, I heard the hint of a smile. "You weren't worried, were you?"

"Yes. I *was* worried, actually."

"Yeah? Now you know how I feel."

I gave a small shake of my head. "Huh?"

He sounded ready to laugh. "Sucks, don't it?"

"God, you are such a…" I didn't even know what to say. My lips twitched. "I suppose you think that's funny?"

"Yeah. Because it is." He paused. "Look, I've gotta deal with something. You gonna be there when I get done?"

It was time to tease him back. "Probably."

"I'll take that as a 'yes.' And how about the time in-between? You going anywhere?"

"No. I ordered pizza."

"Nice." Again, his tone grew teasing. "For Marshall, too?"

My gaze slid to Marshall, who was still blocking my path. Was Jake serious? I doubted it. But still, I couldn't help but wonder, should I invite him?☐

CHAPTER 30

I was up in the penthouse with Steve and Anthony. The pizza had just arrived, and we were digging in.

Steve grabbed a couple of slices and slapped them together, with the topping sides facing each other, like a weird kind of pizza sandwich. He shoved the contraption toward his face and bit off a huge chunk. With his mouth full, he said, "Good thing he didn't want any."

I shook my head. "Huh?"

"I'm just saying." Steve kept on chewing, even as he shoved more pizza into his face. "Marshall. The guy was big. Like he'd eat a lot. You know?"

I gave Steve a look. His pizza sandwich was already gone, and he was reaching for two more slices.

"Yeah," I said. "No one likes a pig, right?"

He slapped the new pieces together and took another huge bite. Chewing around it, he said, "It don't count when the pig's family."

I looked to Anthony. He was reaching for what? His *third* slice? I looked down to the open pizza box. The pizza was almost gone, and I hadn't eaten a single piece.

When I looked up again, Anthony's latest slice was already inside his mouth. And then, with a loud swallow, it was gone.

I couldn't help but stare. How on Earth did he do that? If *I* ate that fast, I'm pretty I'd sure hurt something. I was still staring when Anthony said, "Hey, Luna."

"What?"

He grinned. "Oink."

I had to laugh. I don't know why I was surprised. It's not like I hadn't seen them eat pizza before, even if Steve's pizza-sandwich method was a new development.

My laugher faded as I looked down to my own plate. On it, sat one lone slice, untouched, and if I were being totally honest, mostly unwanted.

Probably, I hadn't wanted the pizza so much as the company. With a heavy sigh, I shoved away the plate and said, "You guys want this?"

Steve gave the plate an odd look. "What am I gonna do with just one slice?" He looked to Anthony and said, "You want it? It's all yours."

Anthony wasted no time. He grabbed the piece and shoved it into his mouth. And then, with a gulp, it was gone.

My own mouth fell open. I looked to the nearby pizza box.

It was empty. Completely empty.

Too late, it occurred to me that I might want a slice in five minutes or so. Okay, I *had* offered it and all. But I guess I hadn't expected them to take me up on it so quickly.

I felt myself frown. They might've asked, "Are you sure?" Or how about, "Hey, is anything wrong?"

I was still frowning when my brothers burst out laughing.

For some reason, it annoyed the snot out of me. "What?" I snapped.

Through choked laughter, Steve managed to say, "Your face."

"What about my face?" I demanded.

"You're like, 'I can't believe they freakin' ate it.'"

He was right. I *couldn't* believe it. But I hated the thought of saying so.

To my continued annoyance, they were still laughing. Anthony said, "Don't be mad. You told us we could have it."

He was right, of course. I tried for a casual shrug. "I'm not mad."

I was a little hurt, maybe, but that wasn't exactly their fault. They were guys. They didn't know how this was supposed to go.

Now, my sister, she would've known for sure. If I'd offered *her* my pizza, she would've asked, "Are you sure you don't want it?" And then, she would've wheedled the truth out of me, and not only about my appetite.

Soon, I would've been telling her everything that had gone wrong today. The list was long. It might've taken a while, but she definitely would've listened. But my brothers? It was like they didn't even care.

Still laughing, Steve said, "Admit it. You're mad."

"Oh, shut up," I told him. "I am not."

Okay, maybe I was a *little* mad, but it was mostly at myself.

Steve and Anthony exchanged a look. It was Anthony who said, "Don't worry. There's another one outside."

I blinked over at him. "What?"

"Another pizza," he said. "We called, had them double the order."

I paused. Now this made zero sense.

But Steve was saying, "Yeah. You never order enough, so we figured we'd teach you a lesson."

I glanced toward the penthouse doors. "When you say, 'outside,' what do you mean, exactly?"

In my mind, I saw visions of crushed pizza boxes strewn across the city-street. Considering my brothers, it wasn't as far-fetched as it sounded.

Steve pushed himself up from the sofa and strode to the penthouse double doors. He flung the nearest one open and reached down into the hall. A moment later, he emerged with another pizza box.

Confused, I stared at the thing. "Wait, where'd that come from?"

Returning, Steve said, "I already told you." He tossed the new box on top of the old box. "From the pizza place."

More confused than ever, I opened the box and looked inside. Yup, there it was, another pizza, exactly like the old one. Suddenly starving, I reached for a slice.

Not taking any chances, I took a bite before I even put it on my plate. When I finished chewing, I gave my brothers a perplexed look. "But I was the one who answered the door. There was just the one."

Across from me, Steve was making a fresh pizza sandwich. "Yeah. I know. But we tipped him double to leave the second one after you shut the door."

"But how could you tip him?" I asked. "You didn't even see him."

"Tipped in advance," Steve said. "Used a credit card."

I stared at him. "You have a credit card?"

Steve shoved his latest pizza sandwich into his mouth. "Doesn't everyone?" He finished chewing and said, "Alright, now, spill it. What's wrong?"

CHAPTER 31

Sitting in Jake's penthouse, I told them everything that had happened since I'd left them a few hours earlier.

There was only one detail I left out, and *that* involved Jake and an elevator.

I could only imagine telling them – not that I ever would. But if I ever *did* get tempted to blab? Well, let's just say we were twenty floors up, and I didn't want them jumping.

I knew my brothers. They'd had more than their share of girlfriends, but that didn't mean they'd relish a blow-by-blow account of their sister having sex on the same elevator that they'd just used to get up here.

I was all too familiar with *that* dynamic. There was this kitchen counter at my mom's place that I was *still* avoiding for reasons that involved my mom, an appliance repairman, and a wine-induced confession on her part.

Plus, my brothers were still eating. So I stuck to details they wouldn't mind hearing over dinner. "It's like, we've been fighting all day," I explained, briefly touching on the main things that Jake and I had been arguing about – Nipple Girl, Jake betting on me getting fired, my ill-fated walk, and the lingering tension about that godawful photo, which I was still refusing to look at.

By the time I finished talking, my brothers were both looking at me like I'd lost my mind. It was Anthony who asked, "About the picture? Why won't you just look?"

Just thinking of that stupid thing made me want to blush. "I don't know," I said. "It just feels like I'm being punished or something."

But Steve was shaking his head. "Nah, that's not it."

"Oh yeah?" I said. "And I suppose *you* know the reason?"

"Sure. It's because you looked like a ho-bag, and now you're all embarrassed."

My face grew a shade warmer. "I didn't look like a ho-bag." I hesitated. "Much."

"Which is why," Steve continued, "those two losers thought you were shaking it for cash."

"Oh, shut up," I said. "I wasn't 'shaking' anything."

"Shaking, showing." Steve shrugged. "If I were Jake, I'd be pissed too."

I stared at him. "You're kidding, right?"

"Hell no." Steve glanced toward the nearest window. "Around here? You go down the wrong street, and you're dead."

"Oh, get real," I said. "It's not that bad."

"Wanna bet?" he said. "Go five blocks, and it's a war zone."

"It wasn't a 'war zone,'" I insisted. "The streets were empty." Looking for support, I turned to Anthony. "You know what I mean, right?"

"Sorry," he said. "I think you're talking out of your ass."

I sank deeper into the sofa. "Thanks a lot."

With a shrug, Anthony reached for the final slice of pizza and practically swallowed it whole.

Well, at least this wasn't ruining their appetites.

"And just for the record?" I told them, "They didn't, as you guys so nicely implied, think I was for sale."

Steve laughed like I'd just said something funny. "Oh yeah? What *did* they think?"

I still wasn't sure, but I didn't want to dwell on it. "I dunno…" I glanced away and mumbled, "They probably just thought I was, you know, a fun time."

Now, Anthony was laughing, too. "Yeah, for twenty bucks."

"Hey!" I said, jumping to my feet. "I'd be worth a lot more than twenty."

As soon as the words left my mouth, I wanted to take them back. Knowing my brothers, I'd never hear the end of this.

Already, they were both laughing their fool heads off.

I flopped back onto the sofa. "You know what? Just forget it."

Steve was still laughing. "In your dreams." He looked to Anthony and said, "Dude, I've gotta say, twenty bucks? You start tapping anything *that* cheap, and things are gonna fall off." He gave a slow nod. "Important things."

Anthony leaned back and said, "Hey, if money changes hands, *I'm* the one getting paid. And not for no twenty bucks neither."

It was all a load of crap. I knew my brothers. Sex for money – whether paying or charging – wasn't remotely their thing.

Thank God.

Steve looked to me and held out his hand, palm-up. "Now come on, let's see it."

I gave him a horrified look. "The picture?"

With a nod, he shoved his hand closer. "Come on. It's on your phone, right?"

"Yeah, but you're not seeing it."

"Why not?"

"Because I don't want *anyone* seeing it."

"Because you looked like a ho-bag?"

"Oh, shut up," I said. "Seriously. Don't *you* have any photos that *you* don't want passed around?"

Steve shook his head. "Not me." He looked to Anthony and asked, "You?"

Anthony shook *his* head, too. "Nope. Sorry."

Inside my pocket, my cell phone buzzed. "Oh, crap," I muttered.

"What?" Anthony asked.

I wanted to groan. "It's probably Rango again."

Steve gave me an odd look. "Again?"

"Yeah, he's been calling me off and on for the past few hours. It's really annoying, actually."

"What does he want?" Steve asked.

"I dunno. He says he wants to get together, but I don't think that's really it. It's gotta be something else."

"Like what?" Anthony asked.

"Well, I have a theory." I leaned forward and said, "I think he's trying to lure me away from Jake, so Bianca can move in for the kill. You know, like they're working together or something."

Anthony glanced toward my phone, still buzzing in my pocket. "Why don't you just block his number?"

"I did," I said. "I've blocked like twenty numbers already, but it's like he's got a million phones or something."

I pulled out my own phone and checked the caller's number. Sure enough, it was another one that I didn't recognize.

Just great.

Anthony reached for his beer. "Oh man, I bet Jake's pissed, huh?"

I winced. "Actually, I haven't quite mentioned it."

Anthony stopped in mid-motion. "Why the hell not?"

"It's been such a crazy day already," I explained. "And I haven't really had the chance." Finally, the phone stopped buzzing. A moment later, I felt the short vibration that indicated a new voicemail.

With a sigh, I swiped the screen and listened. There was no real message, just muffled dance music and the sounds of people talking, not that I could understand a single word.

Probably, Rango was calling from his club again. I deleted the message and tossed my phone onto the nearby sofa. I was so tired of all of this. It was enough to drive a girl to drink.

I stood and went to the fridge, where I snagged a glass of wine for me and a couple more beers for my brothers.

When I returned to the living area, Steve was holding my phone and staring down at the screen while Anthony peered over his shoulder.

I almost dropped the drinks. "What are you guys doing?"

"Looking at the picture," Steve said.

I strode forward and practically slammed the drinks onto the coffee table. "Without my permission?"

"Yeah," Steve said. "You left it there. What do you expect?"

"I expected some privacy. That's what."

Steve shrugged. "Eh, too late for that."

I made a sound of annoyance. "Obviously."

Unsure what else to do, I stalked around the nearby sofa and joined Anthony in peering over Steve's shoulder.

I gazed down at the small screen and paused. Steve had his thumb pressed to the center of the image, covering the portion that contained me.

I had to ask, "Why do you have your thumb on the screen?"

"Because your shirt was see-through. No way I wanna look at that."

Right. I should've realized that.

And, I should've hidden my phone.

Too late for that now.

Next to me, Anthony gave a small shudder. "Yeah. We saw enough already. You're our sister, for cripe's sake."

Yes. I was.

And I was starting to wonder if they'd like a nice elevator story to go with their pizza.

It would serve them right.

Reluctantly, I returned my attention to the screen. "Then why are you looking?" I asked. "Other than the rain, there's nothing to see."

Steve lifted the phone higher. "Those two guys, who the hell are *they*?"

I hesitated. "What two guys?" □

CHAPTER 32

Before Steve could answer, I reached down and snatched the phone from his hand. One look at the screen reminded me why I'd been avoiding that photo in the first place.

Studying it now, I couldn't help but wince. Maybe I did look a *little* ho-baggy, but I hadn't meant to.

From his spot on sofa, Steve turned around to face me. "You see 'em?"

I shook my head. Mostly, I saw a couple of nipples that were obnoxiously perky – and on clear display through the soaked fabric of that thin, white blouse.

Stupid rain.

Steve gestured to my phone. "Upper right corner."

I looked again, but I still didn't see anything. Confused, I enlarged the photo and zoomed in where he indicated. Finally, I saw them, two shadowed figures slinking around the side of a decrepit, brick building.

They wore baggy jeans and dark hoodies, with the hoods pulled low over their faces, probably because of the downpour. Between their hoods and the rain, I had no idea what they looked like, but I could still make out their basic forms. They weren't middle-aged businessmen, that was for darn sure.

My stomach sank. So *that's* why Jake had wanted me to look at that photo again? Was he trying to make a point? If so, he'd succeeded. But why hadn't he just told me?

Trying for a bravado that I didn't quite feel, I said, "Okay. So I wasn't the only one who got caught in the rain. What's the big deal?"

"It looks to me," Steve said, "like they were following you."

"Oh come on," I said. "They were not."

"You sure about that?"

I lifted my chin. "Sure enough."

"Uh-huh." He gave me a dubious look. "You gonna bet your life on it?"

"No. Because that's a stupid bet."

"Except you did."

Okay, this made zero sense. "What do you mean?" I asked.

"The minute you walked down that street, you were betting it would be alright." He snorted. "Now, *that's* a stupid bet."

"Yeah," Anthony agreed. "Talk about a longshot."

I made a sound of irritation. "There was no betting. I hardly even thought about it."

Steve extended his index finger and shot me with an imaginary gun. "Exactly."

Damn it. When did he get so smug all of a sudden? I looked to Anthony and said, "It wasn't a longshot." I summoned up a smile. "See? Here I am. Safe and sound."

Anthony shrugged. "Hey, someone's gotta win the lotto." He turned to Steve and said, "You know what we should do?"

"What?" Steve asked.

"We should find those guys and ask 'em."

Steve gave a slow nod. "Yeah. We should."

Horrified, I looked from Anthony to Steve and back again. "Ask them what?"

"If they were following you," Anthony said.

"Oh, stop it," I said. "That's the worst idea I've ever heard."

"Yeah?" Anthony flashed me a sudden grin. "Why?"

Did I really need to explain this? And why was he smiling? I saw nothing to smile about.

I tried to explain. "Because it might be dangerous or something. You don't even know who those guys are. Or what they might do."

"Uh-huh." Anthony said. "How about you? *You* wanna find 'em?"

"What?" I shook my head. "No. Definitely not."

"Hey, if you wanna get changed," he said, "we'll wait."

I looked down. I was wearing basic jeans and a long-sleeved shirt. "Why would I get changed?"

"I dunno." He laughed. "Like, maybe you wanna put on a bikini or something?"

"Oh, shut up," I said.

"Well, *I'm* sure as hell not gonna wear the bikini." He looked to Steve and asked, "How about you?"

I threw up my hands. Through clenched teeth, I said, "Why does *anyone* have to wear a bikini? And besides, we're not going anywhere."

Abruptly, Steve asked, "Where's Jake?"

Startled by the sudden change of topic, I paused before admitting, "I'm not sure. He said he had an appointment."

"Yeah, I bet," Steve said.

"What does *that* mean?" I asked.

Steve's gaze shifted to my phone. So I looked, too. That godawful picture was still on the screen, taunting me with the stupidity of that whole asinine excursion.

Studying the photo now, it dawned on me that Jake probably knew the exact location of where it had been taken. And, knowing Jake, he might feel the need to learn more about what, specifically, had happened. And maybe, like my brothers, he'd think it was a fabulous idea to pay those two guys a visit.

I felt myself swallow. "You think he's out looking for them?"

"Hell yeah," Anthony said. "The dude's crazy." He said it like it was a good thing.

I didn't bother pointing out that by extension, my brothers must also be crazy, since they'd just mentioned the exact same thing.

Or maybe they were just joking. I sure as hell hoped so. But what if they weren't? I gave them a quick, furtive glance. Well, they were here now, and I needed to keep them here.

My stomach twisted. If only Jake were here, too. Sure, I missed him like I always did. But more to the point, I didn't want him anywhere near those two guys, whoever they were.

Yeah, I knew that Jake could handle himself just fine. He took crazy chances practically every day. But I hated the idea of him taking any chances on my account.

I looked to Steve and asked, "What do *you* think? Do *you* think Jake's looking for them?"

"If you want, we'll check." He flashed me a grin. "Might be fun."

"Fun?" My voice rose. "And *Jake's* the crazy one?"

"Hey, we meant it as a compliment," Steve said.

I looked to Anthony. To my infinite annoyance, he was already walking toward the door. A second later, Steve was following after him. Whatever this was, it was happening too fast.

I scrambled after them and practically threw myself in their path. "But you don't even know where Jake is."

"No harm in looking," Steve said. He sidestepped around me to the left, while Anthony went to the right.

And there I was, facing empty space.

I whirled around to face them. "You can't be serious."

For all I knew, Jake was somewhere perfectly safe. Maybe he was on his way home right now. And even if he wasn't, the thought of my brothers running around Detroit in search of trouble was too scary to consider.

But Steve's hand was already on the doorknob, and I couldn't exactly overpower them.

Crap.

"Wait!" I called. "You *can't* go."

Ignoring me, Steve pulled open the door and walked through it, with Anthony right behind him. Before I knew it, they were like ten steps away from the elevator, and then what?

One short ride, and then disaster. That's what.

I was desperate now. "Hey, dipshits!" I called. "Just so you know…" I winced, and then finished by blurting out, "I had sex in that elevator!"

My brothers froze. For a long moment, neither one of them moved. But then, in unison, they slowly turned around to face me.

Looking more than a little disturbed, Anthony said, "What?"

Damn it. It was too late to turn back now, and considering what was at stake, I wouldn't, even if I could. I extended my arm and pointed straight to the elevator, the one that would carry them to trouble if I didn't do something. "*That* elevator." I crossed my arms and continued. "So I hope you enjoy the ride."

The ride? What the hell? Probably, I could've phrased that better.

Double damn it.

Near the elevator, Steve was looking like all those pizza sandwiches hadn't settled so well. "Son-of-a-bitch," he muttered.

"Yeah," Anthony said, giving me an annoyed look, "It's the same one we used to get up here."

Well, there was that.

I could feel my face, flaming now. But I stiffened my spine and went full-disturbo. "And just so you know..." I swallowed. "The sex was extra-messy."

Messy? I didn't even know what that meant. But from the looks on my brothers' faces, it had the desired effect. They were eyeing the elevator with undisguised horror.

With a muttered curse, Steve turned to Anthony. "Twenty floors up, and *now* she says something?"

"Forget the timing," Anthony said. "It sucks we know at all." He gave me another annoyed look. "Dude, what's with the over-sharing?"

I lifted my chin. "I don't want you leaving."

Anthony glanced toward the stairway, and I could practically see the wheels turning.

Oh, crap. Probably, I should've thought of that.

Looking to head off whatever he was thinking, I announced, "And just so you know, I, uh, had sex in the stairwell, too."

Okay, now this was a slight exaggeration. But Jake *had* kissed me on the stairway. Hadn't he?

Steve narrowed his gaze. "Alright. You wanna play this game?" He glanced to Anthony and said, "It's on." Turning his attention back to me, he said, "So, you wanna swap stories?"

I froze. *Not really.* I mean, I knew that my brothers had sex lives of their own. But I *so* didn't want the details.

Still, trying to look at the big picture, I told myself that anything was better than them leaving. So I braced myself and said, "Sure. I'd, uh, love a good story." Trying not to throw up, I added, "I just, uh, hope it's a good, long one."

A long one?

Heaven help me.

Next to Steve, Anthony muttered, "What the hell?"

As for Steve, he gave me a smile that was pure evil. "Lemme tell you about mom and Bob."

Caught off guard, I shook my head. "Bob?"

"Yeah," Steve said. "The appliance guy." His smile widened. "You know that counter by mom's fridge? Well, I wouldn't be making your sandwiches there, if you know what I mean."

Oh.

Sadly, I *did* know what he meant, and not because of anything he'd told me. "Oh, my God," I said. "She told you?"

Steve and Anthony shared a look. After a long moment, Anthony said, "She told *you?*"

I shuddered. "Unfortunately."

"Shit," Steve muttered. "The way it sounds, she told everyone."

From somewhere behind him, a familiar male voice said, "Hey, she didn't tell me."

CHAPTER 33

I looked toward the sound and spotted Jake, standing in the now-open door to the stairwell.

Thank God.

I breathed a sigh of relief. "You're back."

He moved forward, and the door swung shut behind him. He bypassed Steve and Anthony to join me near the open penthouse doors. He wrapped an arm around my waist and turned to face my brothers. "You coming or going?" he asked.

Steve's gaze drifted to the nearby elevator, and then to the stairwell door. After a long, silent moment, he turned his gaze back to me. From the look on his face, it was obvious what he was thinking. There was no way out of here – or at least, no way that he was eager to take.

I glanced at Anthony. Unfortunately, he had the same look.

Trying to smooth things over, I gave my brothers a tentative smile. "About the stair thing, I might've been exaggerating just a little."

Neither one of them smiled back.

I gave Jake a sideways glance. Talk about awkward. Did he realize what we were talking about? It was hard to tell, and thankfully, he didn't ask.

I looked back to my brothers. They were eying the closed stairwell door with grim resignation.

By now, I was starting to feel almost guilty. "If you want to stay," I offered, "we can order more pizza."

"Screw that," Steve said. "I'm just hoping to keep the *last* pizza down." He looked to Anthony and said, "Twenty freaking flights."

"Yeah," Anthony said as he began trudging toward the stairwell door. "Man, this sucks."

I bit my lip. Probably, I should've retracted the elevator story instead. If nothing else, it would've saved them a walk down the stairs.

But there were two things that stopped me, even now. One – it would've been an outright lie, which would've boosted the odds of my brothers not believing me. And two – if I'd even hinted at anything to do with that elevator, Jake would almost certainly know exactly what we'd been talking about.

Did I *really* want him to know that I'd gone blabbing about our sex life to my brothers? No. Definitely not, even if it *had* been for a good cause.

And then, there was the more serious problem. If my brothers were still heading out for trouble, I needed to stop them.

I turned to Jake and said, "I'll be right back." I left his side and followed my brothers into the stairwell. When the door shut behind us, I lowered my voice to ask, "Hey, where are you guys going anyway?"

"Down," Steve said, not looking too happy about it.

I gave him an exasperated look. "Well, obviously. But you're not gonna go looking for those guys, are you?"

"The ones in that picture?" Steve said. "Hell no. That'd be a waste."

My shoulders sagged in relief. "Good. I'm glad you're being smart about it."

"Yeah, no shit," Anthony said. "You ask me, the dudes are dead. No fun looking now."

I stared at him. "What?"

"Yeah," he said. "Be a waste of time." He turned to Steve and said, "Unless you're up for dumpster-diving. You wanna?"

Steve gave it some thought. "Could be interesting."

I was still staring. "You guys are joking, right?"

"Eh, hard to say," Steve said. "Dumpster-diving..." He made that familiar waffling motion with his hand. "It's kind of hit-or-miss, you know?"

"No, I don't, actually." I gave him a serious look. "You're just messing with me, aren't you?"

"If we are," Steve said, "you deserve it." He glanced down the stairwell. Again, he said, "Twenty freaking flights."

Okay, I felt bad and everything, but couldn't he just drop it already? And besides, what a whiner. "Oh for God's sake," I said. "Just take the elevator then."

"I'll do *that*," Steve said, "when you make a sandwich on that counter."

"What counter?" I asked. But even as the words left my lips, an image of my mom, naked with Bob the Appliance Guy, flashed in my brain.

I couldn't help it. I stifled a shudder. When she'd told me that story, she'd been really, *really* descriptive – with sound effects and everything.

Suddenly, Steve was looking a lot more cheerful. Grinning now, he said, "See how that works?"

Yeah, I did. Unfortunately.

And the image was still there, burning in my brain like a naked clown that I'd been told not to think about.

It's not that Bob was bad-looking or anything, but the image of his privates slapping against my mom's kitchen counter was a little too vivid for my liking.

Damn it.

My gaze slid to Anthony, and I felt myself frown. He was smiling now, too.

Well, that was nice.

In unison, they turned away and started heading down the stairs. I called after them, "Text me when you get back, okay?"

For some reason, they thought this was absolutely hilarious. I didn't get the joke, but then again, I wasn't as crazy as they were either. When they disappeared from sight, I could still hear them laughing, probably at me, although I still couldn't figure out why.

With a sigh, I turned around and headed out of the stairwell. In the hall, I found Jake leaning near the penthouse doors, almost exactly where I'd left him. When I reached his side, he said, "So your mom and the appliance guy, huh?"

Oh great. As if I needed a reminder. There it was again, that same X-rated image – this time, with those dreaded sound-effects. I didn't know what was more disturbing, the mental mom-porno flashing in my brain, or the fact that Jake had overheard me discussing it with my brothers.

How much of it had he heard, anyway? Probably, I didn't want to know.

Deliberately, I changed the subject. "How come you didn't take the elevator up?"

"I did. But I stopped at the office on the way, then took the stairs from there." He flashed me a grin. "Why? You miss me?"

"I might've missed you a little," I admitted.

He reached out and pulled me tight against him. I could hear the smile, lingering in his voice, when he said, "Wrong. You missed me a lot."

I had to laugh. "God, you are *so* cocky." I pulled back to stare up at him. "Did you miss *me*?"

His eyes grew dark and intense. "Always."

"A little?" I smiled. "Or a lot?"

"It wasn't a little." He pulled me closer once again. "You want proof?"

I didn't need proof. I could feel it, hard, pressing against my pelvis. Speaking of things that weren't little. My stomach did a funny little flip, the one it always did when Jake caught me off guard.

Breathlessly, I said the same thing he'd just said to me. "Always."

I heard his voice in my hair, and felt his hands slide down to my ass. "Always," he murmured. "I like the sounds of that."

In spite of everything, I gave a happy sigh. "Me, too." No matter how wrong everything else had gone today, there was something about this that felt so incredibly right.

Jake moved his head and spoke low into my ear. "Wanna know what else I like?"

My voice, when I found it, came out as a whisper. "What?"
"This."

Before I knew it, he'd swooped me up in his arms and carried me through the open penthouse doors. I laughed as he kicked the doors shut behind us and tossed me onto the nearest sofa.

And then, he showed me exactly how much he'd been missing me.

Turns out, it was a lot.

A couple of hours later, we were snuggled up on that same sofa, fresh from the shower and dressed in casual clothes. Wrapped in his arms, I'd nearly forgotten how crappy most of the day had been.

Still, there was something I wanted to get out of the way – tonight, not tomorrow.

Tomorrow, I wanted a fresh start. I wanted to put the events of today behind us – especially that stupid walk and everything that had happened as a result.

So I leaned my face against his shoulder and said, "By the way, I looked at that picture."

"I know."

I pulled back to look at him. "You do? How?"

"I got a text."

"What?" I sputtered. "From who?"

"Anthony."

I sat up. Well, that was great. I felt like I'd been tattled on or something. Trying not to sound as annoyed as I felt, I asked, "What did it say?"

With something like a laugh, Jake reached for his phone and ran a finger across the screen. He turned the phone toward me and said, "This."

I looked. Briefly ignoring what it said, I checked the time of the text. As best I could tell, Anthony had sent it on his way down the stairs.

Maybe *that's* why they'd been laughing. Those asshats.

Jake flashed me a sudden grin. "Hey, they're *your* brothers."

Well, there was that. I looked down to study the text. *Those 2 guys. Did you dumpster them, or what?*

I shook my head. "Dumpster them?"

I knew what it meant. I just wasn't sure of the details. Technically, you could throw a *live* person into a dumpster. Right?

Or maybe – hopefully – nothing remotely like that had happened. I looked back to Jake and said, "You didn't." I hesitated. "Did you?"

"Nah," Jake said. "I saw them. That's it. No dumpsters involved."

"So my brothers were right?" I pulled away and sat up straighter. "That's where you went tonight?"

Jake only shrugged.

Talk about a non-answer.

There was no way I was going to let this go. "How'd you know where they were? Or *who* they were?"

"I got a tip."

Right. And I had a pretty good guess which tip he meant. "It was that text, wasn't it? The one you got in your office."

"You might say that."

"Who sent it?" I held up a hand. "Wait. I know. It was that guy, wasn't it? The one who sent you that picture." When Jake said nothing, I added, "I'm right, aren't I?"

"Does it matter?"

"Yes. It does, actually."

"Why?"

"Because it involves me," I explained. "And maybe, I don't like the idea of some jerk reporting back to you all the time."

"Yeah? Well, too bad."

I drew back. "What's that supposed to mean?"

"You don't wanna know. And I don't want to tell you. So drop it."

"Drop it?" I repeated. If that was supposed to make me miraculously forget the whole thing, he didn't know who he was dealing with. "But why wouldn't you want to tell me?"

"Because, you don't wanna know, just like I said."

"But I do," I insisted.

On the sofa, he said nothing. But the weight of his gaze was feeling heavier with every minute.

Refusing to let him off the hook, I waited in silence.

Finally, he said, "Alright. You wanna know what happened?"

When I nodded, he pushed himself up and stood, towering over me.

I craned my neck to look up at him. "What are you doing?"

He reached for my hand and pulled me up next to him. "Come on."

CHAPTER 34

A moment later, we were standing outside on the balcony. The night was warm and muggy, with a damp wind that made me shiver in spite of the mild weather.

Standing by Jake's side, I gazed out over the urban landscape. From here, I could see the Detroit River and the area that surrounded it. Next to me, Jake was grim and silent, surveying the view with dark, wary eyes.

When he said nothing, I asked, "Why are we out here?"

"Because I've got a question."

"What?" I asked.

"How well do you know this place?"

I gave it some thought. Like Jake, I'd grown up two hours north of here in a town a lot smaller than this. It was true that after college, I'd moved closer to Detroit, but even then, I'd stuck mostly to the suburbs.

Except for a brief stint in a seedy apartment with a skanky roommate, most of the places I'd lived had been a lot less interesting than this. Was *that* what he was getting at?

I glanced over at him. "How well do I know what? The city?"

He looked out over the cityscape. "Everything you see now. The city, the neighborhood, whatever. How well do you know it?"

Obviously, he knew the answer. I'd been living here for just a few short weeks. We spent a lot of time on the balcony and inside the condo. But whenever we went out, it was usually by car and farther than a five-minute drive.

"Not that well," I admitted.

"Well, I do," he said. "And so does Moe."

"Moe? The guy who sent you that picture?"

"Yeah. The guy who *also* saved your sweet little ass."

The statement made me pause, and not because of the compliment. I turned to face Jake head-on. "What do you mean?"

"Those guys who were following you," he said, "you never encountered them. And you wanna know why?"

"Because I outran them?"

"Guess again."

"Honestly, Jake, I have no idea. I never even saw them."

"Right. Because where you grew up—"

"Don't you mean where *we* grew up?"

Jake made a scoffing sound. "Baby, if you think we grew up in the same place..." He stopped and shook his head.

I was almost insulted. "It was the same town," I reminded him. "We even hung out together. Remember?"

For some reason, this made his lips twist into something that wasn't quite a smile. "Uh-huh."

I crossed my arms. "Well, we did."

"Wrong," he said. "You were slumming it. I wasn't."

The more he talked, the more insulted I felt. Growing up, I hadn't had a lot of money, so the idea of me "slumming it" with anyone was ludicrous.

"I was not," I insisted. "And besides, we didn't live that far apart."

"Maybe not in miles. But inside?" He shook his head. "You know what. Forget that. You wanna know what happened? I'll give you the short version."

Gently, he gripped my shoulders and turned me outward again, facing the night cityscape. "Somewhere out there," he said, "are people who like nothing more than fresh meat. And today, wanna know who the meat was?"

"Oh, stop it," I said. "I'm not meat, if that's what you're getting at." Again, I turned to face him. "And you know what? I'm getting a little tired of the lectures. We already talked about this. Can't we just drop it already?"

He gave a wry laugh. "Right."

"What's so funny?" I demanded.

"You," he said. "You want answers. But you don't wanna talk about it."

"Except you're not giving me answers," I pointed out. "You're just giving me a hard time."

"Baby, *I'm* not the one you've gotta worry about." His voice grew darker, harder. "*I'm* not the one who's gonna drag you into some building, make you bleed, and brag about it after."

At the ugly image, I yanked myself away. "Just stop it. You're exaggerating."

He gave that same laugh, but lower and uglier. "It's nice to think that, isn't it?"

"No," I told him. "*Nothing* about this conversation is nice."

"I know. And that's my point." He leaned closer, and his voice grew quiet. "You really wanna know what happened tonight?"

From the look on his face, I suddenly wasn't so sure. Still, I made myself nod.

He leaned a fraction closer. "They're dead."

"What?" I drew back as visions of dumpsters and dead bodies flashed in my brain. "Did, uh, you—"

"No."

I stared up at him, searching his face for clues. Desperately, I wanted to believe him. "Would you tell me if you had?"

"Maybe."

I made a sound of disbelief. "Or maybe not?"

"I dunno. But it doesn't matter, because I didn't touch them." He smiled. "But that doesn't mean I wouldn't have."

"What?"

"If they'd hurt you—"

"But they didn't," I reminded him.

"And now they won't." He shrugged. "See? Problem solved."

His words were so cold, they made me shiver. "None of this is making any sense," I said, recalling what he'd told me just a few minutes earlier. "Tonight, you told me that just saw them."

"I did."

"So, did you talk to them?"

"By the time I saw them?" Jake gave a cold smile. "No point in that, considering their condition."

His words, along with that smile, made me take a step backward. The implication was obvious, and it made my stomach roil. "What are you saying? You saw their bodies?"

"Eh, what was left of 'em."

Okay, that wasn't helping my stomach.

Suddenly, I was glad to be out on the balcony. If I had to hurl, I was in the right place, well, except when I considered the people on the lower balconies.

Obviously, they'd see things differently.

I shook my head. "I don't get it."

"What don't you get?"

"All the inconsistencies." Quickly, I rattled them off. "You know them, but you don't know them. You saw them, but not alive." I swallowed. "They're dead, but you had nothing to do with it."

"Pretty much."

I gave him a hard look. "And how, exactly did they die?"

"Badly."

"Badly? Is that a joke?"

"Eh, just quoting Moe. Although, he didn't put it so nice."

I threw up my hands. "See? That's the kind of stuff I mean. You're quoting him, but you're *not* quoting him."

"Trust me," he said. "The exact quote? You don't want it."

I hesitated. Okay, about this, he might be right. Besides, I had another question. "And how is it that you came home looking so cheerful?"

"I was cheerful because the fuckers killed each other. A nice happy ending. Who doesn't love that?"

I stared up at him. "I doubt *they* loved it."

My head was swimming. It was like there were all these weird puzzle pieces, scrambled around on some giant, dark table. I didn't know how the pieces fit, or what I should do now.

And why was Jake telling me this?

But of course, the answer to *that* question was obvious. He was telling me because I'd demanded to know. In hindsight, maybe I should've dropped the whole thing.

Silently, I turned to look out over the city. From this far up, the view was undeniably beautiful. But down below, things weren't always so pretty. I'd known that, of course, but Jake's story was a cruel reminder of just how ugly things could be.

I let out a long, weary breath, wondering what else I was missing. Next to me Jake shifted, and soon, I felt his arms wrap tight around my waist, holding me gently from behind.

His voice, softer now, drifted down to me. "Don't think about it. It's not worth it."

Probably, he was right. I leaned back against him, suddenly exhausted with the whole sordid situation. Still, I didn't want to wonder later on, so I forced myself to say, "You might as well tell me the rest."

"Why?" he asked.

"Because if you don't," I admitted, "I'll probably be searching the internet tomorrow."

"Trust me. It's not on the internet."

Somehow, I doubted that. It seemed to me that everything was on the internet these days. "Then just give me the short version," I said. "What happened?" I tried to smile. "Starting when I went on that stupid walk."

He lowered his head, and his mouth grazed my ear. In a voice that was almost a caress, he said, "So you admit it was stupid, huh?"

"Oh, stop rubbing it in," I said. "Just tell me, okay?"

"Alright. Here's the short version. It started to rain. You ran off. They ran after you. Moe intercepted them–"

I whirled to face him. "What do you mean by 'intercepted'?"

"Just what I said. Moe pulled up and had a little talk with them. Told them you were hands-off."

"I don't get it," I said. "Why would he do that?"

"Because he owed me a favor. That's why."

"What kind of favor? Legal? Or illegal?"

Jake made that same waffling gesture that Steve had made earlier. "Eh, could go either way."

Oddly enough, I knew what he meant. Jake did a lot of things that weren't quite illegal, but skirted pretty close to the line. I pushed the distraction aside and said, "So then what happened?"

"So then, they took off."

"Just like that?"

"When he wants to, Moe can be fairly persuasive."

From what I'd seen so far, so could Jake. But I'd known that already, hadn't I?

"So what did they do next?" I asked. "Do you know?"

Jake nodded. "The way it sounds, they got pissed off, hit some drugs, ended up with a bad batch."

"So they overdosed? That's what killed them?"

He was quiet a beat before answering. "No. Something went wrong, probably mixed some things that didn't mesh. One of them flips out, tries to chew the other one's face off–"

I drew back. "What?"

"Happens more than you think. So the one shoots the face-chewer, who, believe it or not, has just enough sense to pull out his own gun and shoot back." He shrugged. "A few more shots, and there you go."

I paused. What on Earth could I say to that? Honestly, I had no idea. I couldn't even picture it.

Hell, I didn't even want to.

So all I did was lean closer to Jake and say, "Your life is crazy. You know that, right?"

His voice grew warm. "Yeah. That's why I need *you.*"

I pulled back to gaze up at him. "Oh, like *I'm* supposed to keep you sane?"

"No. What *you're* supposed to do is enjoy the ride." He leaned his head close to mine and said, "About the other stuff, don't worry. I've got it."

He sounded utterly certain. But as for me, I wasn't so sure. Jake's life *was* crazy, and I didn't see it calming down any time soon.

There was a time – a time not too long ago – when I would've embraced the craziness and not given it too much thought. But these days, I was dwelling on everything. What did that mean? Was I growing up? Or growing old?

I sure didn't feel old. But I had to admit that life had seemed so much simpler back when I'd been a little less responsible, a little more carefree, and like Jake, a whole lot crazier.

Now, I didn't know where things were heading. About long-term plans, he'd hinted. I'd hinted. We'd jokingly talked about life as an old married couple someday, with a bunch of kids and maybe a few dogs, too.

But when I closed my eyes, I just couldn't see it. Jake was a bad-ass, a flaming comet that burned hot and fast. What would someone like him want with a nice, normal life?

I turned away and gazed out over the urban landscape. In the distance, I heard police sirens and the low rumble of distant thunder – unrelated, obviously. But it sure fit my mood.

Next to me, Jake said, "Don't."

I turned to him and asked, "Don't what?"

"Don't throw yourself off."

I don't know why, but it made me laugh. A nervous reflex? Maybe. "I wasn't planning on it," I told him.

"Good." His tone grew teasing. "It's a long way down."

I glanced past the balcony rails. It *was* a long way down. Or, if I wanted to look on the bright side, we were a long way up.

Glass half full, right?

"And," Jake continued, wrapping his arms around me once again. "If *you* went? I'd have to throw myself after you."

"Oh stop it," I teased. "You wouldn't."

"Good thing is, we're not gonna find out." He squeezed me tighter and said, "Tomorrow, we're gonna wake up, put all this stuff behind us."

There were other things I wanted to talk about – especially the thing with my car. I needed to know who, exactly, had paid for it. But if I brought that up now, I'd have to bring up Rango, and suddenly, I just didn't have the energy.

I sagged against him, deciding I'd leave that, at least, for tomorrow. We could ponder it then, under the start of a fresh new day.

The more I thought about it, the more I liked the idea. A fresh start, with no fights and no drama. It all sounded so nice.

And it would've been nice – except, as I should've anticipated, it didn't exactly happen that way.□

CHAPTER 35

I woke to the sounds of tapping. Still half-asleep, I rolled over in bed and felt for Jake.

I paused. He wasn't there.

I opened my eyes and sat up, naked and confused. Pale moonlight filtered in through the partially open window blinds, making me squint in confusion.

I heard another series of taps and looked around. The tapping was coming from the closed bedroom door. When the tapping stopped, I heard my sister's voice, just above a whisper. "Hey Luna? You awake in there?"

I rubbed at my eyes. My sister spent half of her time ten hours South in Alabama, and the other half two hours North in our hometown.

What was she doing here? And more to the point, what was she doing here in the middle of the night?

Instantly, I was wide awake. I glanced at the clock on the nightstand. It was past five o'clock, less than an hour before sunrise. Okay, so it wasn't exactly the middle of the night. But it wasn't quite morning yet either.

"Hang on," I called, jumping out of bed and flicking on the lights. I threw on the same clothes that I'd been wearing the previous night and flung open the bedroom door.

And there Selena was, looking surprisingly awake, even if slightly disheveled.

Her long, dark hair was pulled into a loose ponytail, and her clothes – casual shorts and a yellow tank top – were definitely on the rumpled side.

"Is everything okay?" I asked. "What are you doing here?"

She glanced down the hallway, toward the condo's main living area. "I came along for the ride."

It was then that I noticed it, the muffled sounds of male voices. The way it sounded, Jake was talking with Bishop, one of his brothers, who happened to be my sister's fiancé.

I couldn't hear what they were saying, but the conversation didn't sound terribly friendly. No surprise there. From what I'd seen so far, Jake and Bishop didn't exactly get along.

I looked back to my sister and asked, "Are they arguing?"

Selena sighed. "Probably."

"Why? What happened?" I paused. "And what are you doing here *now?* Why didn't you call?"

She gave a small laugh. "What? You're not happy to see me?"

"Oh come on. You know what I mean. This isn't exactly normal."

"Tell me about it." She moved forward and quietly shut the bedroom door behind her. "And just so you know, I did call. You didn't answer. I left a message around midnight. Didn't you get it?"

I shook my head. "Actually, I can't find my phone."

"You lost it?"

"Nah," I said. "I had it here last night. I just kind of lost track of it, that's all."

Just before bed, I'd made a half-hearted attempt to find it. I'd even asked Jake to call my number, hoping to locate the phone that way. Unfortunately, I'd had zero luck, probably because I'd turned off the ringer to avoid Rango's calls.

Still, I wasn't worried. The phone would turn up. It always did, usually within a few minutes of doing whatever around the condo.

Inside the bedroom, Selena sank onto a nearby armchair and stretched out her bare legs. "Would you believe we've been driving all night?"

Well, that explained the rumpled clothes.

"From Alabama?" I said. "Wait, I thought you were spending the summer in Michigan."

"I am," she said, "but I had to run down South for something. It was supposed to be for a few days." She sank deeper into the chair. "Wanna know how long I was there?"

"How long?" I asked.

"A few minutes." She gave a weak laugh. "We'd barely pulled into the driveway when Bishop gets this phone call." She shrugged. "So here we are."

"Who was the call from? Jake?" I felt myself frown. "Funny he didn't mention it."

She shook her head. "It wasn't from Jake. It was from Joel."

"Their brother?"

"Yup, that's the one."

Joel was their youngest brother. Whenever I pictured him, I thought of the quiet kid he used to be, way back in our hometown. But these days, he wasn't a kid anymore.

Now, he was in his early twenties, and from what I'd recently discovered, a bit of a bad-ass – not surprising, considering he was a Bishop.

I sat on the edge of the bed and said, "You know, I saw Joel just a few weeks ago."

She looked surprised. "Really? Where?"

"Here in Detroit. Get this," I said. "This bigtime sports agent..." I paused. "Vince Hammond. You ever hear of him?"

Selena nodded. "You worked for him, right?"

"Yeah, for like five whole minutes. I'm surprised you remember."

"It wasn't just that," she said. "Bishop mentioned him on the drive."

"He did? Why?"

"First, finish your story," she said. "I'll tell mine after."

"Alright. Well, anyway, a few weeks ago, Vince Hammond was trying to sign Joel, you know as a client."

Selena rolled her eyes. "Yeah. I heard."

"From who?"

"From Bishop, who heard it from Joel, in a roundabout way."

I leaned forward. "Well, I didn't *have* to hear about it. I was there."

"No kidding?"

"No kidding. But only for a few minutes, because I wasn't invited. Basically, Jake and I crashed the meeting, hoping to stop Joel from signing. And do you want to know why?"

"Lemme guess," she said. "Because Vince is a crooked snake, who's gonna ruin Joel's life?"

"Uh, yeah. Pretty much. How'd you know?"

"Like I said, Bishop mentioned him."

"Oh, right. So anyway," I continued, "we show up at the restaurant where they're meeting, and Joel's not listening to anything we're saying. He basically tells me and Jake to shove it." At the memory of what happened next, I couldn't help but smile. "But then, Vince starts talking about getting Joel modeling and acting gigs."

"Seriously?"

"Yeah." At the memory, I had to laugh. "You should've seen it. They're sitting around this table, and Vince is talking about modeling and stuff. And suddenly, Joel flips out, knocks over the table, and storms off, leaving Vince covered in his own lunch."

In my mind, I could still see it. "It was like curly noodles and stuff. The guy looked like a total idiot."

Selena was nodding. "Well, that explains a few things."

"Like what?"

Her gaze shifted toward the center of the condo, where Jake and Bishop were still talking. From here, we couldn't see them, but the muffled sounds of their voices were growing louder with every minute.

Selena looked to me and said, "The way I hear it, Joel's changed his mind. He's got a meeting with Vince." She winced. "Today."

"Today? When?"

"We don't know. Sometime this afternoon, maybe?"

"Is that why you're in town? To stop him or something?"

"That's why Bishop's here. As for me, I came to see you." Suddenly, she smiled. "Before I forget, what do you think of turquoise?"

"Turquoise what?"

Her eyes were practically sparkling now. "Bridesmaid dresses."

I couldn't help but smile, too. She and Bishop were getting married next April. To me, it seemed like a long time away. But my sister was one of those planning types, so I guess it fit her personality. Plus, they were building this amazing beach house on the Saginaw Bay, and had timed the wedding for when their home would be fully completed.

Yup, she was a planner, alright. Probably, I could learn a few things from her.

I gave a slow nod. "Turquoise? It's a good color. I like it."

"Good, because—" A crashing sound made her stop in mid-sentence.

In unison, we both turned to look. The sound had come from somewhere near the center of the condo, where Jake and Bishop were still talking, now even louder than before.

Their conversation, if you could call it that, continued as if nothing had happened.

In front of me, Selena gave a worried frown. "Hopefully that wasn't anything of yours."

"Don't worry." I looked around. "Practically nothing in here is mine."

It was true, and now that I thought about it, it was actually kind of depressing.

With a sigh, Selena pushed herself up from the chair. "I guess we should go see." She gave a weak laugh. "We can't let them kill each other, right?"□

CHAPTER 36

Standing near the balcony doors, Jake and Bishop were squared off, facing each other. Neither one of them looked happy. Like *that* was a surprise.

Bishop was telling Jake, "You were supposed to take care of it."

"I did," Jake said. "So don't worry about it, alright?"

Near their feet, I saw a white ceramic lamp, lying on its side. It was broken into at least a dozen pieces, and missing its lampshade. I paused. Nope. There the shade was, lying near the sofa.

That was the good news. In the bad-news category, the lamp itself was a goner. I was pretty sure this was somehow my fault. I had the worst luck with lamps. Unfortunately, that luck seemed to be rubbing off on Jake.

Next to me, Selena called out to Bishop. "We didn't break that, did we?"

We? Meaning her and Bishop? That was just like my sister, taking responsibility for something she had nothing to do with. If things weren't so tense, I might've smiled.

Near the balcony, Jake and Bishop turned to look – not at the lamp, at us.

It was Jake who asked, "Break what?"

I moved forward and pointed. "The lamp."

"Screw the lamp," Jake said. "Bishop's leaving."

I felt myself frown. I hadn't seen my sister in weeks. And seriously, weren't they done fighting already?

On impulse, I said, "He can't leave. We haven't had breakfast."

Jake's gaze shifted to the balcony. "It's still dark out."

"But it won't be for long." I pointed past the balcony doors. "Look, there's the sun, reflecting off that building."

Jake's voice was flat. "That's from the chicken place next door."

He was right, of course. They had this killer neon sign that lit up the whole block. But I wasn't going to let that stop me. "So?" I summoned up a smile. "It'll be light out eventually, right?"

In truth, I wasn't all that hungry. But I *was* tired of them arguing all the time. Selena and Bishop were going to be married. Soon, we'd all be family, in a loose sort of way.

The thought of the two brothers brawling over Christmas dinner wasn't sounding all that festive.

I gave Bishop a quick glance. Speaking of things that weren't festive, he eyed Jake with cold disdain. "You want me to leave?" Bishop told him. "Then take care of it, so I don't have to."

Ignoring Bishop, Jake turned to me and said, "You want breakfast? Fine. I'll take you out."

I smiled. "Great." I turned to Selena and said, "What are you two in the mood for?" Before Jake could object, I added, "There's this great twenty-four-hour breakfast place a few blocks from here. They have killer pancakes." I looked to Bishop and said, "Trust me. You're gonna love 'em."

From the look on his face, he highly doubted it.

I looked to Jake. For someone who definitely loved pancakes, he wasn't looking too thrilled either.

I looked to Selena. At least *she* looked happy.

Twenty minutes later, we were all settled in a booth near the restaurant's window, with me and Jake on one side, and Selena and Bishop on the other. The guys weren't talking, and the tension was thicker than the scent of bacon, but not nearly as pleasant.

Selena and I kept the conversation going, and tried like crazy to include them, but so far, they weren't having any of it. They sat, grim and silent, eyeing each other across the booth's table, and speaking only when the waitress came to take their orders.

After about fifteen minutes, Selena set down her coffee cup and said, "Oh for God's sake." She gestured toward the nearby window. Outside, dawn was finally breaking over the city street. "You guys wanna fight? There's the parking lot. Go ahead."

Bishop gave the window a quick glance. "Who says we wanna fight?"

Next to me, Jake spoke up. "Speak for yourself, dickhead."

I turned to glare at him. "Hey," I hissed. "We're at a family restaurant. Watch the language, okay?"

Jake made a show of looking around. Actually, the place was kind of a dive, and there wasn't a single kid in sight. He lifted an eyebrow and waited for my response.

"Oh, fine," I muttered. "But you know what I mean."

Across from us, Selena tried again. "Alright, if you're not gonna fight, at least talk it out, okay?"

She rested a hand on Bishop's arm. "In fact, let's *all* talk about it." She smiled. "Four heads are better than two, right?"

Jake and Bishop exchanged a look. Neither one looked eager for assistance.

Selena let out a breath. "Alrighty then," she said in a tone I knew all too well. "I'll start with the basics." She looked to me and said, "They're worried that Joel is going to sign with Vince."

Next to me, Jake spoke up. "Wrong. Bishop's worried. I'm not." He turned to Bishop and said, "I've got this, as I already told you."

"Yeah?" Bishop said. "And what happens when it backfires?"

"Nothing," Jake said, "because it's not gonna."

"Your ass," Bishop said. "He's gonna fuckin' hate you."

Selena turned to give Bishop a look. "Hey," she whispered. "Seriously. Watch the language, okay?"

Next to me, Jake's tone grew sarcastic. "Yeah," he told Bishop. "It's a family restaurant, remember?"

"Hey!" I said. "Are you making fun of me?"

Jake shrugged.

"Are you?" I repeated.

Jake flicked his head toward Bishop and said, "Nah, I'm making fun of *him*."

I rolled my eyes. "Nice try."

Across from us, Bishop spoke up. "Just listen," he told Jake. "You do it your way, he's gonna be pissed off."

"It's already done," Jake said, "so drop it."

Confused, I stared from brother to brother. What was already done?

Before I could give it too much thought, Bishop spoke again. "You're gonna get grief. You know that, right?"

"Grief, huh?" Jake leaned back and crossed his arms. "Do I look like I care?"

Bishop's jaw tightened. "You should. You ever hear of blowback?"

Jake grinned. "You ever hear of 'blow me?'"

Bishop looked at Jake for a long, silent moment. "Right." He looked to Selena and said, "You ready?"

She gave him a look. "No. We haven't even gotten our food."

"So, we'll get it to go."

"Nope. Sorry." She gave him a pleading look. "Seriously, we can't leave now."

"Yeah," I added. "And besides, who likes cold pancakes?"

Bishop's gaze shifted to me. "That's what microwaves are for."

Selena made a face. "Microwaved pancakes. That is *so* wrong."

"No kidding," I chimed in. "They're never as good warmed up."

Bishop turned to my sister. In a tone of infinite patience, he said, "Alright, we'll hit a different place. Not a big deal." He flicked his head toward the door. "Now, come on."

"Nope." She crossed her arms. "Sorry. Not 'til you guys work it out."

Next to me, Jake said, "It *is* worked out. Not that dickhead believes it."

Bishop's jaw tightened. "*I'm* the dickhead?"

"Hey!" a scratchy female voice called out from somewhere nearby. "You're both dickheads. Now shut up, so I can read my paper in peace."

We all turned to look. The voice belonged to a gray-haired woman sitting two booths away. When she saw us looking, she slammed down her newspaper and said, "I mean it. Quit bitchin', or go outside. You're ruining my damn breakfast."

Next to me, Jake stood. He looked to Bishop. "You wanna take it outside? I'm game." A moment later, he was striding toward the door, with Bishop striding after him.

So much for a nice, happy breakfast.□

CHAPTER 37

Sitting at the table, Selena and I watched through the restaurant window as they stopped near the street and turned to face each other.

I bit my lip. "They're not really gonna fight, are they?"

Selena gave them a worried glance. "No. Of course not."

I recognized the tone. It was the same one she'd used back in grade school, when she'd assured me that our parents weren't going to get divorced.

A month later, they were living in different houses.

Somehow, the recollection wasn't terribly comforting.

Again, I looked outside. Jake and Bishop were standing within arm's reach of each other, talking, or more likely, arguing. But at least they weren't fighting. Not yet, anyway.

I looked to Selena. "I've gotta ask, do you think Bishop'll hit him?"

"No." She hesitated. "Well, not unless Jake hits him first."

"Oh. That's good."

"Why?

"Because he wouldn't," I said.

She gave me a dubious look. "You sure about that?"

"Yeah. He never does." I paused. "Or at least, not usually." I tried to laugh. "Usually, what he does is piss-off the other person until they take a swing at him. He's pretty good at it, actually."

"Yeah, I noticed."

Again, we looked outside. They still weren't hitting each other. That was a good sign, right?

Just then, our waitress appeared with a huge tray of food. As she started delivering plates, she paused in mid-motion. She was looking out the window, where Jake and Bishop were still facing off, looking like they wanted to kill each other.

"Don't worry," I told the waitress. "We're pretty sure they're not gonna fight."

"If you say so, honey," she said, delivering the rest of the plates and hustling off to the next table.

I looked at the heaping plates and sighed. "Should we tell them the food's here?"

Selena glanced toward the woman who'd complained earlier. She was sipping her coffee while looking down, reading her newspaper.

On the woman's table, I spotted a couple of dirty plates and a wadded up napkin. The way it looked, her food was gone, but in my experience, that didn't mean she'd be leaving any time soon.

She did, after all, have coffee and a newspaper.

In a hushed voice, I told Selena, "Don't get your hopes up. She might be there for hours."

Selena turned and glanced toward the parking lot, where Jake and Bishop were still talking. "If we call them in," she said, "do you think Jake can be nice for once?"

I gave her a look. "I dunno. Do you think *Bishop* can be nice for once?"

"Hey," she said, looking almost insulted. "He's always nice."

"He is not," I told her. "He's especially not nice to Jake."

"That's not true," she insisted.

"Oh really? How would you know?"

"I know because..." She hesitated. "Well, I guess I don't, actually."

"Exactly," I said. "Admit it. You don't even like him."

"Who? Jake?" she said. "That's hardly my fault. It's hard to like him when he's a jerk all the time."

"*He's* a jerk?" I said. "What about Bishop?"

"What about him?"

"He only comes over when he wants to gripe. You know, I've been living with Jake for a few weeks now, and seriously, the only time we ever hear from Bishop is when he comes by to tell Jake what a screw-up he is." I made a sound of annoyance. "Which, by the way, he isn't."

"Luna, come on," she said in her *let's-all-be-reasonable* voice. "Jake pisses people off for a living. You gotta admit that much."

"So what?" I said. "What does Bishop do?"

"What do you mean?"

"For a living. What does he do?"

Her gaze shifted outside, where Jake and Bishop appeared to be engaged in some sort of standoff. They weren't talking so much as glaring.

Was that an improvement? Honestly, I didn't know.

I turned back to my sister. "Admit it. You don't even know."

"What Bishop does?" she said. "I do, too."

"Oh yeah? What?"

"Well, he has some patents, and does some security stuff."

"That sounds awful vague to me."

"It's not vague," she said. "It's passive income. He makes money for things he invented forever ago."

From what I'd heard, he made a lot of money. But that was beside the point. "I'm just saying that I don't appreciate you judging me. Or Jake either for that matter."

At the hurt in her eyes, I softened my tone. "I love him. And he's a great guy. You'd know that if you ever gave him half a chance."

"I *have* given him a chance."

"You have not," I said. "And neither has Bishop."

Selena closed her eyes and said, "I don't believe this."

"What?"

With her eyes still shut, she leaned back in the booth and let out a long, weary sigh. "Why are *we* arguing? *They're* the ones who are mad at each other."

"Yeah, but it's important to me. Can't you at least try to like him?" Thinking of Jake, I turned to look out the window.

I heard myself gasp. "Oh, crap."

Instantly, Selena's eyes flew open. "What?"

I pointed out the window. "Look."

Selena looked. From the expression on her face, she knew exactly what I meant.

Outside, a silver-and-black sports car with dark, tinted windows and flashy silver rims had pulled up to the curb, just a few feet away from where Jake and Bishop were standing.

Hanging out of the open passenger's side window was someone all too familiar. It was Ronnie North, Dorian's younger brother, who'd flipped out at the convention center when he hadn't won that regional sports award.

And since Ronnie wasn't driving, I knew at least one thing for certain. He wasn't alone.

Damn it.

CHAPTER 38

Horrified, I stared through the restaurant window.

From what I could see, Ronnie was spitting mad, literally. He was yelling something to Jake, who, along with Bishop, had turned to look.

I couldn't see their faces, but their stances looked easy and relaxed, like they didn't have a care in the world.

God, they were so damned cocky.

Of course.

I jumped up from the booth, only to collide with a waitress, not ours, who dropped her tray, sending dishes crashing to the floor.

"Oh, my God," I said. "I am *so* sorry." I looked down and saw broken glasses and shattered plates, along with the discarded remnants of scrambled eggs and pieces of syrupy pancakes, obviously from a table that had just been cleared.

At least, I hadn't ruined anyone's breakfast – well, except for the lady two booths over, who was now openly glaring at me.

What? Like I'd done it on purpose? I glared back at her. "Sorry, it was an accident."

And besides, I suddenly recalled, her breakfast was long gone.

But apparently, that didn't matter. With a huff, she returned to her paper, mumbling something that sounded suspiciously like, "Accident, my ass."

Whatever. I had bigger things to worry about. I snuck a quick glance outside, where Ronnie was still yelling, and the guys were still watching.

In front of me, Selena had scooted out of the booth and was now crouching down to help the waitress pick up the mess.

Beside her, the waitress looked ready to cry. "Just stop it, okay? You're gonna cut yourself." She called out toward the kitchen, "Charlie, grab the broom. We got another mess out here!"

Under her breath, she added, "Just great. More out of my paycheck."

I paused. *She'd* be paying for it? I spoke up. "But it wasn't your fault."

If anything, I figured the damage would be added to our bill, and rightfully so. I mean, I didn't expect anyone else to pay for my clumsiness.

The waitress picked up her tray and stood, blinking back tears. Turning to walk away, she mumbled, "Yeah, well tell that to my boss."

I wanted to say something, but before I could find the words, Selena, who'd gotten to her feet, called out, "Hey, wait a second."

The waitress stopped and turned around, but said nothing.

My sister grabbed her purse and yanked out her wallet. She pulled out a few bills and thrust them toward the waitress. "Does this cover it?"

The waitress gave the money a worried look. After a long pause, she said, "Actually, I think that's too much." Wincing, she gave a weak laugh. "I'm an idiot for admitting that, aren't I?"

"No. And it's not too much," Selena said. "It's for the trouble, too." Before the waitress could object, Selena placed the money on the waitress's tray and glanced again toward the window. "Oh shoot, hang on." She pulled out a few more bills and tossed them onto our table, telling the waitress, "Can you tell our server that's for breakfast?"

The waitress looked down at our table, still laden with food that was mostly untouched. "But you didn't eat any of it."

"Tell me about it," Selena said, glancing again toward the parking lot. "Sorry, but we've gotta run."

From a couple of tables away, the woman with the newspaper called out, "Halleluiah!"

Well, that was nice.

I grabbed my purse and, with Selena, rushed for the exit. By the time we pushed through the restaurant door, the situation was already escalating.

I moved to join Jake, but Selena grabbed my arm. "Wait."

I stopped. "For what?"

"If we get too close, we'll distract them."

I gave a quick shake of my head. "What?"

"If we get in the middle of it," she explained, "they'll be more worried about us than themselves."

I paused. It was funny. I'd never quite looked at it that way. But she was right. Still, I had to ask the obvious question. "Then why are we out here?"

Releasing me, she gave a weak laugh. "I dunno. Backup?"

I looked to the street. "Speaking of backups…" I didn't bother finishing the sentence. Selena had eyes. She could see for herself.

Ronnie was still hanging out of the passenger's side window, but now, traffic was piling up behind him.

On the other side of the street, a food delivery truck had claimed the other lane, which meant that until Ronnie moved, no one else could get through.

It was barely dawn, and a Saturday, too, so traffic wasn't even that heavy. Unfortunately, the cars were still stacking up scarily fast. I heard a horn honk, followed by the sound of a male voice yelling out, "Move your ass, dipshit!"

Like so many other times over the past few weeks, I didn't know whether to laugh or cry.

God, what a spectacle.

The only upside was that, for whatever reason, Ronnie didn't seem inclined to actually get out of the car. And for whatever *other* reason, Jake and Bishop didn't seem inclined to do much more than watch, looking – from what I could see now – stupidly amused.

I couldn't say I blamed them. It *was* entertaining, in a freak-show kind of way. And like all freak shows, it had attracted a crowd, not a huge one, but at least twenty people, watching from the sidelines.

Ronnie looked drunk off his ass, which no doubt, explained what he was doing out here so early. To him, it was probably the end of a long night, not the beginning of a new day.

He was still hollering, slurring out toward Jake, "You think you're such a big man. Well, you're not a big anything. You're an asshole, that's what you are."

Jake gave a low laugh. "That's what I hear." He turned to Bishop and said, "Do *you* think I'm an asshole?"

Bishop's voice was deadpan. "Don't ask."

Suddenly inspired, I turned to Selena and said, "Hey, can I borrow your phone?"

"Why?" But already, she was reaching into her purse. "Are you gonna call 911?"

"Actually," I admitted, "I want to get this on film."

She paused in mid-motion. "What?"

"Well, not on film-film," I explained. "I mean I wanna record it. You know. For Jake."

Selena looked at me like I'd lost my mind. "Why? For legal reasons?"

"Does it matter?" I thrust out my hand, palm-up. "Come on. Just hand it over, okay? I'd use my own if I had it."

But I *didn't* have it. The phone still hadn't turned up, and I was starting worry it was gone for good. How or why, I had no idea. It's not like I'd gone anywhere since using it last.

To her credit, Selena handed her phone over without further argument. Hers wasn't terribly different from my own, and within a couple of seconds, I was lifting the phone to capture the action.

I focused in on Ronnie, who was looking like a total idiot. He was now hanging so far out of the car that I started to wonder, was someone hanging onto his legs or something? Whether that was the case or not, it looked decidedly unsafe.

Next to me, Selena asked, "Is this for Jake's channel? This wasn't planned or anything, was it?"

I held up a single finger. "Shhh!"

"Did you just shush me?"

I gave her a look and shushed her again. I almost felt guilty. Like me, she hated being shushed. But I was trying to accomplish something here. She of all people should respect that. Right?

Apparently not. She gave a slow shake of her head and took a half-step away.

Ahead of us, Ronnie lifted both of his fists and hollered out to Jake, "The next time I see you, you're dead meat."

"Why wait?" Jake said. "You can dead-meat me now."

"Oh, suuuuure," Ronnie slurred. "You'd like that, wouldn't you?"

"Hell yeah!" Jake said. "Bring it on, fatso."

"Heeey!" Ronnie bellowed. "I'm not fat!"

I had to agree with Ronnie. He was a big guy, but I didn't see an ounce of fat on him. Then again, I could only see the half that was hanging out of the car. If his ass was big, I'd never know it.

In front of us, Jake gave Ronnie a cocky grin. "If you say so, Tubs."

The crowd laughed. Ronnie sputtered. Somewhere down the street, tires squealed, and something crashed. The crash was followed by the sounds of yelling, not the call-an-ambulance kind of yelling, but the angry, fender-bender kind, filled with profanity and threats to jam a muffler up someone's ass.

As for Ronnie's car, it showed no sign of moving. He glared at the crowd, looking more belligerent than ever.

Amusing or not, this was putting other people in danger. I couldn't help myself. Still holding the phone, I hollered out, "Hey, Ronnie! Just go, okay? You're gonna get people hurt!"

Selena turned to look at me. She flashed me a sudden smile and said, "Shhh!"

"Oh, shut up," I whispered.

From the car, Ronnie was glaring at *me* now. He yelled out, "Shut up! I ain't going nowhere!" But just as he said it, his car lurched forward, only a couple of feet, but enough to throw Ronnie off-balance. He tumbled out of the open window, rolled a couple of times, and landed face-up in the parking lot.

The crowd roared with new laughter.

On the concrete, Ronnie lifted his head. He turned to glare at Jake. "You asshole! You did something! Didn't you?"

"I dunno," Jake said. "Does screwing your mom count?"

Next to me, Selena snickered. When I turned to look, she whispered,

"Hey, you laughed first."

Did I?

Probably.

I did that a lot around Jake, come to think of it.

I looked toward Ronnie's car. A skinny guy with slick hair poked his head out of the passenger's side window. He called out toward Ronnie, "Sorry dude. You okay?"

Before Ronnie could answer, Jake gave the new guy a big thumbs up. "Yeah. I'm good," Jake called. "Thanks, dude!"

With a grunt, Ronnie pushed himself up into a sitting position and yelled out toward Jake, "Asshole! He was talking to me, not you."

"You sure?" Jake asked. "Because I've gotta be honest. I'm pretty sure he was looking at me."

Ronnie leapt to his feet and stood, with his fists clenched and his nostrils flaring. But then, he suddenly froze.

I knew why. It was because of the police sirens that were growing louder with every second. Ronnie's head swiveled toward the sports car, which, a split-second later, squealed off, leaving Ronnie standing there alone, looking like a total doofus.

After a long pause, and a whole lot of profanity, he started running, pretty darn sloppily, given his condition.

When he disappeared around the corner, I lowered Selena's phone and hit the stop button. I looked out toward Jake. He was still standing there, looking like the giant smart-ass he was, with his brother standing next to him.

I don't know why, but I couldn't help but smile. He was obviously insane, but he was all mine.

And suddenly, it was hard to care about anything else.□

CHAPTER 39

Five minutes later, Selena and I were back inside the restaurant, sitting in the same booth. Standing at the end of our table, the waitress gave me a perplexed look. "Excuse me?"

"Our food," I said. "We want to order the same stuff as before."

She shook her head. "It's gone. Nicki told me you were done." Her lips pursed. "You weren't?"

"Yeah, we were," I said. "But now we want new stuff." Trying to sound as reasonable as possible, I said, "Just take the same order, and have them make it again." I gave her a tentative smile. "See?"

But from the look on her face, she obviously didn't. "What? You want free food?"

Across from me, Selena spoke up. "We don't expect it for free. Just pretend we're brand-new customers or something."

The waitress's gaze shifted toward the window, where Jake and Bishop were, once again, talking in the parking lot. They didn't look like best buddies or anything, but at least, they didn't look ready to kill each other.

On the nearby street, traffic was moving like nothing had happened. As for Ronnie, I had no idea where he was. And honestly? I didn't really want to find out.

As I watched, Jake flashed Bishop a grin and said something that actually made Bishop laugh.

For some reason, it warmed my heart. Progress? It would be nice to think so.

I turned back to the waitress and told her, "Don't worry. They're coming back."

A couple of booths away, that dreaded female voice muttered, "Great. Then, *I'm* leaving."

I turned in time to see her slam down her coffee cup, get to her feet, and bustle toward the exit, taking her newspaper with her.

Silently, the waitress watched her go. When the woman walked out the door, the waitress turned back to me and whispered, "Actually, she's been done for hours." She looked heavenward. "Coffee-drinkers. We should charge 'em by the hour, you know?"

As a bartender, I did know. I nodded, and then watched as the waitress turned away to deliver our food-order to the kitchen.

Happily, I was right about Jake and Bishop. They did come back, and managed to have a friendly enough breakfast that didn't involve either one of them throttling each other.

Like I said, progress.

An hour later, the four of us were in the parking lot, standing between the two different cars that had brought us here. When Bishop pulled Jake aside for a quick, private exchange, I walked Selena to her car door.

I hated that she was leaving so soon. In all the commotion, we still hadn't discussed her upcoming wedding. "I wish we had more time," I said.

"Me too," she replied, looking just as disappointed as I felt. But then, she brightened. "I know. Next weekend, let's get together. We can go shopping for bridesmaid dresses or something."

Loving this idea, I gave a happy nod, only to frown when I recalled something that I was dying to know. I lowered my voice. "Uh, that reminds me..." I hesitated, not sure how to put this.

"What?" Selena asked.

I glanced over at the guys, who were still talking. I sidled closer and said, "Do you remember Bob, the Appliance Guy?"

Her face froze, and for a long moment, she said nothing. Finally, in a carefully neutral voice, she said, "Yes. Why do you ask?"

From the look on her face, she knew exactly why I was asking.

I almost groaned out loud. "Don't tell me, *you* know about that, too?"

"That depends." She winced. "Does the story involve that counter by Mom's fridge?"

"Oh, my God. She told you?" I should've known. Selena was a lot closer to my mom than I was. Still, it didn't quite mesh with something that my mom had said.

"I don't get it," I admitted. "She told me that you two never talked about it."

Selena closed her eyes and kept them shut as she said, "Uh, yeah."

I gave a shaky laugh. "Whatever you're feeling, I can totally relate. When she told me, she was *really* descriptive. Was it that way with you, too?"

Selena opened her eyes. Slowly, she shook her head. "I wouldn't say that."

I gave her a long look. Obviously, there was something I was missing. But what? Almost afraid to ask, I said, "Okay, what aren't you telling me?"

"Uh, well…" She hesitated. "I was there."

My mouth fell open. "What?"

"Uh, yeah." She blew out a long breath. "I, uh, walked in on them, actually."

"Oh, my God."

"Yeah," Selena said. "Which is why we never talk about it."

Wow. I didn't see *that* coming. "So she was embarrassed? You'd never guess, the way she talks."

"No. *She* wasn't embarrassed. *I* was embarrassed. You want the truth? I'm still kind of traumatized."

From the look on her face, she wasn't lying.

I couldn't help but stare. "I can't believe you never told me."

"I wanted to spare you. You know, that was like five years ago, and I *still* won't go near that counter."

I wanted to laugh. I did laugh, in fact, but not until Bishop had swept my sister, still looking slightly disturbed, into the car.

Watching them drive off, I could *so* relate.

In Jake's car, on our way back to his condo, he glanced over at me from the driver's seat and said, "When we get back, pack a bag, okay?"

I blinked. "A bag?"

"A bag, a suitcase, whatever."

"Why?" I asked. "For what?"

He grinned. "You'll see."

My own face froze. Desperately, I wanted to smile back, but I couldn't, because I had a sneaky suspicion that he wouldn't be smiling either in another minute or so.

I had to tell him something. And I had the sickening feeling that he wouldn't like it.□

CHAPTER 40

Still driving, Jake asked, "What's wrong?"

"Nothing," I assured him. "It's just that…" I hesitated. "Well, I've got to work."

He gave me a quick glance. "What?"

"Yeah," I said. "For the next three days, actually."

At the next red light, Jake turned his head and gave me a long look. "I thought you were fired."

"Well, I wasn't absolutely *sure* I was fired." I summoned up a smile. "Remember?"

He didn't smile back. "And about the uniform?"

I felt my face grow warm. The last time he'd seen me in my work uniform, he'd literally torn it off my body.

And I'd loved every minute of it.

But now, I wasn't sure what, exactly, he was getting at. The uniform was definitely an issue, especially after that stupid picture.

Hoping for the best, I said, "I have a spare."

When his gaze dipped to my breasts, I could read his thoughts all over his face. The way it looked, his question had nothing to do with torn fabric and popped buttons.

It had to do with the fact that, in my work uniform, I was always one rainstorm away from a girlie show.

Lamely, I said, "I've got a tank top that I'm gonna wear underneath. And honestly, I think we'll be getting new uniforms soon."

I gave a shaky laugh. "There had to be some mistake with the fabric. After all, I can't be the only one who had problems."

Problems – like flaunting my goodies all over Detroit. Yup, that was a problem, alright. But I was hoping Jake would let that slide.

Watching me, he said nothing, and his expression became unreadable. But there was one emotion I could definitely rule out – happiness.

I made a sound of frustration. "In case you don't know, when you keep your job, it's *good* news."

"Yeah? Is that why you didn't tell me?"

"No. It just didn't come up. That's all."

"Right."

"It didn't," I insisted.

"Uh-huh."

Under his penetrating gaze, I started to squirm in my seat. It was true that it hadn't come up, but it *could've* come up. Regardless of what else had been going on at the time, I surely could've spared ten seconds to say something like, "Oh, by the way, my boss is giving me another chance."

So why hadn't I?

I tried to think. Was it because I knew that Jake wanted me to work for *him* instead? Or, was it because yesterday, when I thought I'd been fired, I'd been bucking for sympathy, and had loved it when I'd gotten some?

I recalled Jake's arms, strong and hard, wrapping me up in a warm cocoon of oblivion. It had been kind of nice, actually.

Or who knows, maybe I hadn't mentioned the job thing because it was getting a little embarrassing to be hired and fired all the time. It had gotten so bad, in fact, that my brothers – and Jake, too, come to think of it – had been placing bets on my employment status.

Talk about humiliating.

Jake was still watching me, waiting, apparently, for some sort of response.

I wanted to say something smart, or at the very least something funny, something that would snap us out of whatever this was. But nothing smart came to mind, and my funny bone wilted under his cool, hard gaze.

Desperately, I looked toward the traffic light, and spotted my escape-hatch. "It's green," I told him. "You can go."

He turned to look. "Right." He hit the gas, and we lurched forward.

I forced out a laugh. "You're not trying to launch me out of the vehicle, are you?"

When Jake said nothing, I added. "You know, like Ronnie?" I summoned up another laugh. "That was pretty funny, huh?"

But Jake wasn't laughing. And my own laugh had sounded totally hollow, even to my own ears.

At the next intersection, Jake took a left and pulled his car off to the side. He cut the engine and turned to face me.

I looked around. "Why'd you stop?"

"Because I've gotta ask you something."

"Okay." Trying for a neutral tone, I said, "What?"

"Why will you work for them, but not for me?"

"Them?"

"Hotels, restaurants, whatever." His voice hardened. "Seems to me you're not too picky."

The words stung. "What do you mean by that?"

"I mean, you're a damn bartender."

I stared at him. God, did he have to be such a jerk about it? "There's nothing wrong with being a bartender."

"I know."

"No. You don't." I tried to mimic him. "You're a damn bartender."

"What? You think I look down on it?"

I gave a half-hearted shrug. He'd made his scorn apparent, hadn't he?

"For the record, I don't," Jake said. "With my life? A bartender's a step up."

"That is such a crock," I told him. "You're rich. You own your own company. You're famous, for God's sake. You don't *have* to work as a bartender."

"Yeah? And neither do you."

I was *so* not in the mood for this. "God, what's your deal? Yeah, I work as a bartender. So what?"

His tone softened. "Baby, if it made you happy, that'd be one thing. But you're not happy. You're miserable."

"I am not," I insisted.

"Yeah? You ever listen to yourself?"

I gave another shrug. Okay, so I didn't always come home whistling a happy tune. But who did? "So?" I said. "Not everyone loves their job."

He made a scoffing sound. "So what is it? You love it? Or you don't love it? It seems to me, you want it both ways."

Embarrassingly, I knew exactly what he meant. In truth, I did hate my job. But the situation wasn't as simple as Jake made it sound. "I'm not planning on being a bartender forever," I said. "It's a big company, and now that I have my foot in the door..." I gave him a pleading look, hoping he'd let it drop already.

He didn't. Instead, he made a forwarding motion with his hand. "Go on."

Jeez, did I have to spell it out?

From the look on his face, apparently, I did.

"Well," I continued, "if I play my cards right, I could get into their hospitality department."

"And?"

"And, I'd be using my degree."

"To become?"

God, why was he playing dumb? He knew exactly what I'd been hoping for. We'd discussed it, several times, in fact.

Still, in the most reasonable tone I could muster, I said, "Well, for starters, I could become an event planner or something."

"Right."

I made a sound of impatience. "Why do you keep saying that?"

He looked at me for a long, silent moment. Finally, he said, "So let's recap. Your 'plan' is to work your way up to a job that I'm already offering you."

I glanced away. Technically, this was true. But things weren't quite that simple.

Jake continued, "So, I've gotta ask. Why?"

"You know why."

"Because you'd rather trust strangers than me?" Abruptly, he turned away. "Got it."

I watched, with a sick feeling, as he fired up the engine and pulled away from the curb. Suddenly, I felt like crying. But what would that accomplish? Nothing.

As he drove, I sat, sulking in the passenger's seat. Why couldn't he get it? If I took a job with him, I'd have literally all of my eggs in one basket – the Jake basket. Oh sure, that basket was beyond nice, but how sturdy was it?

Jake loved me. I knew that. And I loved him, too. But what would happen if our relationship ended? I'd have literally nothing – no money, no job, no future. Why couldn't he see how risky that was?

But of course, Jake thrived on risk. He ate it up and went back for more. It was one of the things I loved about him. But unlike Jake, I didn't have gobs of money and hard assets that I could sell if I had to.

I didn't have fame. I didn't have fortune. All I had was him.

Of course, that, in itself, was a very big deal.

I was so damned crazy about him. But I couldn't help but notice that in spite of some hints a few weeks earlier, he'd taken no concrete steps to make the relationship more permanent. I didn't want to rush him. Hell, I didn't want to rush us.

But if our relationship didn't survive, what then?

For the millionth time in the last month, I thought of Bianca. She'd worked for him, too. And now, she was a total basket case.

I sank lower in my seat. Funny, I was feeling like a basket case now.

Suddenly, I was so tired of being on defense all the time. We were now only a couple of blocks away from Jake's building, and I desperately wanted to resolve this before we got there.

I turned sideways in the passenger's seat and said, "Let me ask *you* something. At the conference, center, why didn't you mention that Bianca was there?"

"I wasn't hiding it."

"Yeah. But it still seems odd."

His fists tightened on the steering wheel. "You really wanna play this game?"

"It's not a game," I said. "I really want to know."

"Yeah? Well, there's stuff I wanna know, too."

"Like what?" I demanded.

His voice hardened. "Like, why didn't you tell me that Rango's been hassling you?"

I froze. He knew about that? *Oh, crap.* "Who told you?"

"So it's true." He made a sound of disbelief. "And you didn't tell me."

I squirmed in my seat. "Maybe I didn't want to ruin your night."

He took a sharp turn. With a start, I realized we were pulling into the turnaround of his building. He stopped just outside the main doors and sat for a long, painful moment, looking straight ahead.

Finally, with the engine still running, he turned to face me. His eyes were dark, and his mouth was set. "You've got some guy calling you, giving you a hard time, and you think I don't wanna know that?"

"That's not it," I said. "I just feel bad, you know. It's like you're always riding to my rescue. I feel kind of guilty, like I should be solving some of these problems on my own."

"Maybe I *like* riding to your rescue."

"How could you?" I said. "I'm a mess. It just doesn't seem fair."

His mouth tightened. "Fair is for pussies."

"What does that even mean?"

"It means I don't give a shit about keeping things 'fair.' If somebody's hassling you, I need to know."

Unsure what to say next, I glanced toward the building and saw Pete heading toward us, as if preparing to get my door.

As friendly as I could, I waved him away and turned back to Jake. "Let's talk about this upstairs, okay?"

He shook his head. "I've gotta go."

"What? Where?"

Jake glanced toward the building. "You need me to walk you up?"

Oh, so that's the way it was? Defiantly, I lifted my chin. "No."

"Alright." He turned his head, looking forward now. "Suit yourself."

"When will you be back?" I asked.

"Monday."

I did a double-take. "Monday? That's like two days from now."

"Yeah."

Again, I asked, "Where are you going?"

"Why?" His tone grew sarcastic. "You wanna come with me?"

It was a loaded question, and he darn well knew it. "You know I can't."

"Well, there you go."

It was like talking to that same old brick wall. But if he wanted me to beg, he had another thing coming. With my heart hammering, I opened the car door, stepped out, and shut it quietly behind me. And then, I stood, watching silently from the curb as he roared off to wherever.

A half-hour later, I was back in bed, still dressed, but under the covers. Lying there like the pathetic slob that I was, I tried to tell myself that I was back in bed not because I needed a good place to cry, but because with Selena showing up so early, I'd gotten almost zero sleep.

I tried to tell myself other things, too. I told myself that Jake and I would work it out. He wouldn't really stay away until Monday, and someday, we'd look back at all these stupid fights and laugh.

But for now, I definitely wasn't laughing.

I still wasn't laughing a couple of hours later when the doorbell jolted me out of my jumbled thoughts.

Reluctantly, I got up, trudged to the door, and looked out the peephole, only to see someone I hadn't been expecting.

It was Jake's youngest brother, Joel. And the way it looked, he was mad as hell.

CHAPTER 41

As soon as I opened the door, Joel demanded, "Where the hell is he?"

"Jake?" I stepped back. "Sorry, I don't know."

And that was the painful truth.

Without waiting for an invitation, Joel barged past me and looked around. "Jake!" he yelled. "You asshole! Come out here and face me like a man!"

If I weren't so depressed, I might've laughed. What? Like Jake was hiding under the bed or something? That was *so* not his style. Joel, of all people, should know that.

Trying to keep my tone reasonable, I said, "Joel, listen. Seriously, he's not here." I tried to smile. "Come on. You know Jake. He's not afraid of anything."

"Yeah? Well, maybe he should be."

I stared up at him, wondering if I should be worried for my safety. Right now, he wasn't the Joel I thought I knew. His dark hair framed that familiar, angelic face – a face that might've lulled me into a nice sense of security, except for the fact that his eyes were flashing with unfamiliar rage.

I'd known Joel since he was a kid, since both of us had been kids, actually, even if I *was* slightly older than he was. But now, I was having a hard time reconciling the skinny kid I'd known back then with the muscular adult who stood, quaking with anger, in front of me.

If he were a stranger, I'd be smart to run. But he wasn't a stranger. He was Jake's little brother, and obviously, he was hurting in some way that I didn't quite understand.

I pushed aside my own misery and said, "Joel, seriously, what's wrong?"

He made a scoffing sound. "Like you don't know."

Of course, I had a vague idea. Just this morning, Jake and Bishop had been discussing the situation involving Vince Hammond.

To me, their concerns had been entirely justified. If Joel ended up signing with Vince, it wouldn't end well. I just knew it.

True, Vince repped some of the top names in sports entertainment. But Joel was Jake's brother. There was no way on Earth that Vince would ever do right by him.

If Joel could only see that, he'd walk away from Vince on his own. He'd tell Mister Hotshot Agent to shove it, and he wouldn't look back.

But something told me that a decision of any kind had been, very recently, ripped out of Joel's hands.

I recalled something that Bishop had told Jake, just a few hours earlier. *He's gonna fuckin' hate you.*

The way it looked, Bishop had been right.

I reached out and touched Joel's arm. "Is this about Vince Hammond?"

Joel yanked his arm away and said, "Quit playing me, alright? You think I don't know?"

"Know what?"

His breathing was ragged, and his fists were tight. "What you two did."

Two? Confused, I shook my head. "Who? Me and Jake?"

He glared down at me. "You had no right."

I shrank back, surprised to realize that he was angry with me, too. "But I haven't done anything."

As if looking to gain some semblance of control, Joel took a deep, unsteady breath. In a slightly calmer voice, he said, "Look, I'm not pissed at you, alright?"

"Good," I told him. "Because I didn't do anything wrong. In fact, I don't even know why you're so mad, not specifically anyway."

His lips twisted into a pale imitation of a smile. "Right."

"It's true," I said. "So just tell me. What happened?"

He looked at me for a long, serious moment, as if trying to decide if I was lying.

Again, I reached out and touched his arm. When he didn't pull away, I gave his arm a gentle squeeze. "Just tell me, okay?"

I glanced to the nearby sofa. "Why don't you sit down? We'll talk it out. Can I get you a drink or something?"

"I don't need a drink," he said. "I need Jake to fix this."

"Fix what?"

Through clenched teeth, he said, "Vince dropped me. And I know Jake was behind it."

I let out a long, weary breath. I should've seen this coming. A dozen small details drifted into place, giving me a pretty good idea of what had happened.

I recalled that strange meeting yesterday, where Vince and Jake had hammered out some sort of truce. Obviously, the truce had something to do with Joel.

But what exactly were the terms? If Vince agreed to drop Joel as a potential client, what would Vince want in return?

Instantly, the answer popped into my brain. Of course. For months, Jake had been messing with Vince's clients, costing them endorsement deals and who knows what else. It slowly dawned on me that over the past week or so, Jake hadn't been messing with a single one of them.

In fact, other than those encounters with Dorian and Ronnie North, Jake hadn't really been messing with anyone.

Had he given all of that up to save Joel from Vince?

In front of me, Joel said. "See? You know what happened. Don't you?"

"Actually, I don't know anything for sure, honest." In a weird sense, it was true. Yeah, I had some pretty good guesses, but until I had confirmation, there was no way I'd be throwing more gasoline on the brotherly fire.

Joel's gaze hardened. "You know more than you're saying. I can see it all over your face."

I resisted the urge to look away. "Honestly, I'm really not sure. Things have been kind of crazy lately. Have you tried calling him?"

Joel practically snorted. "You think he'd answer?"

"I know he would." And I did. Jake was a lot of things – a trouble-maker, a smart-ass, a royal shitlord. But in his own crazy way, he loved his brothers, and he was no coward. If he was available, he'd answer.

With something like a laugh, Joel reached into his pocket and pulled out his phone. He scrolled through the screen, pressed whatever, and waited. A moment later, I heard Jake's voice. Unfortunately, it wasn't the live version. It was just his voicemail greeting.

As the greeting played, I looked to Joel and said, "You're gonna leave a message, right?"

With a cold smile, Joel waited for the greeting to end, and then he spoke into the phone. "Hey, asshole. Call me. I'll be waiting." He disconnected the call and said, "There. You happy?"

Actually, I wasn't, and not only because of this. But it seemed insensitive to say so. Whatever was bothering me, it paled in comparison to what was going on with Joel.

Again, I glanced to the sofa. "Sure you don't want to sit down?"

Joel gave me a hard look. "What I want is for *you* to call him."

I hesitated. "Me?"

"Yeah. Are you gonna do it or not?"

I looked past his anger and saw the kid I used to know. He was hurting. That much was obvious. So I ignored his rudeness and said, "Sure, um, yeah. I'll do it." I held out my hand for his phone. "What do you want me to say?"

"Not from *my* phone," he said. "From *your* phone."

I blinked up at him. "What? Why?"

"Because if *you* call, he'll answer."

Somehow, I wasn't so sure. For all I knew, Jake had blocked my number.

Okay, I didn't really believe that, but after this morning, Jake wouldn't be jumping to take a call from *me* – at least not until he cooled down.

But Joel didn't need my problems on top of his own, so I summoned up a smile and said, "He'd answer for you, too."

"Except he didn't."

"Well, I'm sure he's just tied up or something."

"Yeah? Prove it." With slow precision, he added, "Go get your phone, and give him a call."

Stalling, I said, "You mean now?"

"Yeah. *Now*. I'll wait."

I tried to make a joke of it. "I'm afraid you'd be waiting a long time." When he said nothing, I added, "Because actually, my phone is kind of missing."

He stared down at me, obviously not believing a single word I was saying.

When he finally did speak, his voice had a bitter edge that hurt to hear. "Yeah, I bet."

"It is," I insisted, glancing around. "But you know what? It's gotta be around here somewhere."

In truth, I wasn't so sure. But I *was* desperate. I gave Joel a hopeful look. "Wanna help me look for it?"

"Nice try."

"I'm not 'trying' anything. I'm telling you the truth. And if we had a landline—"

"But you don't." He glanced toward the still-open penthouse door. "This is such bullshit."

"It is not," I insisted.

"Uh-huh." He eyed me with obvious loathing. "When you call him, as in the minute I walk out the door, you tell him that I'm looking for him."

And with that, he turned away and strode out of the penthouse, heading toward the elevator.

Desperately, I called after him. "Wait! At least give me a minute to look for it."

But he didn't wait. And he didn't look back. Already, he was pushing the down button.

Watching, I didn't know what to do.

Unless I was willing – and let's face it, able – to physically restrain him, I had no way to make him stop. And, in more frustrating news, I also had no way to contact Jake.

After the elevator carried Joel away, I tore through the condo, frantically looking for my phone. I doubted that I'd find it, but I *had* to try.

Turns out, it was all for nothing. After fifteen frantic minutes, I gave up. All I was doing was wasting time.

I bolted out the condo, took the elevator down to the lobby, and found Pete at his usual station. "Can I borrow your phone?" I asked, pointing to the landline on his desk.

A moment later, I was standing alone behind his station, gripping the receiver as I punched in Jake's number.

It rang once, twice, and then – *damn it* – went to voicemail. When Jake's greeting ended, I spoke into the receiver. "Jake, listen. Joel was here, and he's really upset. I don't know where you are, but you *really* need to get ahold of him."

After a brief pause, I heard my voice soften. "And wherever you are, I hope you're okay." I bit my lip. "See you Monday?"

I was just hanging up the receiver when I looked up and spotted a familiar male figure striding through the building's glass double doors.

Unfortunately, it wasn't Jake.

It was Bishop. And right behind him was, of all the people I *didn't* want to see, Bianca. □

CHAPTER 42

From behind Pete's desk, I looked from Bishop to Bianca. Had they arrived together? Or was it some sort of weird coincidence?

When Bishop spotted me, he strode over to the desk and said, "Is Jake around?"

I shook my head. "I wish."

A couple of paces behind him, Bianca called out, "What? He's not? After I made a special trip?" She stomped over to me and said, "Well, this is just great."

No. Actually, it wasn't. I turned to Bishop and said, "You're still in town? I thought you left."

"I did," he said. "And now, I'm back."

I did the math. They'd been heading back to our hometown. That was a two-hour drive. They'd left how long ago? Not even four hours. Unless I was mistaken, the math didn't add up. What had he done? Tossed my sister out the window and done a quick U-turn?

As if reading the expression on my face, he said, "Don't worry. I walked her to the door and everything."

"You must be a fast walker," I said.

Bianca claimed the spot next to him and said, "Doesn't anyone care why I'm here?"

Why lie? "I don't," I said, turning to Bishop. "Do you?"

Bianca followed my gaze, and then, as if noticing Bishop for the first time, she did a double-take. A slow smile spread across her face, and she ran a nervous hand through her long, dark hair.

In a surprisingly sultry voice, she said, "Are you Jake's brother?" Her gaze drifted down his body and back up again. "Oh, my God, you could be twins."

Watching this, I made a sound of annoyance. "Yeah. But they're not."

Ignoring me, she sidled closer to him and practically purred, "So, what are *you* doing here?"

I couldn't help but roll my eyes. "Forget it," I told her. "He's engaged."

Bianca drew back. "I don't know what you're implying, but I don't appreciate it."

Well, *I* didn't appreciate her drooling over my sister's fiancé. Had she no shame?

Apparently not. Undaunted, she once again leaned closer to him and said, "So, engaged, huh?"

I spoke up. "Yeah. To my sister."

Bianca's smile disappeared. She turned to me and said, "You can't be serious."

"Yes." I smiled. "I can."

I looked to Bishop. Showing zero interest in Bianca, he looked back to me and said, "Where is he?"

"Jake?" I bit my lip. "I wish I knew. You're the second brother to come looking for him."

Bishop cursed under his breath. "Joel?"

I nodded.

Next to him, Bianca said again, louder this time, "Doesn't anyone care why I'm here?"

If I didn't care the first time, why would I care now? I looked to Bishop, who told her, "That depends. You a friend of Luna's?"

Bianca pursed her lips. "Not particularly."

"Then I don't care," Bishop said.

Suddenly, I felt all warm and fuzzy. In spite of everything, I had to smile.

As for Bianca, she was definitely not smiling. "I'm a friend of Jake's," she told him. "Doesn't that count?"

"No," he said.

"Why not?" she demanded.

"Because you're lying."

She gave a huff. "I most certainly am not."

"Yeah. You are," he said. "If you were his friend, you'd be nicer to his girl."

Bianca's eyes narrowed. "In case you didn't know, *I* used to be his girl, and nobody was nice to me."

Bishop shrugged. "Might be a reason for that."

I felt myself nod in agreement. "And besides," I told her, "you were never his girlfriend. You went out a couple of times. That's it."

She gave me an annoyed look. "You don't know anything."

"I know you're a fibber," I said. "Does that count?"

"No, it *doesn't* count. And I'm *not* a fibber, whatever that is."

Ignoring our exchange, Bishop turned back to me and said, "About Joel, how long ago did he leave?"

Next to him, Bianca gave another stomp of her foot. "Oh, for God's sake, I'm here about Joel, not that either of you seem to care."

That made us pause. Together, Bishop and I turned to look. It was Bishop who said, "What?"

"Yes," Bianca snapped. "As I've been trying to tell you, there's a reason I'm here."

Bishop said, "Which is…?"

Bianca straightened. After a long dramatic pause, she said, "About an hour ago, Vince met with Joel and told him that the deal was off. And, as you can imagine, Joel didn't take it so well."

From what I'd seen, that was a massive understatement. I looked to Bishop and said, "I can vouch for that. When he stopped by, he was *really* mad."

Bianca gave us a smug smile. "See? So here I am, trying to warn Jake, not that anyone seems to appreciate it."

Bishop asked, "Warn him of what?"

"Apparently," Bianca said, "Joel thinks that Jake had had something to do with it."

Before I could stop myself, I asked, "Did he?"

"Of course he did," Bianca said, "not that Joel was supposed to find out."

Bishop studied Bianca's face. In a carefully measured tone, he said, "So how *did* he find out?"

"How should I know?" Bianca said.

I spoke up. "I know how. Vince told him." I looked to Bianca and said, "I'm right, aren't I?"

"No," she said. "You're not." She glanced away. "Not exactly."

"Not exactly?" I repeated. "What does *that* mean?"

Looking slightly uncomfortable, Bianca mumbled, "He just didn't deny it when it came up. That's all."

Right. Vince the Snake strikes again.

Thinking of the whole sorry situation, I had such mixed feelings. On one hand, I could totally see why Joel was angry. But on the other hand, he'd been walking straight into a trap, whether he realized it or not.

Across from me, Bishop said, "Joel's no fool. Of course he'd know." He gave me a serious look. "As I told Jake this morning."

Feeling overwhelmed, I asked, "What should we do now?"

"You?" Bishop said. "Nothing."

"But—"

"I'll handle it," he said. "When Joel left, did he say where he was going?"

I shook my head. "Sorry. I wish he had. But basically, he just stormed off."

"And what about Jake? Where is he?"

Something in my heart twisted. "Honestly, I have no idea."

Next to him, Bianca gave a little smirk. "Trouble in paradise?"

I felt my body stiffen. Her words hit too close to home, not that I'd ever admit it, well not to Bianca, anyway.

I gave her my snottiest smile. "You'd like to think so, wouldn't you?"

"Me?" She put a delicate hand to her chest. "Of course not. I wish you all the best."

"Sure you do." I looked to Bishop and asked, "So what's your first step?"

"First, I've gotta find him."

"Which one?" I asked. "Joel or Jake?"

"Whichever one turns up first."

I gave him a sympathetic look. "There must be something I can do to help."

"There is one thing," he said. "You got your phone? You can give Jake a call."

I glanced down to the nearby landline. "I already did." I frowned. "But he didn't answer."

"Not from *that* phone," Bishop said. "From your cell. So he knows it's you."

I almost groaned. If only I *had* my cell.

"I wish I could," I said, "but my phone's missing." I tried to smile. "But if I find it, I'll call him right away. I promise."

And then, there was the thing I *didn't* say. For all I knew, Jake wouldn't be answering *any* of my calls today, no matter what phone I was calling from.

We had, after all, parted on a pretty sour note.

After a quick goodbye, Bishop turned away, preparing to leave.

Bianca lunged for his elbow. "Wait! You'll tell Jake I warned you, right?"

Watching, I felt my gaze narrow. "Why *did* you tell us, anyway?"

Bianca hesitated. "Maybe I'm a nice person."

"Or maybe," Bishop told her, "you're hedging your bets, playing both sides."

With a huff, she dropped her hand. "Jeez, why is everyone so cynical? Maybe I'm just trying to do the right thing."

I almost laughed. "Yeah. And maybe I'm the Queen of England."

Already, Bishop was heading toward the doors. Bianca turned to scramble after him. Across the distance, I heard her say, "I'll help you look."

He didn't even pause. "No. You won't."

Silently, I watched until they disappeared from sight, and then, I checked the clock on Pete's desk.

Just as I'd suspected, it was time to get ready for work. I tried to look on the bright side. If nothing else, it would be a break from all the drama, a place to pass the lonely hours while waiting for Jake, a chance to forget all about missing cell phones and rocky relationships.

Or so I thought.☐

CHAPTER 43

Parked in the employee lot, I'd just cut the engine and was preparing to go into work when a familiar male figure appeared just outside my driver's side window.

Startled, I gave a little jump and felt my heart practically leap from my chest.

It was Rango, the ex-boyfriend from hell. I glanced around, wondering where on Earth he'd come from. Around me, I saw plenty of vehicles, but none that could belong to him.

Those other cars were all too old, too dirty, or too modest. When it came to Rango's taste in anything, only the best would do.

But then again, who was I to talk? I was driving one of Jake's cars. It wasn't exactly an old rust-bucket.

Reluctantly, I returned my attention to Rango. His dark spiky hair was styled in its usual disarray, and he wore the same kind of designer clothes that he always wore. Through the glass, he flashed me the same boyish smile that he'd used on me the first time we'd met.

Back then, I'd been utterly charmed. Now, I wanted to whack him in the face.

With what, I didn't know, but I was willing to get creative. I looked to my right. Surely, there was something in the glove compartment.

The sounds of tapping on glass made me turn to look.

Rango called through the driver's side window. "Hey, open up."

Sure, like *that* was a good idea. Instead, I demanded, "What are you doing here?"

He made a circular motion with his hand. "Roll down the window, and I'll tell you."

I stared at him. "No way."

"Why not?" His lips thinned. "I'm not gonna hurt you, if that's what you think."

Honestly, I didn't know what to think. But I wasn't going to take any chances. "Then what *do* you want?"

"Like I said, I just wanna talk."

"Yeah? Well maybe you should've called first." As soon as the words were out, I realized how incredibly stupid they were. One – I didn't want him calling me. And two – even if I did, I no longer had a phone.

It was still missing, probably forever.

Outside my car, Rango said, "Very funny."

Confused, I squinted through the glass. Why was that funny?

Before I could even think to ask, he said, "You've made your point, so lay off, alright? That's why I'm here. To ask you nicely." He hesitated. "As a friend."

Okay, now I was really confused. For one thing, Rango was no friend of mine. And for another, what so-called point had I made?

I had to ask. "What are you talking about?"

"The phones," he said. "They're not mine. So stop calling, alright?" With an obvious effort, he summoned up a stiff smile. "Truce?"

I still had no idea what he meant. I studied his face, wondering what I was missing.

He gave me a pleading look. "Will you please roll down your window? It's really hard to talk like this."

He was right. It was hard. But after everything he'd done to me, I couldn't bring myself to care. "So what?" I said. "I don't want to talk to you at all."

He paused, as if thinking. "Okay. I can deal with that." He gave me a hopeful smile. "Then you're gonna stop calling me?"

"No. Because I haven't *started* calling you. There's nothing to stop. See how that works? And besides, you're a fine one to talk. You called me like a hundred times yesterday."

"I know." Mumbling now, he added, "And I'm sorry. Okay?"

Funny, he almost looked like he meant it. But with his voice so low, I could hardly hear him.

Screw it. I rolled down the window and said, "And why *were* you calling me, anyway?"

"Maybe I missed you."

I gave him a dubious look. "Or maybe, Bianca put you up to it."

"So what if she did? It wasn't the *only* reason I called." With an obvious effort, he plastered on that same boyish smile as before. "Come on. Admit it. Don't you miss me at least a little?"

Why lie? "No."

The smile disappeared. "Yeah? Well, tell me that again after you and Jake split up." His lips curled into a sneer. "The way I hear it, things aren't going so good."

His words found their mark. It was true. They weren't going so good. I still had no idea where Jake was. And stupid or not, I missed him like crazy.

Did he miss me?

Pushing that question aside, I managed to tell Rango, "Well, you heard wrong."

"Yeah, sure," Rango said. "Call me when it's over. *Maybe* I'll give you another shot."

I looked toward the glove compartment. And maybe *I'd* find a nice, thick crowbar within grabbing distance.

Hey, it could happen.

I turned back to Rango and said, "Don't hold your breath."

"Yeah. Whatever." His jaw tightened. "So about that truce, is it a deal?"

Okay, I was no expert in military terms, but I knew enough to know that truces were only a thing when both sides had been fighting. As for me, I hadn't been doing anything other than answering my phone.

And now, I couldn't even do that.

If this was some sort of war, I was in serious trouble. By rights, Rango shouldn't even be here.

Abruptly, I asked, "And what about your dad? Wasn't he supposed to keep you away from me?"

Rango snorted. "My stepdad? The asshole?"

I gave a non-committal shrug. Whether the guy was an asshole or not, I had no idea. But he *had* agreed to keep his stepson from bothering me.

Rango was frowning now. "Shit, he's not even my stepdad anymore. Would you believe he dumped my mom?"

I blinked. "What?"

"Yeah." Rango made a sound of disgust. "Catches her *one* time with the gardener, and he flips the hell out."

Suddenly, Rango looked almost ready to cry. "Makes her move and everything." In a small, pathetic voice, he added, "And, he cuts off *my* allowance."

I stared at him. Rango was like thirty years old. "You have an allowance? Seriously?"

"Not anymore. Weren't you listening?"

I gave a little shake of my head. "But you *did* have an allowance?"

"Hey, I've got expenses," he said. "Who are you to talk?" He made a show of looking at the car I was sitting in. "Is that *your* car?"

"No." I gave him the look of death. "Because some idiot *crushed* my car. Remember?"

"Hey, you got paid. What are you griping about?"

How stupid was he, anyway? He'd crushed it for fun. He'd thrown a party and everything. If that wasn't gripe-worthy, I didn't know what was.

And then, there was the other thing. "Yeah, I got paid," I said. "So what? You weren't even the one who paid me."

"Sure I was," he insisted.

"Yeah, right." Didn't he remember? "Just yesterday, you told me you *didn't* pay for it."

"Yeah, well I did some digging. Turns out, I did." Looking distinctly annoyed at the discovery, Rango continued. "The asshole paid Jake, and deducted it from *my* allowance. You happy now?"

Oddly enough, I was – especially because Rango looked so *un*happy about it.

Did that make me a bad person?

Did I care?

Apparently not. Because I was actually smiling. "Poor baby."

"No kidding," Rango said. "Hey, uh, that reminds me. I've gotta ask you something."

"What?"

"So, uh, can I borrow some money?"

I almost laughed in his face. "You can't be serious. And if you are, the answer is no."

He gave me a pleading look. "But I really need it," he whined. "I've got expenses, you know?"

As someone who had never gotten an allowance, not even as a kid, I was no stranger to expenses – or how they were generally paid.

Again, I smiled. "Yeah? Well, the restaurant's hiring."

Rango drew back like I'd just spit in his face. "What? You want me to work as a—" He swallowed. "—waiter?"

I shook my head, enjoying this way more than I should've. "Not as a waiter. That requires experience." I brightened. "But you could always work as a busboy."

He looked utterly horrified. "A busboy?"

"Or a dishwasher," I helpfully added.

I knew Rango. There was no way on Earth he'd be caught dead in a service job. I started to wonder about all those businesses that he supposedly owned. Maybe he didn't own them after all. Maybe he'd been merely running them for his stepdad.

If that was the case, Rango was in some serious trouble. But that wasn't my problem, and the way I saw it, some humility would do him a load of good.

I was still mulling this, when I heard a cell phone ring somewhere outside my car.

With a muttered curse, Rango reached down and retrieved a black satchel from somewhere near his feet. As I watched, he rummaged through the bag and pulled out a small silver cell phone. He studied the display and frowned.

A moment later, he looked to me and demanded, "Alright, how'd you do that?"

"How'd I do what?"

Abruptly, he leaned forward and stuck his whole head inside my car.

Caught off guard, I leaned back to avoid contact. "What the hell are you doing?"

His head swiveled from side to side. "Alright, where is it?"

"Where's what?"

He pulled back and practically spat the words, "Your fucking cell phone."

CHAPTER 44

Talk about nerve. Sitting in the driver's seat, I considered the absurdity of his question.

Where was *my* phone? Maybe he should worry about his own phone. It was, after all, still ringing.

Rango looked to my lap. "What? Are you sitting on it?"

"No, I'm not…" I hesitated as something slowly dawned on me. "Wait a minute. Are you implying that *I'm* calling you? Like right now?"

As an answer, Rango shoved his phone – or, more accurately, *one* of his phones – practically into my face.

I felt my eyebrows furrow. On the display, sure enough, I saw my own name, as clear as day.

How was that possible?

His phone was still ringing. I snatched it from his hand and hit the answer button. And then, silently, I waited.

A moment later, I heard the sounds of – What the hell? – a porno movie, playing on the other end of the line.

Or at least, it sure sounded like a porno movie, unless – heaven forbid – it was the real thing. I heard grunting and groaning and naked skin slapping together in ways I could only imagine. And then, I heard – I paused. No, that couldn't be right – a cow?

Sure enough, there it was again. A distinct mooing sound.

I swallowed. Oh, my God. It wasn't just a porno. It was, well, I didn't know what it was exactly. But overall, it was pretty darn disturbing.

And then, I heard something else. A snicker.

And not just a generic snicker. A *familiar* snicker.

Damn it.

I yelled into the receiver. "Hey! Ass-munches!"

Suddenly, the movie – if that's what it was – stopped playing. A moment later, I heard Steve's voice say, "Gee, that's pretty rude."

"Rude?" I wanted to throttle him. "Not as rude as animal porno." My voice rose. "Seriously, what the hell? You stole my phone?"

"Nah, we just borrowed it."

"I don't freaking believe this." I lifted my gaze to Rango, who stood, staring down at me from outside the car.

Deliberately, I turned away, looking to avoid eye-contact. In a much quieter voice, I told Steve, "Well, I need it back. *Now.*"

"Get real," Steve said. "We can't bring it back *now.* We're working."

"Oh, for God's sake. You're not working. You're making obscene phone calls."

"Hey, we're doing both," he said. "It's called multi-tasking. You ever hear of it?"

Multi-tasking? Like slapping him silly *and* yelling? On that front, I was feeling highly motivated.

From somewhere in the background, Anthony called out, "And besides, we're on break."

Steve said, "See?"

I *so* didn't have time for this. Through gritted teeth, I said, "Tonight then. Nine o'clock. Bring the phone, or else."

"Oh, alright," Steve said, not sounding too happy about it. "But just so you know, *you're* buying the pizza. And don't be skimpy this time. We want two – no *three* – pizzas. With everything." He paused. "And beer, too. Bottles, not cans."

"Fine," I snapped. "But you'd better have the phone."

I ended the call and looked up. Rango was still waiting, looking nearly as disturbed as I felt.

In worse news, I was already late for work. Silently, I grabbed my purse and pushed open the car door, nudging Rango out of my way.

He was still looking a little shell-shocked. "So, uh, about that truce…"

"Fine," I said. "Whatever. A truce. Just stop calling me, okay?"

He gave a nod so vigorous, I was surprised he didn't break something.

I shut the car door behind me, locked it with the remote, and hustled toward the restaurant, leaving Rango staring after me.

I know, because I looked.

So much for my newfound self-control. □

CHAPTER 45

"Hey, don't be mad," Steve was saying. "We did it for you."

"Yeah," Anthony agreed. "You should be thanking us, not griping about it."

I gave them a look. "You stole my phone."

"Nah," Steve said. "We just borrowed it, like I told you."

Did I really need to point out the obvious? "It's not borrowing if you don't ask permission."

Sitting across from me in Jake's penthouse, Steve was making another pizza sandwich. "Hey, you got it back, didn't you?"

Yeah. I did. And I wasn't letting it go. Even now, I was clutching it so tight, I was half-surprised that it didn't shatter.

I looked to my brothers. "About Rango, how many times did you call him, anyway?"

Steve grinned. "A lot."

Stupidly, I couldn't stop myself from grinning back. The look on Rango's face had been so priceless I almost wanted to giggle.

How twisted was that?

"See?" Steve said. "You liked it. We knew you would."

"I wouldn't go *that* far," I told him.

Steve shoved the pizza sandwich into his face and started chewing. "Sure you would. You just don't wanna admit it."

I was still smiling. "Oh, shut up." I paused as a new question popped into my head. "And why wouldn't he just block my number?"

"Good question," Steve said. "Want us to call and ask?"

"No," I blurted out. "Definitely not." Deliberately, I changed the subject. "But about those sounds…" I hesitated, unsure how to put this. "Was it, like, from a movie or something?"

If so, I definitely didn't want to see it – or hear it again, for that matter.

Next to Steve, Anthony laughed. "Not *one* movie. *Two* movies."

I gave him a confused look. "What?"

"Yeah," Anthony said. "We took a regular porno, and threw in some bits from this old farm show. A cartoon, actually."

He leaned back, looking unusually proud of himself. "We got Trey to help us. He got a total kick out of it."

No surprise there. Cows did have nipples, right?

Still clutching my phone, I sank back onto the sofa, trying to pretend that everything was okay. I wasn't eating, and this time, I didn't care one bit whether they saved any for me.

I didn't want pizza.

I wanted Jake.

It was just past nine o'clock, and my bartending shift had ended an hour earlier. Even at work, I'd gone through the motions with a distracted mind and an aching heart.

Where *was* Jake?

And how pathetic was I, sitting around waiting for him to return, like the sad sack that I was? If I had any dignity at all, I'd probably be packing my bags and moving my stuff out of his place.

But then again, I had no stuff, or at least, not enough stuff to matter. Probably, I could throw everything I owned in one big suitcase and walk out with very little trouble.

Should I?

Maybe that's what Jake wanted me to do, move out to save him the trouble of throwing me out. I didn't want to think that, but maybe I'd be foolish not to.

I glanced down at my phone, praying for it to ring.

It didn't.

Had Jake even gotten my message? And if he had, why wasn't he calling me back?

I was so lost in my thoughts that it took me a moment to catch Anthony's next words. "Oh, by the way, Jake called."

Jolted back to reality, I said, "What? When?"

"Around four."

"*Five* hours ago? Why didn't you say something?"

"Hey, don't be pissed," he said. "It's not like we could call you."

Through gritted teeth, I reminded him, "Only because you had my phone."

Anthony nodded. "Exactly."

"But why didn't you tell me in person?"

"I did. Just now."

Why was I wasting my time arguing about this? Jake had actually called. That was good news. Right?

I mean, he wasn't calling to tell me to pack my bags. Was he?

I leaned forward to ask, "What did he say?"

Anthony reached into his pocket and pulled out a wadded napkin. He tossed it in my direction and said, "He said he doesn't have his phone, left it in his car or something. Wanted you to call him at that number."

"So you talked to him?"

"Nah," Anthony said. "He left a message."

Confused, I looked down to my phone. "But there *were* no messages. I checked."

"Right," Anthony said, "because I got them for you." He reached for another slice of pizza. "There was this other one from your dentist, says you're due for a cleaning or something."

Right now, I didn't care one bit about dental work. All I cared about was Jake.

I was dying to call him back, like now. But my brothers were still eating. I didn't want to be *that* girl, the one who ditched her dinner companions to jump the instant a guy called.

But this wasn't just any guy. It was Jake. And we'd parted on such awful terms.

Trying to be subtle, I picked up my phone and checked the time.

Mentally, I added a half-hour to eat, an hour to visit, and then what? It was a Saturday night. What if they wanted to watch a movie or something?

Maybe I could give Jake a quick call, and arrange to talk later?

Steve's voice interrupted my thoughts. "Just call him. We don't care."

I perked up. "You sure? You won't be insulted or anything?"

"Shit, it would take a lot more than *that* to insult us," he said, reaching for the TV remote.

Well, there was that.

He started flipping through the channels and stopped three channels in. He looked to Anthony and grinned. "Kung fu."

Anthony gave a slow nod. "Yeah. We could do that."

A second later, they were lost to everything, well, everything except for the ninja-looking guys, scaling the side of what looked like an ancient monastery.

Soon, I was in the bedroom with the door shut. I called the unfamiliar phone number and waited, praying that Jake would answer.

Finally, he answered with an unenthused, "Hey."

I froze. The greeting wasn't exactly warm and fuzzy, was it?

My heart sank. Maybe I'd be packing my things, after all. □

CHAPTER 46

Clutching my cell phone, I hesitated. "Jake?"

Instantly, his voice warmed. "Luna."

I gave a weak laugh. "You weren't expecting anyone else, were you?"

"Actually, I was."

My face fell. "Oh."

"Not like that," he said. "Baby, I am so glad you called."

I let out a long, relieved breath. "Really?"

"You have no idea."

"Actually, I'm pretty sure I do."

"Listen," he continued, "I am so fucking sorry. This morning, me, running off like that, it was a dick move, and I don't blame you if you're still pissed."

His words, as rough as they were, made my heart go all soft and gooey. Still, I couldn't let him take full responsibility. I wasn't exactly blameless in all of this.

I had to say it. "Jake?"

"Yeah?"

"I'm sorry, too."

"Why? You weren't the dick. I was."

"I've been doing some thinking," I said. "About the job thing, you made a lot of good points."

"I know."

I had to laugh. "Cocky much?"

His voice warmed a few more degrees. "Wouldn't *you* like to know?"

My stomach gave that familiar flutter. "Maybe."

"Maybe, huh? When I get back, I'm gonna turn that 'maybe' into a 'yes.'"

I felt myself smile. "I have no doubt."

"Me neither."

The way it sounded, he meant it, too. And suddenly, I was even *more* eager to see him.

Determined to put our argument behind us *before* that happened, I made myself say, "About my job, I don't know if I agree with everything you said, but I can see why you were mad."

His tone grew teasing. "Yeah? Me, too."

I rolled my eyes. "Oh, stop it." After a brief hesitation, I asked, "You're not *still* mad, are you?"

"Nah. I'm too busy missing you."

"I miss you, too," I said. "But I've gotta ask, if you miss me, why didn't you come back? Where are you, anyway?"

"Long story. You don't wanna know."

"Actually, I do."

On the other end of the phone, Jake said nothing.

"Seriously," I said, "just tell me, okay?"

"I will. But not now."

Disappointment coursed through me. "Why not?"

"Because it's not a phone type of conversation. But I'll tell you later. I promise."

It was vintage Jake, with the old, "I'll tell you later," routine. In spite of my warm feelings, I didn't like it.

How could we ever have a relationship, a real, long-term relationship, if he was so secretive all the time?

It was so frustrating that I didn't know what to say. I was silent so long that Jake finally asked, "What's wrong?"

"Nothing."

"No. Tell me."

I sighed. "I don't want to fight."

This was a huge understatement. For some reason, I didn't think I could stomach yet another argument, at least not now.

"No fighting," he said. "Whatever it is, just say it."

"Alright. I'm just wondering, I guess, why you won't tell me where you are."

Now, it was his turn to be silent. As the silence stretched out, I felt that sad, sinking sensation replace the warmth from earlier.

We'd been talking for how long now? Less than a minute? And already, we were on the verge of another fight? This was definitely a bad sign.

Jake's voice, softer now, broke into my thoughts. "Is it that important to you?"

"Well, yeah, actually."

"Alright. I'm in Vegas."

I almost dropped the phone. "Vegas?" Other than stupid bets with my brothers, Jake wasn't a gambler, at least not that I knew of. So what was he doing there? "Why Vegas?" I asked.

"The truth? I was hoping you'd be here with me."

In a flash, I recalled what he'd mentioned this morning in the car, something about packing a bag and going away for the weekend. I also recalled that a few weeks earlier, I'd made a passing remark about how much I'd like to go to Vegas someday.

"Oh, my God," I said. "Was it supposed to be some sort of surprise vacation?"

"Not a surprise anymore." He gave a wry laugh. "And without you? Not much of a vacation either."

"So *that's* why you didn't want to tell me?" I winced. "I ruined the surprise, didn't I?"

"Not *all* of it."

Now, that got me thinking. "There was more?"

"Wouldn't *you* like to know."

This time, I wasn't so quick to say yes. In truth, I *did* want to know, but if there was another surprise, I didn't want to ruin that one, too.

Deliberately, I switched gears. "Did you get my message? About Joel, I mean?"

"Not directly. But I heard from Bishop."

"You did? Did he find Joel?"

"Sort of."

"What do you mean 'sort of'?"

"He talked to him. That's it."

"How'd it go? Did you hear?"

"Oh, I heard about it," Jake said, sounding like the conversation had been less than friendly.

"From Bishop?"

"*And* from Joel. Let's just say, I got an earful."

"I can believe it," I said, recalling my own encounter with his brother. "Is Joel okay?"

"He will be," Jake said. "He just doesn't know it yet."

"How about you?" My voice softened. "Are you okay?"

I heard a smile in his voice as he said, "I am now."

Soon, I was smiling, too. And I'd be smiling even more when Jake returned.

Still, I had to ask, "About Joel, what are you gonna do?"

"Nothing."

I don't know what I expected, but his answer caught me off guard. "Nothing? Why?"

Dark humor crept into his voice. "Because, in Bishop's words, I've done enough."

"Since when do you listen to Bishop?"

"Hey, there's a first for everything." He paused, and his tone grew more serious. "And Bishop's right. Joel needs some time to cool off. Me chasing after him? Not gonna help."

I felt so bad about everything that I had to sigh. "True."

"Hey, don't worry. Bishop's on it. Joel isn't *quite* so pissed at him."

"And what about Vince?" I asked. "Are you really gonna leave his clients alone?"

"Not just *his* clients."

"I'm not following."

"Then lemme put it this way." Jake was quiet a beat before saying, "I'm done."

CHAPTER 47

I wasn't quite following. "Done with what?"

"The fights," he said. "Messing with people. All of it."

I was so shocked that I could hardly speak. To me, this was good news. *Very* good news. The way I saw it, Jake was thrilling enough without all the fights and drama.

Still, I had to ask, "Why?"

He was quiet for a long moment. "You know my dad, right?"

I'd never been introduced, but coming from the same hometown, I knew enough to grasp the basics.

Jake's dad was mean, half-crazy, and notorious for all kinds of things that made normal people run in the other direction.

Growing up, I'd seen him around town, but it's not like I'd ever spoken to the guy.

"I don't know him personally," I said, "but I know that he's um…" I searched for the right words, and settled on, "…a bit of a character."

"Yeah. That's one way to put it."

"But I don't get it," I said. "What does your dad have to do with all this?"

"I don't wanna be him."

"But you could never be him," I pointed out. "You're totally different."

"Am I?"

"Yeah. Totally."

"Well, then I'm gonna *stay* different." He made a scoffing sound. "When *I* have a family? I'm not gonna be that guy, brawling on the front lawn, taking one too many hits to the head." His voice hardened. "Embarrassing the shit out of my kids."

"But you don't even have kids."

"Yeah?" In his voice, I heard the hint of a smile. "Neither do you."

"But–"

"Chew on that a while," he said. "We'll talk when I get back."

Now, I was totally dying to see him.

Who was I kidding? I'd been dying to see him the moment he'd left.

Still, one thing confused me. I'd known Jake for years. Nothing embarrassed him. Or at least, that's what I'd always assumed.

Was I that clueless?

Trying to understand, I said, "But wait. So your dad embarrassed you?"

Jake laughed. "Me? Nah."

"But you just said…"

"Not me. Joel. And maybe the others, I dunno."

I saw what he meant. A house like Jake's would've been hard to grow up in.

Even Jake, maybe he didn't embarrass easily, but he still had his scars. And I wasn't thinking of the physical kind.

When he returned home, I vowed, I'd kiss some of those scars away and remind him just how amazing he was.

I only wished I didn't have to wait. Trying not to sound as desperate as I felt, I said, "So when *are* you coming back?"

"Monday night. Late."

"How late?"

"Past midnight, maybe later."

"Oh." My shoulders sagged. "Because you can't change your flight?"

"No. Because, like a dumb-ass, I promised Bishop a favor."

"Really? What?"

"To spend some time with our brother."

I wasn't following. Based on what he'd already told me, I knew it couldn't be Joel. So who?

"Which one?" I asked.

"Lawton."

The answer surprised me, mostly because it hadn't even been on my list. Obviously, he meant Lawton Rastor, who, in addition to being Jake's half-brother, was practically a household name.

Jake never talked about him. And I had to wonder, why was that?

As far I knew they weren't remotely close. But Jake *had* gone to his wedding, and it wasn't *that* long ago.

Unfortunately, I'd missed the whole thing, but only because Jake and I had the bad luck to be broken up at the time.

I hated that – and not because I missed the wedding, even if it would've been nice to go.

Turning my thoughts to the present, I said, "So, he lives in Vegas now?"

"Nah," Jake said. "He's out here for a sports thing." He gave a humorless laugh. "I think Bishop wants us to 'bond' or something."

"You don't want to?"

"Eh, it's complicated. Family. You know."

I did know, as evidenced by the sounds of Kung fu fighting, coming from other room. Over that noise, I heard a knocking sound, not on my end, but on Jake's.

With a muttered curse, Jake said, "Baby, I hate to say this, but I've gotta go. Call you tomorrow?"

I hated that he had to go, but I liked the fact that he was spending time with his brother. Who knows? Maybe it would do him good.

I sure hoped so.

Besides, I had my own brothers to think of. Suddenly, a Kung fu marathon was sounding like the perfect way to end the evening.

Smiling into the phone, I said, "Until tomorrow then." In a quieter voice, I added, "I love you."

"I love you, too. And when I get back, I'm gonna prove it."

I wasn't sure what he meant by that, but I was definitely looking forward to it.

After the call ended, I practically floated into the main living area where I gorged on pizza, Kung fu, and the company of my brothers, who stayed until nearly midnight, watching two movies back-to-back.

When the movies ended, I watched, still smiling, as they opened the penthouse doors and strode out with the promise to return Monday evening for Kung fu, part two.

My smile faltered when I saw them turn to take the stairs.

"Wait," I said. "Don't you wanna take the elevator?"

They stopped moving. Steve said, "Yeah. Soon as you make a sandwich on Mom's counter."

I rolled my eyes. "Oh come on. That's not a fair comparison, and you know it."

"Your ass," Steve said.

Next to him, Anthony said, "Dude, watch the phrasing, okay. I don't need the reminder."

"No shit," Steve said, pushing through the stairway door. Just before it swung shut behind him, I heard his voice, loud and clear, say, "Twenty freaking flights. I'm telling ya. She's gotta move." □

CHAPTER 48

I was making a Long Island Iced Tea when I heard Robert say, "She's here."

I looked up. Robert was standing just to my left, looking tense and uneasy. He didn't need to say who *she* was, or why he was frowning.

It was Monday at three o'clock. Apology time.

I dug deep and summoned up a smile. "Great." I glanced toward the entrance, but didn't see her. "So, she's...?"

"Near the far wall." His frown deepened. "Table for ten."

I paused. "Ten?"

Okay, I knew I needed to apologize. And I knew it would be unpleasant. But nowhere in my wildest dreams had I envisioned myself apologizing in front of nine other people who had nothing to do with this.

Robert summoned up a smile of his own. It looked as fake as mine probably did. "Don't worry. It's just her." His smile faltered. "For now."

Again, he glanced toward the far wall. From this angle, neither one of us could see her table, but I knew exactly where it was.

"Oh," I said. "That's good."

We were in the middle of the afternoon lull, and the restaurant was barely half-full. The way I saw it, this was a good thing. The smaller the crowd, the better.

"Yeah," Robert was saying. "She got here early to hold the table. The way she talked, she's having a meeting or something after."

Meaning, after my apology, of course. Suddenly, I was more than eager to get this thing over with. Better to do it fast and early rather than wait for an audience.

As if reading my mind, Robert said, "If you wanna go now, I'll man the bar."

He didn't need to ask me twice. Working faster now, I put the final touches on the Long Island Iced Tea and set it in the waitress pick-up spot. "That's for Melanie," I said, lifting the small divider that separated the bar from the dining area.

Over my shoulder, I said, "Wish me luck."

As I left, I swear I heard him mutter, "Yeah. You're gonna need it." My steps faltered, but I didn't turn back. Choosing to believe he said something else, I moved purposely past the other sparsely occupied tables and into the section that he'd indicated.

I spotted the woman, sure enough, sitting alone at a table for ten. Breathing a sigh of relief that no one else had yet arrived, I moved toward her with my heart thudding in my chest.

I don't know why. I mean, I was no stranger to apologies, and the woman looked harmless enough. She was a soft-looking professional type, maybe forty years old, with a no-nonsense haircut and a blouse buttoned up to her neck.

And yet, I knew from our last encounter that she could be highly unpleasant when she wanted to be. I recalled the last time I tried to apologize. The more I told her how sorry I was, the more irate she became, until practically everyone in the whole restaurant had stopped to listen.

But now, sitting alone at that huge table, she had out her cell phone and was quietly looking down at the screen, as if checking email or something.

When I reached her side, she didn't look up. Instead, she turned slightly away and kept scrolling on her phone.

I paused. She *had* seen me, right? Filled with new uncertainty, I said in the most pleasant voice I could muster, "Excuse me? Um, ma'am?"

She gave an irritated sigh, but said nothing. She didn't even look up.

I hesitated. Was the sigh directed at me?

Obviously, she knew I was here. She *had* to know. Even if I hadn't said anything, here I was, standing right next to her chair – I felt my jaw clench – within slapping distance, as coincidence would have it.

I waited for a long, awkward moment, and when she still didn't look up, I tried again. "Excuse me. I'm sorry to interrupt, but—"

With another irritated sigh, she raised her arm and lifted her index finger, as if indicating I should wait one moment while she finished.

I waited, feeling my face burn with embarrassment. I don't know why. It wasn't that embarrassing, but it made me feel incredibly awkward just the same.

Fearful that she'd think I was reading over her shoulder, I took a small step sideways, only to hear her say, "Going someplace?"

She was still looking down, and *still* scrolling. I felt my shoulders tighten and my blood pressure rise.

But I swallowed my irritation and said, as nicely as I could, "No. Of course not. I was just trying to give you some privacy. That's all."

"Oh," she said, still looking down. "I guess that's okay."

"But if you'd like," I said, "I can come back in a couple of minutes."

Her voice sharpened. "In a hurry, are you?"

"Uh, no," I stammered. "I just don't want to rush you."

And, I don't want to be standing here like an idiot.

"Oh, don't worry about *that*," she said, her tone growing decidedly snippy. "Believe you-me. I don't intend on being rushed."

Yeah, and *I* didn't intend on slapping her silly. But sometimes, these things just happened, didn't they?

I felt my palms grow twitchy, and my mouth grow tight. I started glancing around, wondering how long I'd be standing here.

It was then that I spotted them – my brothers, a few tables away. They had drinks and menus placed in front of them and amusement written all over their faces.

I felt my gaze narrow. What on Earth were they doing here?

And why were they looking so amused? I saw nothing funny about this whole experience.

Deliberately, I looked away, doing my best to ignore them.

Finally, after several long minutes, the woman stopped scrolling and set down her phone. She lifted her head and smiled – except it wasn't at me.

Looking past me, she called out, "Yoohoo Sarah! Over here!"

I turned my head to see a young woman around my own age, or maybe a couple of years younger. She had a colorful book-bag slung over her shoulder and a smile that looked a little strained.

She approached the table and took a seat next to the woman, whose name, I suddenly realized, I didn't even know.

But then again, I hadn't expected this to be such a long-term relationship.

Sarah looked up, meeting my gaze. "Uh, hi." She looked around. "So, uh, could I get a ginger ale?"

Eager to kill some time, I chirped out, "Sure thing," and started to turn away.

Before my escape was complete, Miss Table-for-Ten said, "Hold on." Finally, she looked at me. "You *are* coming back, I assume?"

Unfortunately.

"Of course," I assured her with what I hoped was a smile. "I'll be back in a minute."

On my way back to the bar, I stopped at my brothers' table. In a hushed voice, I demanded, "What are you guys doing here?"

"What else?" Steve said. "Watching to see how it goes."

"How *what* goes? The apology? How'd you know it was now?"

"You told us Saturday," Steve said. "Don't you remember?"

"No." It was true. I *didn't* remember. After talking with Jake, I'd been too high on love to remember anything. That was two days ago, and I was *still* a little buzzed.

"Well, you did," Steve insisted.

"So?" I said. "That wasn't an invitation."

Anthony chimed in, "But we've got this bet. We want to see who wins."

"A bet?" I hissed. "Again? On what, this time?" I shook my head. "You know what? Never mind. I'm sure I'll hear about it later."

Not that I wanted to. In truth, this was all kind of depressing. They weren't here to offer sympathy or support. Instead, I was just fodder for their entertainment.

Tonight, at Kung fu, part two, no doubt I'd be hearing all about it. I tried to look on the bright side. After that, I'd be seeing Jake, finally.

Reluctantly, I glanced toward Miss Table-for-Ten. She was facing away from us now, talking to Sarah about who-knows-what.

Following my gaze, Anthony said, "Get this. We spotted that lady in the parking lot. She drives this big, black van. It took her like twenty minutes to park."

"Yeah," Steve added. "And she got all mad when this guy parked next to her, told him that he was 'crowding her space.'" Steve gave a low laugh. "Made him move his car. I shit you not."

I gave the woman another quick glance. In a low voice, I said, "I can't say I'm surprised."

"You know what you should do?" Anthony said, "Tell her you're 'sorry' you pissed in her drink."

I shook my head. "What?"

He grinned up at me. "It's an apology, right?"

I stared down at him. The plan was seriously flawed. For one thing, I hadn't "pissed" in her drink. For another, the whole point of apologizing was to keep my job, not be escorted out by security, or worse, prosecuted for food-tampering.

"I'll think about it," I muttered, turning away to fetch the ginger ale.

"On your way back," Steve called after me, "bring us a couple of beers, will ya?"

No. That wasn't going to happen. They had a waitress, whoever it was. And there was no way I'd be calling any more attention to them, or to me, for that matter.

Back at the bar, Robert asked, "How'd it go?"

In my frustration, I forgot to be diplomatic. "Terrible."

He frowned. "How so?"

"Sorry," I said. "Actually, it hasn't even happened yet." I went on to explain how she'd been deliberately ignoring me, but wanted me to return.

By now, a sickening realization was settling over me. She wanted an audience, hand-picked by her, no less.

As I considered this, I couldn't help but wonder, what on Earth was I doing here? □

CHAPTER 49

With quick, jerky movements, I filled a tall glass with ice and ginger ale. As I went through the motions, I was conscious of Robert watching me, and I couldn't help but wonder what he was thinking.

As for me, I was thinking that probably I *was* stupid for working here, when I had a perfectly good job-offer with someone I loved and trusted.

Jake.

I glanced toward the door, half-tempted to walk out now.

But I couldn't.

If I walked out now, I'd never know if I'd quit because it was the smart thing to do, or because I couldn't stomach the thought of apologizing to some ninny.

Melanie's voice interrupted my thoughts. "Hey Luna, that lady's asking for you."

I looked up. She didn't need to tell me which lady. I gave her a sympathetic look. "So that's your table, huh?"

Melanie glanced at Robert and said, "Unless *you* want to wait on her."

It was a joke, obviously. I didn't even know who she meant – me, or Robert. Either way, it wasn't going to happen. I hadn't had the training, and Robert already looked scared shitless.

And poor Melanie. She'd been the lady's waitress the last time, too, when my stupid drawing had caused all that trouble.

I turned to her and said, "I'm sorry you got stuck with her twice. Talk about bad luck, huh?"

"It wasn't luck," she said, giving Robert an annoyed look. "*He* made me do it."

I turned to Robert, wondering what he would say.

"You passed along the note," he told her. "The way I see it, you're getting off light."

He meant *my* note, obviously, with that stupid butt-cartoon. Melanie's gaze shifted to me, and I could tell exactly what she was thinking.

This was all my fault.

The sad thing was, she was right. I winced. "Sorry. If it makes you feel any better, I'm sure she's gonna put me through the ringer."

"Let's hope so," Melanie muttered, and then turned away. Over her shoulder, she called out, "And don't make her wait, alright? I don't need any more trouble."

I let out a long sigh. If Melanie was angry, I had only myself to blame.

Next to me, Robert said, "Don't feel bad. She called *me* a ferret-faced weasel."

"Who?" I turned to face him. "Melanie?"

He shook his head. "Not Melanie. The customer." He glanced toward the dining area. "And Melanie's right. You'd best not keep her waiting."

Hurrying now, I put the ginger-ale on a tray and started making my way out there. When the table came into view, I stopped dead in my tracks.

There it was, the table for ten. And there *they* were, ten customers, including the lady who I owed that apology to.

Well, this was just great.

From what I could see, the rest of the customers were all young women, around Sarah's age, maybe in their late teens or early twenties. Near their chairs, I spotted backpacks and book bags, like they'd just come from class or something.

My gaze zoomed in on the group's leader, the woman I'd be

groveling to. As I watched, she gave a tittering laugh and announced to the whole table, "Of course, it's better to learn by *other* people's mistakes, don't you think?"

I sucked in a breath. *My* mistakes?

It sure sounded like it.

She went on to say something about field trips and extra credit. I started to wonder, was she their professor or something? And was *I* today's lesson?

Reluctantly, I started moving again. While my legs carried me forward, my mind churned with uncertainty. Why was I putting myself through this? Even with tips, my income was nothing spectacular.

And what about those so-called advancement opportunities? Did they really exist? Or was that all just a sham? Something to sucker in rubes like me, who were desperate to use their college degrees for something other than low-level service jobs?

I'd just passed my brothers' table when Steve called out, "Oh, Miss! Can we get a couple of Moon Pies over here?"

God, they were such asshats.

"No," I hissed and kept on moving.

"Gee," Steve muttered. "Talk about rude."

Ignoring his comment, I approached the table for ten and delivered Sarah's ginger ale before looking to the group's leader.

With a thin smile, the woman said, "We're so glad you came back." She looked around the table and said, "We were getting worried. Weren't we?"

I scanned the group. None of them looked particularly worried. Even Sarah, who'd been waiting for the ginger ale, looked more confused more than anything.

Determined to play it safe, I managed to say, "I'm sorry that took so long."

"I doubt *that*," the woman said, getting to her feet. She looked to the rest of the table and announced, "Anyway, this *bartender* here has something she wants to say." Her lips formed a smirk. "And I wanted you all to witness it."

I swallowed. Witness it?

My stomach was roiling now. Of course, I'd already known that she'd intended to make an idiot of me. But I hadn't expected her to be quite so blatant about it.

Again, I thought of Jake and his offer. If I wanted to, I could quit this place right now, and this whole thing would be over. I could tell the lady to shove it. And then I could run, fast and hard, for the exit.

It was so very tempting.

But that was the old Luna, the one who'd jump at the easy way out, only to regret it later. Who knows? Maybe I *would* end up quitting. And maybe, I'd be quitting today.

But I wasn't going to do that without knowing for absolute certain that it wasn't merely to avoid something unpleasant. So I stiffened my spine and tried to keep my voice steady as I looked the woman straight in the eye, and said, as sincerely as I could, "I'm *really* sorry about what happened the other day."

When she made no response, I added, "It was a mistake, and I hope you can forgive me?"

The woman stared at me. "Is that it?"

Was it?

I didn't know what to say. My face was burning with new embarrassment. What did she want? Better words? Me on my knees? A kiss on her ass?

I was willing to apologize, and I wanted to do a decent job of it, but I wasn't willing to beg, if that's what she had in mind.

When I said nothing, the woman looked heavenward and said, "Why don't you tell us what, *specifically*, you're sorry for."

Us? I glanced toward the table's other occupants, who eyed me with expressions ranging from sympathy to contempt.

The woman's words echoed in my mind. What, specifically, was I sorry for?

Well, right now, I was sorry that I didn't have a club, because I'd very much like to beat her with it.

My gaze shifted toward the exit. From here, I couldn't see the door, but I knew exactly where it was. In thirty seconds, I could be out of here.

I felt my jaw tighten. And let that woman get the best of me?

And then there was the long-term problem. If I messed this up now, and things with Jake didn't work out, what then? My job-history was already shaky, and I was a year past college graduation.

As it stood now, my resume was a mess, and it wouldn't get any cleaner by screwing this up, too.

I recalled my brothers, sitting a few tables away. Knowing them, they were laughing their asses off. As for me, I felt like crying.

I was being stupid, taking this way too personally. It wasn't like the lady had slapped me or anything.

I paused.

Yet.

Damn it. Suck it up, Luna.

Reluctantly, I tried again. "I'm sorry about that drawing." My voice was shaking. I hated that it was shaking. This wasn't a huge deal. It really wasn't. Trying to rein in my emotions, I continued, softer now, "It was a joke, but it wasn't meant for you."

She pursed her lips. "Oh really? So it was meant for *another* customer?" Her voice rose. "What kind of place do you run here, anyway?"

I stared at her, unsure what to say. I wasn't running anything. I was just a stupid bartender, thinking I could get my foot in the door of a larger company and, oh, I don't know, actually use my college degree – the one I'd beggared myself to get.

It wasn't supposed to be like this.

Thinking of everything – the college loans, my own stupidity, and all of my poor choices, not just since graduating, but for as long as I could remember – I felt the first sting of tears.

With an effort, I blinked them away.

I wasn't going to do this. I wasn't going to cry in front of a low-level bully and her captive audience.

This *wasn't* a big deal. Really, it wasn't.

I squared my shoulders and tried again. "I am *really* sorry," I told the woman yet again. "That drawing, well, it was meant for my brothers, who come in here sometimes." As I spoke, I snuck a quick glance in their direction and paused.

They were gone.

On their table, I saw a handful of bills, tucked under one of their drinks, payment for lunch, obviously. But wait, had they even *had* lunch?

Either way, they were missing a wonderful show.

I stumbled over the rest of my latest apology, and finished by admitting, "I don't know what else you want me to say, but I *am* really sorry."

God, how many times had I said that? It felt like a million, and I seriously doubted my ability to say it even one more time.

Finally, after a long moment, the woman gave me a thin smile and announced, "I guess that'll do."

My shoulders sagged. With relief? Or defeat? I didn't know, and I didn't want to speculate. Somehow, I managed to say in an embarrassingly weak voice, "Thank you. I'm glad to hear that."

Had I no pride?

Shit. Apparently not.

To my infinite relief, Melanie arrived with a tray full of drinks, giving me the chance to make my escape. Walking on auto-pilot, I trudged back to the bar, where Robert was waiting.

One look at my face, and he frowned. "That bad, huh?"

"It was fine," I lied. "She accepted my apology, so…" I shrugged, reluctant to continue. For some stupid reason, I still felt like crying.

God, I was being such an idiot.

He gave me a sympathetic look. "If you want to take a break, I'll cover for you."

I glanced toward the door, wondering if I should say exactly what I wanted to say. I'd done it. I'd apologized. I'd kept my job. So why wasn't I happy?

But I knew why.

And suddenly, I knew what I had to do. In a weird twist of fate, it happened to be exactly what I wanted to do.

How often did *that* happen? ☐

CHAPTER 50

After my shift, I returned to Jake's building and entered the lobby like I usually did, from the parking garage. Most of the time, I made a beeline straight for the elevator.

This time, I didn't. Instead, I stopped and stared. I couldn't help myself.

Standing just inside the lobby's front entrance was a sleek-looking blonde in a tailored business suit. At first glance, she might've been an accountant, or maybe a high-powered attorney of the corporate variety.

Whatever her real profession was, I had no idea, because I knew her by a different name.

Nipple Girl.

And the way it sounded, she was here to see Jake.

She and Pete were facing off just inside the lobby's glass double-doors. From where I stood, I could just barely make out what she was saying.

Her voice was surprisingly cool with a vague upscale accent. "Perhaps I can wait in his office then?"

Whatever Pete said in response, I couldn't make it out. His back was to me, and his words were too low to hear. Besides, I was so focused on *her* that I barely noticed anything else.

The last time I'd seen her, she'd been wearing a sequined dress that showed plenty of skin. Her voice had been high and giggly – all baby-doll, zero business.

Even her hair was completely different. At the convention center, it had been big and bouncy with long, flowing curls. Now, it was styled into a simple, elegant twist.

Who *was* she, anyway?

As I watched, she looked toward a nearby seating area and said, "Surely, you can't object to my waiting *there?*"

Pete turned to study the cluster of chairs. His eyebrows furrowed, and he looked uncertain.

She lifted her hand and touched his elbow. When Pete turned to look, she gave him a dazzling smile and said, "Don't worry. I'll behave. I promise."

Pete looked around, only to stop in mid-motion when his gaze landed on me. His face froze in an expression that practically screamed, "Oh, crap."

Well, that was nice.

I liked him. I'd even defended him. So why was he looking at me like *I* was the problem? Before I knew it, I was striding straight toward them.

When I reached their side, Pete looked from me to her. He swallowed and glanced toward the doors, as if tempted to bolt.

I suddenly realized something. I'd probably had the same look on my own face just a few hours earlier, when Miss Table-for-Ten had been treating *me* like dirt.

The realization was the cold splash of reality that I needed. It wasn't Pete's fault that I was desperate for answers and unafraid to seek them head-on. But that didn't mean I had to run away either.

With an effort, I summoned up what I hoped was a reassuring smile. "Don't worry," I told him, giving Nipple Girl a sideways glance. "*I'll* behave, too." My smile felt too thin and too fake, but I kept it plastered there anyway, for Pete's sake, not hers.

Pete's gaze bounced from me to her. Finally, he gave a short nod, and turned away. As I watched, he walked out of the building and stood near the curb, facing away from us.

To give us some privacy? Or to wash his hands of the whole sorry situation?

If the latter was the case, I couldn't say I blamed him.

I was still staring after him when I heard Nipple Girl say, "So, do you work for Jake, or…?"

I turned to look at her. Her expression was friendly enough, but I couldn't return the favor. I wasn't feeling friendly, and I didn't see any reason to fake it.

Her question hung in the air, and I didn't know what to say. For a such simple question, it was insanely complicated, so instead of answering, I lobbed back a question of my own. "Do *you*?"

I was pretty sure I knew the answer to that, but hey, it would get the ball rolling, right?

Her brow wrinkled. "Do I work for him?" She shook her head. "Not yet." She flashed me a sudden smile. "But I'm hoping to." She glanced around. "In fact, that's why I'm here. I was hoping to talk to him."

Talk to him, huh? I snorted, "Yeah, I just bet."

The last time I'd seen her, in that video, she'd been trying to do a lot more than talk. A snapshot from that whole sorry scene flashed in my brain. She was clutching Jake's legs, and had her face plastered to his crotch.

If she'd been hoping to talk to his privates, she'd been in the perfect position.

Her smile faded. "Oh, no. You're his girlfriend, aren't you?" She looked heavenward and added, "Oh fiddlesticks. I should've known that."

Fiddlesticks?

The scene was starting to feel eerily familiar. Just a few weeks earlier, another strange – and yeah, obscenely attractive – girl had shown up in a hotel room that I'd been sharing with Jake. She'd played Miss Nicey-Nice, all the while giving me the obvious impression that she and Jake were doing the naked pretzel on the side.

It had almost destroyed our relationship. But of course, that had been the intention all along, hadn't it?

I gave Nipple Girl a long, cold look. That *last* girl had been a low-level actress hired by Vince Hammond.

Was he up to his old tricks? It sure as hell looked like it.

God, what an idiot. Like I'd fall for the same trick twice. How stupid did he think I was, anyway?

In front of me, the girl gave a nervous laugh. "I saw he had a girlfriend, but I was hoping that wouldn't be an issue."

Oh, for crying out loud.

I was getting a little tired of this whole stupid scene. How many actresses would Vince be sending my way before he got the message? And why on Earth was he doing this at all? Didn't he and Jake have some sort of truce?

Then again, why should I be surprised? Vince wasn't exactly the honorable type, was he?

Maybe it was time to play this differently, to show Vince that his crazy schemes wouldn't work on me, not anymore.

I felt myself smile. Maybe it was time to give him – and any actresses he sent – a taste of their own medicine.

CHAPTER 51

Standing in the lobby, I considered her last statement. *"I saw he had a girlfriend, but I was hoping that wouldn't be an issue."*

Right. Because when it came to Jake, I'd just love to share, and who knows, maybe join in the fun. The more the merrier, right?

At the thought of Jake with anyone else, I felt my fingers clench and my mouth go dry. But of course, that was supposed to be my reaction, wasn't it?

Obviously, her words were scripted to get under my skin, to cause friction between me and Jake, to start yet another argument, and cause Jake trouble.

But that wasn't going to happen. Not this time.

With new resolve, I kept my smile in place. "Oh, he *does* have a girlfriend, but you're right. We can't let *that* stop us." I leaned close and lowered my voice. "Tell me, do you still have that dress?"

She took a half step backward. "What dress?"

"You know, that sexy, sequined thing." I licked my lips and practically purred, "It looked *so* hot."

She hesitated. "Why, uh, thank you. It was supposed to, actually." She gave a little wince. "I hope you're not angry about that."

I gave an exaggerated eye-roll. "Angry? Why would I be angry?" In a breathy voice, I said, "You know what *I* want?"

From the look on her face, she didn't really want to know. But I had to give her credit. After the briefest hesitation, she managed to ask,

"What?"

"A repeat performance."

She blinked. "I'm afraid I'm not following."

I gave a breezy wave of my hand. "Oh, don't be coy. We're all adults, right?" I leaned even closer and said, "Tell me, what do you think of mayonnaise?"

She hesitated. "Uh, it tastes fine, I guess."

"Oh, please." I gave a little giggle. "We don't want you to *eat* it. We want you to roll in it. We've got this big room upstairs that we cover in plastic..." I gave another hand-wave. "Well, you know, you've probably got one of those, too, right?"

From the look on her face, she apparently didn't.

When she said nothing, I asked, "Don't tell me you're more of a mustard girl?"

She gulped. "Mustard?"

Her gaze shifted toward Pete, who was still standing outside, near the curb. The way it looked, she was praying for some sort of rescue, or maybe just a distraction.

Oh, I had a distraction for her. "If you like him," I said, "we can ask him to join us."

She turned back to me and said, "Pardon?"

"The doorman," I said, giving her a sloppy grin. "You like his uniform. Am I right?"

"Uh, yeah. It's um, really nice."

I leaned toward her. "I know what we'll do. We'll make him wear it." I gave a dreamy sigh and gushed, "I *just* love a man in uniform, don't you?"

"Uh–"

"Oh hey, a quick question... Do you have glasses?"

"Uh, glasses?"

"You know, like reading glasses."

She hesitated. "Actually, I wear contacts. Why?"

I made a show of looking disappointed. "It's just that, well, if you wore glasses, you could fling them off, all sexy like, you know, like that slutty librarian in my favorite porno." In a loud stage-whisper, I added,

"Speaking of pornos, you don't care if we film it, do you?"

She croaked, "It?"

Even through her perfect makeup, I could see the color rising, hot and fast, to her cheeks. I recalled the last actress that Vince had sent. She'd been a local girl who'd mostly done bikini ads for her family's car dealership.

This new girl was definitely more upscale, and a better actress, too.

I had to give credit. She'd pulled off the drunken bimbo act perfectly. And now, she was doing a pretty good job of acting all horrified.

Or, who knows? Maybe that part *wasn't* an act. After all, there was a big difference between acting like a drunken bimbo and actually following through on the sort of things I was suggesting.

Obviously, the script had called for *me* to be horrified. Probably, I was supposed to be upstairs by now, sobbing into my pillow or pacing the floors, waiting for Jake to return so I could let him have it.

At the expression on her face, I almost wanted to laugh. Yeah, maybe she was just doing a job, but didn't she know? Real people could get hurt.

And not just me. Jake.

If I had my way, she'd never be pulling crap like this again, not on Jake, not on me, and not on anyone else either.

And if this worked out the way I thought, she'd run straight to Vince and tell him that his latest scheme hadn't worked.

She might give him details. Or she might not.

At this point, I hardly cared. I just wanted this to end, already.

Knowing Vince – that snake – she wouldn't be the last girl he sent. But eventually, if I kept doing this, he'd surely get the message.

I felt a real smile spread across my face. The next girl he sent, maybe I'd whip out some celery and offer to spank her ass with it. At the thought, I almost laughed out loud.

In front of me, she'd gone still and silent. Her gaze shifted to the lobby doors.

Yeah, that's right. Run. And don't come back.

Looking to drive the point home, I asked, "So, do you charge by the hour, or…?"

To my surprise, she didn't run. Instead, she did something that I should've seen coming.

She slapped me. □

CHAPTER 52

I stood, dumb-struck, as she pulled back her hand and gave a little gasp. "Oh, my God. I'm so sorry."

And the way it looked, she meant it.

Well, that just sucked. I wanted to slap her back. But could I?

I mean, she'd just apologized for it. It seemed terribly unsporting to slap someone who'd just said they were sorry.

Damn it.

I could still feel it, the heat of her hand, burning across my cheek. My fingers twitched with pent-up frustration and the urge to strike back.

Maybe I could follow her lead, do the quick one-two slap-apology combo. Then, she'd be in *my* shoes. See how she felt then.

Take that, Nipple Girl.

In front of me, her breathing was ragged, and her eyes were glistening.

Looking at her, my shoulders sagged.

Oh, crap.

The way it looked, she was ready to cry.

Well that made two of us. I mean, it's not like my day had been so terrific either. And who invited her here, anyway?

No one. That's who.

In front of me, she was making an obvious effort to pull herself together. She swiped at her eyes, rubbing away unshed tears.

Or maybe, that was all just part of the show.

I gave her a hard look. "Who *are* you, anyway?" Before she could answer, I held up a hand. "Wait. Better yet. Who sent you?"

"No one." She gave me a shaky smile. "But I *am* a friend of Jake's P.R. director."

Huh?

Jake didn't *have* a P.R. director. Did he?

"Who do you mean?" I asked. But even as I said it, I knew the answer. I gritted my teeth and said it out loud. "Bianca."

The girl in front of me nodded. "You know her?"

"Oh, do I ever."

Her brow wrinkled. "Is that a problem?"

I had no idea what to say. Yes, it was a huge problem for too many reasons to count. "So Bianca put you up to that?"

"To what? Hitting you?" She winced. "No. Sorry. That was all me." She squinted toward my cheek and asked, "Is your face okay?"

"Forget that," I told her. "I meant that scene at the convention center. Was that Bianca's doing?"

She hesitated. "Well, not *all* of it. I mean, I like to think I put my own touches on it, you know?"

Touches? If she meant touching Jake's crotch with her face, she'd certainly accomplished that.

In front of me, she perked up. "But Bianca *did* pick out my dress."

I felt my jaw tighten. Bianca and dresses – I knew exactly how that went. When she'd helped *me* pick out a dress, I'd ended up looking like a prairie lady.

But at least my nipples hadn't been popping out all over the place.

The tears long-gone, she leaned forward and asked, "So, did he like it?"

"What? The dress?"

"Well, that too. But I meant the audition."

I gave a little shake of my head. "What audition?"

"At the convention center. Bianca said he was looking for a co-star. Or maybe a recurring character?" Her eyes brightened, but this time, not with tears. "Someone really sexy and flamboyant."

Well, she had been *that.*

"So," she continued, "what did he think?"

I couldn't recall his exact words, but I knew exactly what he'd thought. According to Jake, she'd been drunk, nauseous, and stinky, well, as far as her perfume, anyway.

I didn't smell any perfume now. But who knows? Maybe that was Bianca's brainchild, too.

It would be just like her.

The more I thought about it, the more I decided that the person who really needed slapping was Bianca.

When I saw her next, maybe I would.

And I wouldn't be apologizing for it either.

Take that, Bianca.

The girl's voice broke into my thoughts. "Oh, no. You're mad about my performance, aren't you?"

Was I?

Definitely.

But somehow, I didn't think I was mad at her. Not anymore. "Actually," I admitted, "I'm not sure."

She bit her lip. "I'm sorry I got carried away. It was supposed to be just an act, but..." She licked her lips. "He is *so* hot. Once I got started, I just couldn't stop myself."

I watched, in new horror, as she started fanning herself, even as her voice became husky. "When he carried me out of there, I thought, 'Oh yeah, baby. Take me to heaven. I'm ready to go.'"

At something in my face, she drew back and cleared her throat. "But, of course, I was just a *little* tipsy."

Tipsy? More like drunk off her ass. But from the look on her face, she already knew that. Why rub it in?

"And," she continued, "in my defense, I didn't know beforehand that he had a girlfriend." Her brow wrinkled. "Funny that Bianca didn't mention that."

"Yeah. Funny."

She gave a shaky laugh. "Thank goodness for the internet."

"Uh. Yeah."

She lowered her voice. "Can I tell you a secret? I was so nervous, I came *this* close to throwing up on him. Pretty embarrassing, huh?"

Listening to this, all I could think was, *more embarrassing than the nipple? Really?*

But I didn't say it, because I was coming to a startling realization. I actually liked her. She was refreshingly honest, especially for a friend of Bianca's.

But I still felt like I was missing something. "About today," I asked, "did Bianca send you here?"

"Not exactly." She glanced around. "But about the co-star thing, she never got back to me. And now, I can't seem to reach her. I didn't have her home-address, so I figured I'd come here, straight to the source."

By now, I was actually feeling sorry for her. "And you said Bianca's a *friend?*"

Some friend.

She considered my question. "Well, we *are* members of the same theatre group."

Curious, I asked, "What kind?"

She gave a dismissive wave of her hand. "Just a local thing. But hey, you never know when you'll catch that big break, right?" She smiled. "And once I learned of the co-star job, I was all in."

I recalled the scene from the convention center.

All in?

Not so much.

As nicely as I could, I said, "I'm really sorry to tell you this, but there's no co-star job."

Her smile faded. "There isn't?"

I shook my head. "And there never was."

"But Bianca said…" Her words trailed off, like she didn't know where to go from there.

Hoping to spare her some grief, I said, "Bianca doesn't even work for him."

Her face froze. "She doesn't?"

"No. And they're not even friends. Not really."

She was frowning now. After a long moment, she muttered, "That bitch."

And the way it looked, she didn't mean me. □

CHAPTER 53

I'd been upstairs for less than an hour when the doorbell rang. Through the closed condo doors, I heard Steve call out, "Hurry up. I'm sweating my ass off out here."

When I opened the door, Steve, with Anthony on his heels, barreled into the condo and said, "You got the beer, right?"

"Yeah," I said, watching as they strode toward the kitchen. "I picked it up yesterday."

With Jake gone, I'd been working like crazy to get everything else done, including shopping for this little pizza and Kung fu party.

At the thought of Jake, I couldn't help but smile. In just a few short hours, he'd finally be home, and I was dying to see him.

Over the last two days, we'd been talking plenty on the phone, but it was poor substitute for the real thing.

In the kitchen, Steve yanked open the fridge and started rummaging around inside. He emerged a few seconds later with a bottle of beer in each hand.

He tossed one to Anthony and opened his own. He took a long pull and said, "Man, I'm sweating my ass off."

"Uh, yeah," I said. "You kind of mentioned that." I moved forward for a better look. He did, in fact, look kind of sweaty.

"What happened?" I asked. "Is the air on the fritz again?"

"In the truck? Nah." Steve glanced vaguely toward the condo doors. "We had to take the stairs." He practically shuddered. "Remember?"

Warmth flooded my face. Mental note – traumatizing my brothers with details of my sex life might work fine in the short-term. But in the long-term? Well, let's just say it wasn't the smartest plan.

"Hey, I know," I said. "What you *could* do is take one of the *other* elevators—"

"They don't reach this floor," Steve reminded me.

"Yeah, I know," I said. "But you could get off—"

"Stop." He gave me an annoyed look. "Get off? Really?"

"Oh, shut up," I said. "What I mean is that you could take another elevator to the eighteenth floor, and then, you'd only have to walk up two flights." I offered up a shaky smile. "What do you think?"

Steve looked to the fridge. "I think I need more beer."

It was definitely time to change the subject. As Steve went to the fridge, I turned to Anthony and said, "Just so you guys know, you need to leave by eleven, okay? Jake's returning sometime after midnight, and I want to have the place cleaned up by then."

Anthony looked almost insulted. "What are saying? That we're messy?"

I didn't bother answering. They weren't just messy. They were total slobs. But in reality, it wasn't the mess I was worried about. It was the fact that I was dying to see Jake alone.

Makeup sex.

I wanted it. Bad.

And unless I wanted to send my brothers straight into therapy, it would be a good idea to send them on their way before that sex actually got started.

Returning with a couple more beers, Steve glanced around. "So where's the pizza? You ordered it, right?"

"Don't worry," I told him. "It should be here any minute."

"Good," he said, "because I'm starving. I haven't eaten since breakfast."

"Liar," I said. "You had lunch."

"Did not," he insisted.

"Sure you did. I saw you at the steakhouse. Remember?" I gave him an annoyed look. "And thanks a lot for coming in to gawk at my apology. Did you guys enjoy the show?"

Suddenly, Steve was grinning. "Oh yeah. It was freaking awesome."

Well, that was special. It was nice to know that my brothers got such a kick out of seeing my humiliation. But in light of the whole elevator thing, I didn't want to make a big stink about it, so all I said was, "So, who won the bet?"

"What bet?" Anthony asked.

"At the restaurant," I reminded him, "you said you had a bet."

"Oh, *that* bet," Anthony said. "Eh, we both lost."

"Yeah," Steve said, "it kind of sucked, actually."

I shook my head. "What do you mean?"

Steve cracked open his new beer and tossed the other one to Anthony. Turning back to me, he said, "Well, *I* bet that you'd hit her with something, and Anthony here—" Steve lifted his beer-bottle in Anthony's direction "—bet on a food fight."

I stared at them. Okay, I hadn't always been the most mature person in the world. But even I had my limits. I was still staring. "How old do you think I am?"

Steve shrugged. "Hey, we were just thinking what we'd do."

I paused. Now, that made a weird kind of sense.

"And just so you know," Anthony said, "Steve was right. We didn't get the chance to eat."

"What happened?" I asked, recalling how they'd left so suddenly. "Did the inspector call or something?"

"For work?" Anthony said. "Nah. That's not it." He looked to Steve and said, "You wanna tell it, or should I?"

Knowing my brothers, I was almost afraid to ask. "Tell what?"

"About that lady," Anthony said. "The one who gave you such a hard time."

Oh. Her.

After my apology, she'd spent the next hour running Melanie ragged, while she proceeded to lecture her younger dinner companions about choosing the right career, so they didn't end up working, as she had put it, a dirty, low-level service job.

Melanie, who had a bachelor's degree in philosophy, hadn't been amused.

But at least *I* didn't have to deal with that woman ever again. After my apology, I'd kept myself firmly behind the bar, where I made drinks on auto-pilot while contemplating my next career move, which I wasn't willing to discuss just yet.

Right now, I had a more pressing topic of conversation. With growing nervousness, I asked my brothers, "What about that lady?"

They were both grinning now. Steve said, "You hear about her van?"

Okay, now I was really nervous. In my mind, I saw visions of spray paint and punctured tires, courtesy of my brothers. True, vandalism wasn't exactly their style, but their smiles were definitely on the evil side.

Speaking slowly and carefully, I said, "What about her van?"

Steve laughed. "It was stolen."

CHAPTER 54

Looking at my brothers, I froze. "Oh, my God. Don't tell me you guys stole it?"

"Oh, get real," Steve said. "We didn't steal it. Jeez."

Just when I started to relax, Anthony said, "Yeah. We borrowed it."

Of course.

Horrified, I asked, "Where's the van now? Oh, my God. Please don't tell me you drove it *here*."

At this, they both burst out laughing. Steve said, "How stupid do you think we are?"

I stared at them in disbelief. "You sure you want an answer to that?"

Steve studied my face. "Eh, probably not."

Next to him, Anthony spoke up. "Hey, don't worry. She got it back."

"Yeah," Steve said. "It wasn't a big deal. All we did was move it."

"Yeah," Anthony said. "And we only drove it for like thirty seconds."

I was almost afraid to ask, "So where'd you drive it to?"

Steve grinned. "You know that adult book store, just around the corner?"

I gave a confused shake of my head. "There's a book store?"

Steve nodded. "Yeah. Like a block away from the steakhouse. You never saw it?"

Silently, I shook my head.

Anthony spoke up. "It's not just books. They've got videos, sex toys, you know, the usual stuff." He took a long pull of his beer. "Great movies, too."

Next to him, Steve laughed. "Your buddy Rango can tell you about those."

I tried not to laugh. "So *that's* where you got that porno?"

"Yeah," Anthony said. "It's not like we keep them laying around, for cripe's sake. How desperate do you think we are?"

"No kidding," Steve added. "We like the real thing."

Okay, now *I* was feeling a little traumatized. Desperate to change the subject, I said, "That's funny. I thought all you guys liked was Kung fu."

Steve gave me a solemn look. "Hey, don't mock the Kung fu."

Curious in spite of myself, I asked, "So what happened? With that lady, I mean?"

"Well," Anthony said, "when she's done eating or whatever, she comes out of the restaurant, and she's got all these students trailing after her, like she's got paperwork to give them or something."

He grinned. "But surprise, surprise, when she gets to her spot, her van's like gone."

"Yeah," Steve added. "So she flips out, starts yelling, makes like she's gonna call the cops." He shrugged. "You know, the usual stuff."

I swallowed. "The usual stuff?"

How often did they do stuff like this? Probably, I didn't want to know.

Anthony picked up the story. "So we come along and say, 'Oh hey, what's wrong?' And she starts blubbering that her van was stolen, and we're like, 'Oh, no way. What does it look like?'"

Steve broke in by saying, "So she gives us the description, and we're all like, 'Oh wait, didn't we see that van at the sex shop?'"

I tried not to laugh. "You didn't."

"Sure we did," Steve said. "And she gets all mad, like—" Steve did a poor imitation of a woman's voice. "—How dare you suggest such a thing? What kind of woman do you think I am?"

Steve flashed me a grin. "Which of course, we don't answer, because we think she's a freaking goblin. No point in telling her *that*, right?"

I paused. "Uh, right?"

"Exactly," Anthony said, "So we're all like, 'Hey, don't be embarrassed. We shop there too.'"

I just had to ask. "Did that make her feel better?"

"Hell no," Steve said. "'She huffs her goblin-ass over there, looking to prove us wrong. But sure enough, there's her van, in a prime spot, too. And the van's fine, exactly like she left it."

Anthony snickered. "Well, not *exactly* how she left it." He turned to me and said, "We tossed that porno onto her passenger's seat."

I stared at them. "You're kidding."

Anthony toasted me with his beer. "Nope."

In spite of myself, I had to know. "Did her students see it? The movie, I mean?"

"Eh, hard to say," Anthony said. "She took off pretty fast." He shrugged. "So, there you have it."

I was still staring. "Why would you guys do such a thing?"

"Oh, cut the crap," Steve said. "You know why."

I felt my lips twitch at the corners. "Because she was mean to me?"

"Hell yeah," Steve said. "I was kind of wishing you'd kick her ass."

"I was tempted," I admitted.

"Next time," he said, "don't be tempted. Just go with it. That's what I'd do."

"Or," Anthony chimed in, "do the food fight thing, like, hit her with a pork chop. That's what *I'd* do."

I rolled my eyes. "I'll think about it."

We were interrupted by the sound of a muffled bump against the penthouse doors. "Pizza's here," I said, heading toward the condo entrance.

But when I opened the door a moment later, I didn't see any pizza. All I saw was Jake.□

CHAPTER 55

I rushed forward and fell into his arms. "You're back."

When his arms closed tight around me, I sighed against his chest, lost in the feel of his hard body against mine.

I heard his voice, low in my ear. "Yeah. I couldn't wait." He gave a low chuckle. "But you wouldn't believe the flights."

I pulled back to gaze up at him. "That bad, huh?"

"You don't wanna know." He smiled. "I left Vegas ten hours ago."

I blinked. "You did?" Non-stop it was a four-hour flight. Based on what he'd just said, I could only imagine the layovers. I smiled up at him. "But you didn't tell me."

"You ever hear of a surprise?"

"But what about Lawton?" I asked. "Was he bummed you left early?"

"Nah."

"Are you sure?"

"Hey, his 'bride' showed up to surprise *him*. Trust me, he's not wasting time missing me."

The way it sounded, there was a lot of surprising stuff going on. And, as Jake would soon find out, I had a few surprises of my own.

But for now, I leaned forward again and molded my body against his. His chest was rock-solid, and his arms were firm and strong around my back. With him so close, I felt like I could stand there forever, just soaking up the feel of him.

And who knows? Maybe I would've, except for the sound of the elevator dinging, followed by another sound, a whole lot less cheerful.

It was Steve muttering, "What the hell is *that?*"

I pulled away and whirled toward the sound of his voice. He was standing with Anthony, just inside the condo doors. Both of them were staring, looking equally disturbed.

Alright, I'd been a reasonably good sport about the whole elevator trauma. But seriously, couldn't they just give it a rest already?

I glared over at them. "Oh for God's sake. What? You've never seen two people hug before?"

"That's not it," Steve said, pointing past me, toward the elevator. I turned and saw what he saw – a burly man in a bunny suit, holding a stack of three pizza boxes.

The man trudged forward and stopped short when he saw us looking. In a glum monotone, he said, "I lost a bet."

I had to ask. "With who?"

"My brother." He sighed. "Don't ask."

I snuck a quick glance at Steve and Anthony. I could *so* relate. And the way it looked, they could, too.

Trying not to laugh at the guy's misery, I pulled away from Jake and reached into the pocket of my jeans, retrieving the bills that I'd tucked in there earlier. Looking at the amount, I hesitated, wondering if I should add a few extra dollars to what was already a generous tip.

Before I could make any such move, Jake reached into his own pocket, and peeled off a hundred. He strode forward and handed it to the man, saying, "Here. Keep the change."

The man brightened considerably. "No kidding?"

"Hey, you earned it," Jake said, taking the pizzas and heading into the condo, with Steve and Anthony trailing after him.

Jake set the boxes on the kitchen counter, only to see Steve snatch the top two boxes and begin heading toward the condo door, while Anthony reached into the fridge and snagged a full six-pack of beer, before turning to follow after Steve.

Confused, I called after them. "Hey, where are you going?"

Over his shoulder, Anthony said, "Back to the hotel."

"But why?" I asked.

He laughed. "Because we got what we came for."

Insulted now, I sputtered, "What? The pizza?"

"Nah," he said, "to make sure you're alright." And then, he exited the condo, pulling the door softly shut behind him.

On my face, I felt the beginnings of what became a big, stupid smile. I was still smiling when I turned to Jake and said, "Can you believe those guys?"

Jake was smiling, too. "What *I* can't believe is their sister."

I couldn't help but tease him, just a little. "You mean Selena?"

"Yup."

My jaw dropped. "What?"

He flashed me that familiar cocky grin. "Nah. The other one."

I reached up with both hands and gave him a mock shove to his chest. With lightning speed, he caught my wrists and held them tight.

Laughing, I tried to pull away. "Stop! No fair."

"Screw fair," he said. "Where's the fun in that?"

I gave another mock tug. "But you've been so bad lately."

"Oh yeah," he said, looking maddeningly unconcerned. "How so?"

I searched my memory bank and blurted out the first thing that came to mind. "Well, there was that bet with my brothers."

"Yeah? Which one?"

"That last one," I said, "where you bet on me getting fired last Saturday."

"Nah. That wasn't the bet."

"Yes, it was," I insisted. "You told me so yourself."

"Wrong," he said, gently turning my wrists inward. He lowered his head and kissed the left one, softly, just above my palm.

My breath caught. "Fibber."

"No fib here." He turned and kissed the other wrist, making my pulse give a maddening jump. With his lips still grazing my skin, he said in low, seductive voice, "The bet was on you leaving your job, *not* on you getting fired."

With him so close, I was finding it hard to think. "Huh?"

"Maybe I was betting…" His lips moved higher, trailing up the inside of my lower arm."…or should I say, *hoping*, that you'd quit."

"Actually," I breathed, "I did."

He pulled back. "What?"

At the look on his face, I had to smile. "You're not the only one with surprises."

"When?" he asked.

I couldn't help but feel at least a *little* smug. "Today."

I didn't bother with the details. I could fill those in later. But basically, I'd quit almost immediately after apologizing to that awful woman. And, in more responsible news, I'd even finished my shift.

In hindsight, I was actually pretty proud of myself.

Watching me, Jake's lips curved into an amused smile. "And you didn't call to tell me?"

Probably, he'd been in the air at the time. But that wasn't the point. I smiled back. "You're not the only one with secrets."

His expression turned thoughtful. "Hmmm."

"Hmm what?"

His hands were still on my wrists. He pulled me closer, tucking my hands between our chests. "I have a surprise, too."

I could feel the surprise, raging hard against my pelvis. Unable to stop myself, I pressed my hips closer, loving the feel of his erection, pulsing now, through our clothes.

And then, before I knew it, I was swept up in his arms, laughing as he carried me toward the bedroom. "Wait!" I giggled. "Don't you want pizza?"

He didn't even pause. "Nope. All I want, I've got right here."

I was still laughing. "But what about me?"

"Why?" he asked, as he carried me through the bedroom doorway. "Are you starving?"

"Definitely." I smiled. "For you."

"Yeah?"

I leaned my head against his chest and said, softer now, "Definitely." □

CHAPTER 56

Breaking with tradition, Jake didn't toss me onto the bed. Rather, he moved forward and lowered me gently until I was resting, face-up, breathless and eager, on the thick bedding that covered his king-size mattress.

Wordlessly, I stared up at him, loving the fact that he was finally home. He wore dark slacks and a gray button-down dress-shirt. The clothes were rumpled, but his eyes were warm as they drifted over me in a leisurely caress.

When I reached out my arms in a silent bid for him to come closer, he gave a slow, deliberate shake of his head.

Breathlessly, I asked, "Why not?"

His gaze locked on mine, and I saw the hint of a smile as he said, "I think we need a blindfold."

Instantly, my body responded, growing hot and eager under his newly secretive gaze.

Somehow, I managed to say, "We?"

He didn't answer, but his look said it all. It wouldn't be *him* wearing it.

We'd never done the blindfold thing, and in spite of my body's obvious enthusiasm, I wasn't quite sure how I felt about that idea.

It wasn't that it was too kinky. We'd crossed *that* bridge plenty of times. It was the fact that I absolutely loved looking at him, no matter what he was wearing, or what we were doing.

For days, I'd been missing the sight of him, but for some reason, it felt like years. And depriving myself now felt needlessly cruel, especially with him so achingly close.

And yet, thinking of what he'd just said, the warmth was building deep in my core.

How messed up was that?

As I watched, Jake turned and walked purposely toward the tall dresser where I'd been keeping a few of my things. He pulled open the top drawer, rummaged around for a few seconds, and emerged with a familiar dark satin scarf.

He'd purchased that scarf for me a couple of weeks earlier, during one of our impromptu shopping trips. Now, I couldn't help but wonder if he'd been planning something like this all along.

That would be just like him, and I loved him all the more for it. For all his impulsiveness, he had a cunning streak that was almost kind of scary.

Slowly, he turned to approach the bed, with the scarf now wadded up in his right hand.

At the mere sight of him, my heart gave that familiar little flutter. Still, I heard myself say, "Wait."

His lips curved into the whisper of a smile. "For what?"

"I miss seeing you," I admitted.

"Oh yeah?" He grinned. "Too bad."

"What?" I laughed, even as a new thrill coursed straight through me.

With the scarf still in-hand, he moved toward me, looking so perfect that I felt like I could watch him forever.

But soon, I wouldn't be watching him at all.

I had to say something, even if it meant repeating myself. "Wait."

An eyebrow lifted. "Again?"

Desperate now, I managed to say, "Yeah. At least, um..." I felt my tongue dart across my upper lip. "...until you take off your shirt?"

He paused, looking down at me with warm amusement written all over his face.

As for my own face, it was feeling a lot warmer now, too. But why be coy at this point? "If you want," I offered, "I could take it off for you." I smiled. A helpful smile? Probably not.

Probably, it was the same kind of smile that all those groupies gave him, just before flinging their undies, or hell, even themselves, straight at him.

Trying to be at least a *little* reasonable, I added, "But if you'd rather take it off yourself, um, while I watched, that would be really nice, too."

"Yeah?" He looked almost ready to laugh. "Good to know."

Was he making fun of me?

If he was, I couldn't bring myself to care, because soon, he was standing near the bed, reaching his free hand toward the collar of his button-down shirt.

Never taking his gaze from mine, he deliberately unfastened the top button and then slowly went for the second.

Button by button, he progressed lower, until the shirt fell open, giving me a glorious view of his muscular pecs, his lean torso, and those spectacular washboard abs, firm and tight, visible just above the waistband of his dark, tailored slacks.

I felt myself smile. *Yup. Pure perfection.*

But then again. I'd known that already, hadn't I?

As I watched, he slid the shirt off his shoulders, and let it hang, as if momentarily forgotten, while he gazed down at me.

Mesmerized, I drank in the sight him – his eyes, his face, and his nearly naked torso, with all those finely chiseled muscles and exotic tattoos. Soon, the shirt was sliding to the floor, where it fell in a gray, rumpled heap.

Bare-chested now, Jake prowled forward, slowly and deliberately, until he leaned over me and brushed my lips with a kiss so light, it only made me hungry for more.

But there *was* no more. He pulled back, unwound the scarf, and then, leaned over me again to fasten it firmly over my eyes, making everything go surprisingly dark.

It was almost funny, because I hadn't realized the scarf was so opaque. Again, I couldn't help but wonder how much of this was planned, even inside that boutique, when he'd insisted on buying me that scarf, in spite of its outrageous price tag.

I recalled his smile as he'd draped it over my shoulders and whispered, "I'll be seeing you in that later."

And now, he was. But I couldn't see him.

Still, through his motions, I could sense what he was doing – tugging the blindfold tighter, tying it with some sort of knot, and then, once more, brushing his lips softly against mine before pulling back, as if seeking a better view.

Desperately, I reached out with both hands, seeking, and finding, his chest. Hungry for the feel of him, I trailed my fingers over the lines and ridges of his torso, until he pulled slowly away, leaving my fingers brushing only air.

Missing him, I whispered, "Jake?"

Soon, I felt his fingers working the button of my jeans, and then my zipper, which he slid down with one leisurely motion. I then felt his hands on my hips, gripping the thick fabric of my jeans and tugging downward until the cool air kissed my pelvis, and then my thighs, followed by my calves.

Lastly, he tugged off my socks, one-by-one.

And then, he was gone.

I didn't know where to, until – obviously from somewhere beside the bed – he started working the buttons of my blouse, unfastening them slowly, as if we had all the time in the world.

At the thought, I felt myself smile. We *did* have all the time in the world. He was home, and the way it sounded, he wasn't going anywhere, at least not any time soon.

His voice, soft and seductive, drifted over me. "I love that smile."

"I love *you*." I paused. "Even if I can't *see* you."

His tone grew teasing. "Is that a complaint?"

"Uh, yes?"

"Uh-huh," he said, obviously unconvinced.

I almost laughed. "You are *so* cocky."

"Yeah?" I felt a finger lightly brush my bottom lip, and then drift lower, down my chin, past my throat, between my breasts, down my stomach, past my navel, and then lower.

It paused on the lacy waistband of my skimpy panties. Skimpy or not, I was wishing I hadn't worn any, because when his finger moved lower, brushing my clit, I was already dying for the feel of his skin on mine.

My hips rose, and I think I might've whimpered.

His voice, still low, drifted over me. "If you want, *I'll* show you cocky."

His meaning was obvious. And I *did* want that. Very, *very* much.

In fact, I wanted him so bad that I was finding it almost hard to breathe. He'd barely touched me, and yet, I was more than ready. I knew exactly what I wanted. I wanted him inside me, and the thought of waiting one more minute seemed impossible to bear.

"When?" I breathed. "Like soon?"

I heard a low chuckle as he pulled away, leaving my hips rising into nothingness. And then, I felt a hard yank, as my panties were pulled off and tossed away to wherever. Finally, I felt his finger, brushing the same spot as before, now, with nothing in the way.

When his motions quickened, I ground against him and whimpered for more. "Seriously," I breathed, "I don't wanna wait. I've been missing you like crazy."

His voice was low. "Me, too." And yet, he made no move to come closer.

Desperately, I reached out with both arms, wanting to pull him tight against me.

"Nice try," he said, moving his fingers slower now, as if teasing me with the wait.

But then, I felt one long finger slip inside of me, and my arms fell, loose at my side, as I lost the ability to protest anything, even as my thighs parted, and my hips rose.

His voice, filled with warmth, drifted over me. "You know what I missed?"

Barely coherent, I managed to say, "What?"

"Seeing you like this."

Somewhere in the back of my mind, I realized the sweet irony of his statement. I missed seeing him too, and I might've protested, except that speech had suddenly become impossible, as my stomach clenched, and my body shuddered.

I couldn't see him, but I *could* feel him, teasing the orgasm out of me with his blissfully expert touch. I was so lost in the rolling, shuddering sensations that, at first, I almost didn't notice when the bed shifted, and I felt the weight of his hard body, poised above mine.

His lips brushed my ear. "So I'm cocky, huh?"

Unable to speak, I only nodded.

I was hot and slick, and dying to feel him inside me. With growing desperation, I reached down and was thrilled to discover that he was now fully naked – naked and massively hard in my warm, soft hand.

With blind anticipation, I guided him to my opening and lifted my hips, wanting, with all my being, to have him inside me, at last. He paused, holding his own hips motionless for a long, intense moment before surging forward, filling me so completely that I cried out with the pure bliss of it.

And then, we were moving together, with our hips rising and falling against each other, providing the closeness that I'd been craving – and missing – for days.

I felt his hands wrap themselves around mine, and then move my wrists upward until they were captured just above my head.

When his lips found my ear, I heard his voice, low and intense, "I love you."

"I love you, too," I breathed, lost in everything except the feel of him so blissfully close.

His long fingers intertwined with mine, and I felt his teeth graze my earlobe, just before he said, "Luna?"

"Hmmm?"

"Marry me." □

CHAPTER 57

His words felt like part of a dream. I was so lost, I could hardly think. "What'd you say?"

"You heard me." As if to drive the point home, his hips surged forward, claiming me as much with his body as with his next words, said with so much love, they burrowed deep into my soul. "Now, say yes."

My voice, when I found it, came out as a happy whisper. "Yes."

His body stilled for the briefest instant. And then, with words of love and promises of forever, he surged forward yet again.

I was soaring, as we rode together toward sweet oblivion, until, with another long series of shudders, we collapsed together into a warm, blissful heap.

His fingers, still intertwined with mine, gave a gentle squeeze. "Yes, huh? I'm gonna hold you to that."

I was so lost in contentment that it took me a moment to realize that I was still blindfolded. And for some reason, that struck me as incredibly funny. I started to giggle, and once I started, I couldn't bring myself to stop.

With insane happiness, I squeezed his hands right back, only to pause and grow suddenly still.

Something was different.

There was something new on the ring finger of my left hand.

I rubbed at it with my thumb. Sure enough, there it was – a ring where there hadn't been one before.

And not just any ring. From the feel of it, it was a ring with an insanely huge stone.

Unable to resist, I moved my hands and yanked at the blindfold. A moment later, I was staring over Jake's bare shoulder at a gorgeous diamond engagement ring, glittering on my ring finger.

I felt my eyes widen and then grow suddenly misty. "Oh, my God."

I heard Jake's voice, warm in my ear. "See? You're not getting out of it now."

I gave another happy laugh. "As if I'd want to."

Shifting his body, he moved to the side, and then wrapped his strong arms around me, cradling me against his chest.

I placed my palm on his naked torso, admiring the ring, almost as much as I admired him. I heard myself say, "It's too much."

"What's too much?"

"This. I don't know. Everything." I pulled back to look into his eyes. "Is there such a thing as being too happy?"

"Nope." And then, his tone grew more serious. "Later on, we'll do this right, okay?"

I wasn't following. "What do you mean?"

"I mean," he said, brushing his lips against mine, "that we'll go out, have dinner, flowers, whatever. And then, I'll get down on one knee and ask you the right way, in a room-full of strangers, the way I planned."

It was almost funny. For all his crazy ways, Jake had a traditional streak that was surprisingly appealing. But on this particular thing, he had no idea what he was talking about.

"No," I whispered. "That was absolutely perfect, just the way it was."

"Yeah? Well, just say the word, and I'll make it *more* perfect next time." He cracked a smile. "Even if this *was* my third try."

That made me pause. "I don't get it. Your *third* try?"

"You don't wanna know."

Didn't he know who he was dealing with? "I do, too," I insisted.

After a long, suspenseful pause, he said, "The first time was the day you *thought* you got fired."

I blinked. "Really?"

"Really. I had this big thing planned for after that meeting with

Vince."

"What kind of thing?"

"Dinner, flowers." He gave a small laugh. "Some guy with a violin." His voice softened. "And, the ring. I'd just picked it up when I saw you with Trey in my office."

His story was so sweet that I felt my insides go even *more* warm and gooey, as if that were remotely possible.

"But wait," I said, recalling something Trey had told me that very same day. "I thought you were shopping for a car."

He grinned. "Engagement present."

"Wait. Do you mean, uh…"

"For you."

It wasn't the first time Jake had tried to buy me a car. And I had the flattering feeling that it might not be the last.

Still, I hear myself say, "Isn't that a little extravagant?"

"Yup."

I laughed. "Honestly, I'm not sure what to say to that."

"Good," he said, "because it's in your parking spot right now."

He looked so happy, and yeah, just a little bit smug, that I couldn't bring myself to object.

Still, I did feel a little guilty. First there was the ring, and now the car, and then, the best thing of all – him.

What was *I* bringing to all this?

I had to say it. "But I didn't get you anything."

"Wrong," he said. "You got me you."

"But that's nothing, I mean, not in the gifty way."

"Wrong again." His voice grew softer. "It's everything."

I felt myself smile. "No. *You're* everything. Everything I ever wanted."

But then, I felt my smile fade as I recalled everything else that had happened on that horrible day – multiple fights, my stupid walk, and the tension afterward.

Had all of that caused Jake to have second thoughts? I didn't want to ask, but I didn't want to wonder, either.

I tried to make a joke of it. "So, you almost changed your mind, huh?" I forced a small laugh. "With all our fighting, I guess I can see why."

But Jake wasn't laughing. "Let's get one thing straight," he said. "The only thing that changed was the timing."

Relief washed over me. "Really?"

"Really." He gave me a playful squeeze. "After all, I wanted you to say 'yes.'"

Laughing now in earnest, I gave him a mock push to the chest. "As if there was any doubt." I paused. "So about that bet with my brothers, *that's* the reason you picked *that* day?"

"For you to leave your job? Maybe. A guy can hope, right?"

I just had to tease him. "So, you had inside information, huh? My brothers might call that cheating."

"You kidding? They'd call it smart."

"Well, there is that." Recalling him saying that this was his *third* attempt, I had to ask, "But what about the second time? When was that?"

His answer was one word. "Vegas."

"You mean that impromptu vacation?"

He nodded. "When I thought you were fired, I figured, 'Hey, I'll take her to Vegas, make it a night to remember.'"

My voice grew softer. "Jake?"

"Hmm?"

"Just so you know, this *was* a night to remember." I burrowed against him. "And I wouldn't have changed a thing."

"Yeah?"

"Definitely." I paused. "But I *am* curious."

"About what?"

Cautiously, I said, "You weren't hoping to get married in Vegas, were you?"

"That would've been up to you." He smiled. "In fact, it's still up to you. Say the word, and we'll catch the next flight out."

The idea was almost tempting, not because I wanted to get married in Vegas, but because I was so embarrassingly eager to make it official.

Still, Vegas wouldn't be my first choice. Apparently, I had a traditional streak too. Go figure.

Tentatively, I said, "And if that's *not* what I want?" Quickly, I added. "I mean, what if I want a big traditional wedding with family there."

His lips lifted at the corners. "Your family? Or mine?"

I knew what he was getting at. His family was a fragmented mess. Still, I wanted to be hopeful. I smiled with as much confidence as I could muster. "Both of our families."

His tone became teasing. "Yeah, good luck with that."

"Seriously," I said. "You wouldn't mind, would you?"

His gaze met mine. "Luna, I'd marry you anywhere, any time and count myself lucky."

At this, I felt a big goofy smile spread across my cheeks. "Awwww."

After a long, quiet moment, I pulled back to ask, "Are you really going to quit?"

"With the videos?" His voice grew quieter. "Yeah."

"So you'll be retired, huh?"

"Me?" he said. "Hell no."

More curious than ever, I asked, "So what are you gonna do?"

"I've got some ideas." He stroked my back, and his voice softened. "Does it matter?"

"Not to me," I said. "I'm just happy you're mine." And I meant it, too.

"Luna?"

"Hmm."

"It's a serious question. Let's say I was just a regular guy. Would you still feel the same way?"

I had to laugh. "Jake, I've loved you since I was twelve." I leaned my forehead against his. "And I'll let you in on a little secret."

"What?" he asked.

I gave him my brightest smile. "You'll never, ever be just a regular guy."

CHAPTER 58

A half-hour later, I was still smiling, cradled in Jake's arms, when the sound of the doorbell jolted me from my blissful state.

When it rang again, I made a move to sit up, only to feel Jake tighten his grip and ask, "Where do you think you're going?"

I had to laugh. "Don't you hear that?"

"Nope."

"Liar," I teased. "Are you expecting someone?"

"Nope."

"Well, don't you think we should get it?"

"Nope."

"Oh come on. Is that all you can say?"

He paused for a long moment before saying, in a tone of absolute sincerity, "I love you. How's that?"

With a happy sigh, I let my head fall back onto his bare chest. "Actually, that's pretty wonderful."

He ran a lingering hand across my bare hip. "And?"

"And, I love you, too."

"That's my girl."

I curled myself tighter against him, enjoying the feel of his body so close to mine. Yes. I was his girl. And I was going to stay his girl. Always.

I was still enjoying that happy thought when the pounding started. Whoever the visitor was, they'd obviously given up on the bell and were taking a more violent approach. The way it sounded, they were willing to bust the door down, if that's what it took.

At the sudden realization of who it might be, I bolted upright, and this time, Jake didn't stop me.

I said, "What if that's Joel?"

I mean, I knew they talked and everything. But with Jake back in town, maybe Joel was looking to confront Jake in person.

They *were* brothers, after all.

As if thinking along the same lines, Jake was already out of the bed and tugging on his pants. No underwear. No socks. Just the pants.

Skipping the shirt, he strode toward the bedroom door and said, "Wait here, okay?"

I almost protested. After all, I wanted to be there for him. But probably, Jake had the right idea.

This was a brother-to-brother thing. And, as much as I'd like to help them resolve things, odds were pretty high that I'd only get in the way.

Still, I wasn't going to just lay around naked either, so when Jake shut the door behind him, I crawled off the bed and threw on the same clothes that I'd been wearing earlier.

I'd barely finished buttoning my blouse when the sounds of yelling made me pause in mid-motion.

Oh, crap.

It wasn't Joel.

It was Bianca.

Her voice, high and shrill, echoed off the walls. "Where is she?"

Unwilling to let Jake handle *this* alone, I scrambled toward the bedroom door and flung it open wide, just in time to hear Jake say, in a surprisingly calm voice, "None of your business."

But already, I was striding toward them.

At the sight of me, Bianca shrieked, "You!"

I stopped and glanced around. "Me?"

"Yes, you! *You* gave her my address, didn't you?"

I blinked. "What?"

Through clenched teeth, Bianca said, "Did you, or did you not, give Claire my home address?"

"Ohhhh," I said, as realization dawned. "Is Claire the girl from the convention center?"

Bianca looked like she wanted to kill someone, me in particular. "As if you didn't know."

"I didn't know her name was Claire," I said, surprised to realize that I'd never even asked her name.

But I *had* given her Bianca's home address, because, after all, fair was fair.

I looked to Jake, whose gaze was drifting between me and Bianca, as if assessing the need for some sort of intervention.

Funny, I didn't think one would be needed.

For too many reason to count – the amazing sex, the sight of Jake standing there shirtless, and yes, most of all, the fact that we were now officially engaged, I couldn't seem to make myself care that Bianca was throwing yet another hissy-fit.

By now, it felt like old news.

I gave her a cheery smile. "Sorry, I figured you'd like the surprise."

She was still glaring daggers at me. "Well, I didn't."

"Oh well. You win some, you lose some."

Bianca's voice rose to a new crescendo. "She slapped me!"

I gave a half shrug. "Eh, she slapped me too. That's the way the cookie crumbles, huh?"

Jake's head snapped in my direction. "Someone slapped you?"

I waved away his concern. "Yeah, but it turned out okay."

From the look on his face, he wasn't so sure.

A sudden gasp made me look to Bianca. She was staring, horror-stricken, at my left hand. In a voice quivering with anger, she demanded, "What. Is. *That?*"

I looked down and spotted, of course, the ginormous engagement ring, glittering on my finger. I gave it a little wave, watching cheerfully as it sparkled under the overhead lights. "Oh, this?"

She was eying the ring like it might jump from my finger, and bite off her face. "Yes. *That.*"

Awful or not, I couldn't help but giggle. "I dunno," I said, letting my happy gaze land on Jake. "You'll have to ask my fiancé."

But she never did. Instead, with a string of profanity, she turned and stomped out the open condo door, and then, slammed it shut behind her.

As for me, I looked to Jake, expecting to see a face filled with amusement. Instead, I saw a face – the face I loved more than life itself – filled with obvious concern. "If someone hurt you," he said, "I need to know."

The darkness in his eyes hurt to see. I loved him. And I wanted him to be whole and happy, just like I felt.

So I wiped that darkness away with laughter and kisses, and the promise of a lifetime of more where that came from.

Because Jake was mine. And he was going to stay mine. Forever.

THE END

Other Books by Sabrina Stark

Unbelonging (Unbelonging Book 1)

Rebelonging (Unbelonging, Book 2)

Lawton (Lawton Rastor, Book 1)

Rastor (Lawton Rastor, Book 2)

Illegal Fortunes

ABOUT THE AUTHOR

Sabrina Stark writes edgy romances featuring plucky girls and the bad boys who capture their hearts.

She's worked as a fortune-teller, barista, game-show contestant, and media writer in the aerospace industry. She has a journalism degree from Central Michigan University and is married with one son and a pack of very spoiled kittens. She currently makes her home in Northern Alabama.

ON THE WEB

Learn About New Releases & Exclusive Offers
www.SabrinaStark.com

47368570R00196

Made in the USA
Middletown, DE
23 August 2017